NIGHTSCRIPT

VOLUME FIVE

EDITED BY C.M. Muller

CHTHONIC MATTER | St. Paul, Minnesota

NIGHTSCRIPT: *Volume Five*

Tales © 2019 by individual authors. All rights reserved.

FIRST EDITION

Cover: "Erlkönig" (1887) by Julius Sergius von Klever

Additional proofreading by Chris Mashak

Nightscript is published annually, during grand October.

CHTHONIC MATTER | St. Paul, Minnesota
www.chthonicmatter.wordpress.com

CONTENTS

Mother Sylvia

Patricia Lillie

———◆———

TWO CHILDREN STAND at my door. Their upturned faces reflect the moonlight. The boy's is pale and unformed, like over-risen dough. The girl's is golden and crisp, baked to perfection.

"Please," she says. "We're hungry." Her immense eyes brim with tears. I think they should stir sympathy, but they don't. If I feel anything, it's fear.

"Where are your parents?" I am accustomed to knocks at my door, although they seldom come after sunset. When they do, they are made by adults—harried servants, frightened mothers, worried farmers, tearful maidens—seeking brews to ease pain, to vanquish fevers, to save a favorite sow, or worse, philters. No combination of herbs can arouse love, but I provide one anyway. The trek to my cottage is long. Only the desperate undertake it at night, and the desperate pay well.

"Well?" They haven't answered. The girl stares up at me with inhuman eyes. The boy stares at his feet.

"We don't know," she says. Her voice is low and musical, but I can't tell if the notes are sad or joyous.

I have little experience with children. It's possible I don't like them.

"You'd better come in," I say. My reputation in the village is tenuous at best. The people need me, but they fear me. Turning away a pair of hungry urchins would do me no good.

I GIVE THEM buttered bread with honey and fruit—the last of my apples, stored and carefully rationed since last harvest. I tell myself the latter is a selfless act and feel virtuous.

The food vanishes so fast it might not have existed.

The boy grins at me. His lips glisten with apple juice. Flecks of red skin are caught in his uneven teeth.

I go to the cupboard and take down the cake I made that afternoon. There is nothing selfless about sharing the cake. I can and will bake another. But it is my treat, my late-night comfort, and setting it before them takes more out of me than parting with the last of my apples did.

I slice a meager piece and give it to the girl. The boy yanks the platter to him. He stuffs the gingerbread into his mouth by handfuls and gulps it down, not bothering to chew. I wonder if he will choke and find the thought doesn't bother me. I am more horrified by my reaction than by the possibility of his death. Maybe I have been alone too long. Maybe that is why the children are here.

When the cake is gone, the girl places a sticky forefinger on the blade of the knife I still hold.

"Thank you," she says.

"You will sleep in the barn tonight. Tomorrow, we will walk into town. Father Jacob will know what to do with you."

I do not want them in my house.

I WAKE TO the smell of baking. The sun is up. I have overslept, and someone is in my house. My chest tightens. I cannot breathe. I remember the children. I try to picture them, but they are vague, a half-remembered dream. A crash from the kitchen tells me they are real.

in prayer. He appears brighter than last night. A hint of pink stains his doughy cheeks. His features are still ill-defined, spongy. Unlike the girl's, his eyes are tiny and hard, currants buried in a soft bun. His smile makes me queasy.

His sister—I assume she's his sister although they look nothing alike—is on her hands and knees before the hearth, a bucket at her side and scrub brush in her hands.

My kitchen is so clean I barely recognize it. The floor is swept. The crockery gleams on the shelves. The table is covered with a clean cloth on which sits a basket of eggs and a mug overflowing with flowers. To my relief, the blooms are nothing I need. Just the honey-suckle that covers my cottage.

"Oh!" The girl jumps up and pulls a pan from the oven.

Gingerbread.

"How did you get in?" I ask.

"The door was open," she says. Her brother nods. I have yet to hear him speak.

I am sure I bolted the door. It's second nature. I am a woman alone, far from the nearest neighbor, and contrary to the rumors, my skill with plants does not extend to other magics.

The girl takes two eggs from the basket, leaving only two behind.

"Sit," she says. "I'll make you breakfast."

"What about you and your brother?"

"Oh, we've eaten. Long before the sun came up."

The boy's smile stretches to show his teeth.

I am dizzy. I sit.

IN THE MORNING light, I see their clothing, though well made, is filthy and ragged. The boy's trousers are too short. His bare ankles are scratched. The girl's skirts are mud-covered and torn.

"How far did you travel?" I say.

"We came through the woods," she says.

I go to the linen box. Under the bedsheets and quilts, I find a child-sized apron. It's clean and unstained. A faint yellowing of the fabric is the only evidence of age.

"Were there children in this house?" The girl ties the apron around her waist over her ruined skirt.

"I wasn't born an old woman, you know. These should fit." I pull a shift and kirtle from the chest and toss them at her feet. The shift is patched, but it will do.

She snatches them from the floor and buries her face in the deep green folds of the kirtle.

I hand a pair of trousers to the boy. He holds them to his waist. The length is perfect.

"Did you have a brother?" The girl clutches her new garments to her chest.

"I am not going to take them from you," I say. "They're yours to keep." I suspect Father Jacob will look more kindly on clean and well-dressed children.

"Did you have a brother?" she repeats.

"I don't remember." It is the truth. I recall a boy, but he was gone long ago. I've forgotten who he was and where he went, if I ever knew.

In the juniper tree outside my window, a bird sings. I don't recognize the song.

In the bottom of the box is a red velvet cap. It would fit the girl. I bury it beneath the bedclothes.

A rap at the door tells me it's later than I thought. "Go. Draw water from the well and wash yourselves before putting on those clothes. I have business to attend to."

"I'M SORRY. YOU needn't have stopped. I have nothing to send with you today," I say. Brother Wilhelm, from the monastery, is on his way to market. "The hens haven't been laying. Maybe eggs next week, or maybe dyes or herbs."

He looks concerned.

"The hens will start laying again—or else they're for the pot," I say.

"Are you well? You look tired." His concern is not for the chickens.

"Yes." I cannot think what else to say. I don't tell him about the children.

"I will check in on you next week," he says.

I thank him and wish him a good day at market.

After he leaves, I realize I could have—should have—sent the children to town with him. He would have gladly delivered them to Father Jacob. Now, if I take them myself and he sees us, he will think it odd.

They will have to stay one more night.

I TAKE THE children to the gardens with me. I don't want them alone in my house. The boy I set to weeding the root vegetables. He is silent but compliant. I leave him among the beets. He can do little damage there.

The girl I take to my herbs. There, among the sages, I question her. Where are they from? Why did they come to my door?

She is a storyteller.

She spins a tale of loving parents fallen on hard times. Of hunger and deprivation. Of a mother who convinces a father to take the children into the woods and abandon them so that the parents may eat, and of a father who agrees.

I do not question the last. If I were hungry enough, I might do the same.

"The first time, Hans saved us. He left a trail of little white stones and we found our way home. But the second time…" A tear rolls down her cheek.

A single tear. I am skeptical.

"Hans is your brother? The boy with you?" It's hard to believe that potato of a boy could engineer a rescue.

"Yes. He's ill now, but he'll be well soon. You'll see." She looks like she's trying to produce another tear, but none comes.

"If he is called Hans, what are you called?"

"Greta. What is your name?" She widens her eyes and parts her lips.

A chill creeps over me, and I shudder.

"Frau Trude. Mother Holle. Walpurga. Berchta. Take your pick. It doesn't matter to me." I have no intention of giving this child my true name.

"I shall call you Mother Sylvia."

The name is strange, but so is the girl. I shrug. One name is as good as another to me, and tomorrow I will be rid of both brother and sister.

In the afternoon, two visitors arrive at separate times. The first is a woman hoping to conceive, the second a woman wanting to rid herself of a child already conceived. I supply both with packets containing the required ingredients and instructions on the brewing and drinking of their teas. Neither appear to notice the children in my gardens. Considering the nature of their errands, I decide it's willful blindness. They pay me and hurry away. Many have need of my skills, but few linger once their transaction is complete.

We work until the sun is low, when I hurry the children inside. I don't want Brother Wilhelm to spot them on his return trip.

They sleep in the barn again. I make sure to bolt the front door.

I HAVEN'T YET opened my eyes when I hear them. The children, who wandered in and out of my dreams all night, are in my house. Angry, I want to jump from my bed and confront them.

I can't.

I ache. My neck, my limbs, my head. I move and my back spasms, my legs cramp. Inch by inch, I creep from my bed and stand tall. The effort makes the room spin. My vision dims. I stand still, draw deep breaths, and push the pain down until it is buried inside me. One foot, then the other, I tell myself.

By the time I make it to the kitchen, my joints have somewhat loosened and the ache in my head has faded, but I am exhausted.

"Mother Sylvia!" The notes in Greta's voice are those of joy, but her face is unreadable. She drops her broom and runs and takes my arm and leads me to the table. Her unearthly eyes are pools of black. I fear that if I look into them for long, I will drown. Still, I am grateful for her support. As she lowers me into the chair across from her brother, I know there will be no walk to town today.

The mug of honeysuckle still sits in the center of the table. The blooms are shriveled. One falls, a tiny brown corpse robbed of its sweetness. The basket contains no more eggs than it did yesterday.

"Two of the chickens are missing," Greta says.

Hans brushes something from the corner of his mouth. A feather? No, it must have been a crumb. He has no doubt already eaten some of the honey-covered bread Greta places in front of me.

Or not. A starving dog sits across from me, tongue hanging to the table, salivating. I hear a low growl. I scrabble for my plate, pull it as close as I can, nearly in my lap, and eat quickly before the beast can seize my food.

When I finish, all I see is the boy, silent and placid as ever. His features have changed, jelled and hardened. The slight curve of an aquiline nose. A suggestion of sharp cheekbones. A hint of handsomeness to come—other than his eyes which are still small and hard, buried in the flesh beneath his brow. How did I ever think him a potato? He smiles.

I rise, doing my best to appear strong and graceful despite the pain.

"Out," I say. "We have work to do."

I cannot show weakness in front of these children.

HANS STRIDES AWAY and disappears.

Before I can call out, Greta says, "He is fine. I told you he would be well."

I cannot decide which disturbs me more, having him near me or not knowing what he is up to, so I let him go.

"You shiver," she says.

"A chill. It will pass." In truth, despite the blazing sun, I am cold. More than cold. I am chilled to my core.

"Wait." Greta runs to the cottage.

"No," I shout. She doesn't hear me.

She returns with a piece of thickly woven fabric and drapes it over my shoulders.

I pull my grandmother's shawl close, but it doesn't warm me. How did she know where to find it?

We go to the herb bed. If I kneel in the dirt or even bend to the plants, I may not be able to stand again, so I give the girl a lesson.

Feverfew for headaches and infertility. Coriander for fever. Wormwood and mint for the stomach and comfrey for the lungs. Rose, lavender, and sage for aching joints. Tansy, rue, and pennyroyal, the downfallen maiden's friends. I catalogue the herbs and their uses. She repeats my words in a singsong voice, a child repeating a nursery chant.

I do not take her into my workshop. I do check the door. It remains locked, just as I left it. We avoid the small garden, the dark bed behind the workshop. I do not show her the belladonna, the foxglove, the others. They have their value, but they have more than one use. Uses I am loath to share with the girl. She is, I reason, just a child. She has no need for such knowledge.

A steady stream of visitors comes and goes. All seek salves or sachets, cures or prophylactics. Many comment on my appearance. I am moving slow. I am wrapped in a woolen shawl on a stifling August afternoon. Others are too immersed in their own woes to see mine. Not one questions or even mentions the presence of the children.

When Hans reappears, a chicken dangles from his hand. Its neck is wrung and its feathers plucked.

Greta squeals. "Shall we roast it or shall I make a stew?"

"Do that again and it will be you in the pot." My rage has no effect on the children.

"Silly Mother Sylvia." Greta pats my arm. Hans passes her the dead fowl and shows me his teeth.

Later, I go to bed before the children. I don't know where they will sleep, nor do I care. I don't bother to bolt the front door.

I WAKE BEFORE the sun rises. *Today*, I think. *Today I will take the children to Father Jacob. Today I will be rid of them.*

My body betrays me. My bones are ice. My joints are frozen. I struggle to sit up. My grandmother's shawl lays across my legs. A tree limb—stripped of its branches and bark, polished, and topped with a knot—leans against the bed. I know it was cut from my juniper. I reach for it.

My fingers have turned to talons and my knuckles swollen to the size of walnuts. I want to cry out. This withered hand is not mine. Ice fills my throat and freezes my voice.

I heave myself from the bed but cannot stand straight. I am hunched. Bent like a fishhook. I claw at the shawl. It has grown during the night. I drape it over my head and wind it around my body. The edges puddle around my feet.

Supported by the juniper crutch, I hobble from my room. I do not make it to the kitchen. In the front room, a fire blazes. I sink into my chair by the hearth. The flames provide no warmth.

"Drink this." Greta stands before me. She hands me a steaming mug.

The hot liquid sears my frostbitten lips and throat. I taste honey, chamomile, lemongrass, and something else. I should know what it is, but I don't.

The girl sinks to the floor at my feet and leans against my legs. She whispers words my frozen ears can't take in. My teeth chatter.

She rises.

"Don't leave me," I say. Or maybe I just think it. She retreats to the kitchen.

I want to sleep but know I shouldn't. I fight to keep my eyes open. I think I succeed.

When Greta returns, she is no longer a child. She is a young woman, tall and beautiful. Her enormous eyes remain pools of darkness, but they are changed too. Or I am changed. I am willing to drown in their depths.

She bends and kisses my forehead. "Come, Mother Sylvia," she says. "I've lit the oven. It will warm you."

THE BRAMBLES

David McGroarty

————◆————

IT WAS THE life's ambition of Ellie Litchfield to pack everything in and move out of the city, to some suburban avenue with broad grassy verges and rows of mountain ash, populated by happy couples and retirees and people with roof boxes on top of their cars. There she might slacken, perhaps even grow fat, relax into the space like a plant that is taken out of its pot and allowed to take root in a garden. There she hoped to stay forever. She moved, finally, on retirement, aged only 55. It was too late for her husband, Jack, who had died young, and had never in any case shared the dream with her. The house was semi-detached, mock Tudor, named "The Brambles" by its former owners (both now deceased), and when she saw it, she loved it.

There had never been anyone in the dream but Ellie. Even when Jack was alive. In the suburban home of her fantasy, she had always been alone. The imagined population of that tree-lined avenue had been silent characterless figures, like background actors in a film, or automata in a museum. So well-rehearsed was the dream that when she moved to The Brambles, the people—the neighbors—stood out at first as aberrations, imperfections in the landscape: boys on bikes who did not just pedal up and down the street but around and around in tight circles, smoking and swearing loudly at one another; dog-walkers whose animals left wet turds on the pavement. And it struck Ellie, within days of her relocation, that the dream would, in some respects, remain a dream, until she died.

She discovered also that in her decades of living at elbows with the wider human race in inner-city London, she had become cocooned, and that the cocoon would now need to fall away, or she would have no choice but to think of herself as a hermit. She felt exposed in those first weeks. She retreated regularly to the house's back garden, which, penned in by wooden fences on either side and by a brick wall and a row of overgrown laurels at its rear, offered her a sort of refuge, a decompression chamber in which gradually to acclimatize to suburban life.

But the garden was wild and unwelcoming. The grass was two feet tall in places, and that was the least of it. Vines latticed what must once have been a lawn, and there were tall thistles and clumps of nettles. It was one impenetrable mass of green beyond the patio, and the patio itself was being taken over by the snaking boughs of a wisteria, which had burst monstrously out of a large clay pot, its roots penetrating and shattering the concrete slabs while its limbs spread up and across the rear end of the house and onto the roof. For those first few weeks, she would sit on the back doorstep, and rarely made it further.

Ellie was there on the step, a month after the move, when her neighbor chose to introduce herself by mounting a stepladder and stretching her neck so that her head appeared above the tangled clumps of jasmine that topped the fence. She was younger, twenty years younger, at least. Ellie had heard her calling her two daughters in from the garden for school or homework. She had a sharp, educated voice, with some of the darkness of the North in the vowels. She introduced her family first: "We're the Scotts." And then she said her name was Kate, and her husband was Mike, and the girls were

Sian and Gracie.

"I meant to say hello sooner," she said. "You feel like you ought to, you know?" And she pulled a face like a chastised child and said, "Bad neighbor."

"Oh, don't worry," Ellie said. She thought to get up and go to Kate at the fence, but the wisteria and the jasmine barred her way. "It's good to meet you now. I'm Ellie."

Kate nodded and then scanned Ellie's garden jungle. She sighed, opened her mouth as if to speak—to comment on the state of the place, Ellie felt sure—but then stopped herself, and nodded again.

"It's a mess, I know," Ellie said. "I do mean to get around to it. I don't know where I should start."

"Start with the patio, I should say. And then work your way forward."

It was spring, and the wisteria that dominated the patio was blooming. Despite its overbearing size—its stem was as broad as her own thighs—Ellie had grown fond of it. Its purple flowers framed the window of her bedroom at the back of the house and gave a pastoral flavor to the morning view from her bed. Of all the plants she might have killed off or pared back, it would have been the last. She noticed, though, that its growth had been stymied, wherever it tried to cross the dividing line between the property that was now hers, and the Scotts' house. And she could well imagine Kate, on her stepladder, armed with shears or perhaps a petrol-chugging chainsaw, attacking the wild wisteria wherever it threatened to encroach.

"Maybe I should just leave it all," Ellie said, not entirely joking. "Have my own wild space."

Kate frowned. "That's what the Jacksons called it."

Jackson had been the surname of the man and woman who lived in the house before her. It had not occurred to her that the old couple might have let their garden grow wild deliberately. Ellie had heard that they had been ill, had, in fact, died within weeks of each other. She had assumed that they were just too frail to manage it.

"I'll give you a hand if you like," Kate said. "It's a big job."

"That's very kind, but perhaps not today."

"Of course, any time." Kate went behind the fence for a second, then came up again. "Come round for a cuppa some afternoon and we'll make plans. I work at home but I'm usually done by lunchtime. Lazy!" She made her naughty-girl face again and disappeared, and this time she did not pop back up.

BESIDES THE WILD space at the back, there were other traces of the Jacksons in the old house. In the loft, Ellie found a box of books that had belonged to them, mostly military history books with monochrome covers of wrecked urban landscapes. There was a rotten old blanket there too, and some sort of ledger, with entries that were mostly indecipherable. She remembered that the old man had run a small shop in Harlow, and then could not recall how this information had come to her.

Her most unexpected find came when she stripped the wallpaper in the smallest bedroom. Beneath it, a mural had been painted onto the wall: a cartoon scene. She had seen similar affairs on the walls of the children's ward she had all but lived in when, as a child, her son Thomas had been desperately ill with Hodgkin lymphoma—anthropomorphized animals and inexplicably sexed-up fairies—though this painting was immeasurably more crudely done. She was both appalled and fascinated by its artlessness. It was impossible to tell if the figures in the mural were cats or dogs, partly because they were so badly drawn, but also because from the neck down they resembled nothing so much as seventies hippies, in long robes and garlanded with flowers, holding hands and apparently dancing. There was something about the collision of outmoded counterculture and childish cartoon that seemed obscene to her. She wondered why the Jacksons had covered it with paper and not paint, had not wanted to obliterate it entirely.

She painted the mural over, but later she described it to Kate and asked if the Jacksons had had any children in their lives. Kate said that they had not, and nor had she ever seen or heard any children, and then quickly changed the subject to the garden and how she could help Ellie to tame it.

ELLIE HAD NEVER been inclined to nurture friendships. She was glad for the help with the garden, but found Kate tiring. Kate talked endlessly, about herself usually, or about her husband whom Ellie never saw. Ellie listened but found it hard to absorb much information. It was like listening to the shipping news.

Together, they weeded the patio and scrubbed it clean of moss. The lawn took several more days of effort, and Ellie learned that Kate's husband worked in retail, and was often overseas, and that the two children were not doing well enough at school. They cut down the vines with shears, uprooted the thistles, the nettles, and the dock weed.

Beneath all of that, around their fourth day of work on the garden, they found a layer of something else growing. Kate said it was probably chickweed, but then confessed that she likely wouldn't know what chickweed was if she saw it, and that she certainly had never seen anything like this. Perhaps it was a lichen, she said. Whatever the weed was, a dense mesh of it covered the entire lawn and would not be easily shifted. It had many tough roots that seemed to go deep and its fibers were like copper wire. Ellie tried at first just to yank it out, but even in gloves, her hands were soon bruised and tired. She and Kate finally turned the whole patch over with a spade, and raked up the remnants of weed and tossed them in a heap.

The last of the strange weed covered a large ornament in the center of the garden. It had grown so thick and entwined upon itself that there was no way of knowing what the ornament was. It stood chest-high and was vaguely person-shaped. Ellie had the impression that it was a statue, a cherub, but it could as easily have been a birdbath. There was no way of removing the weed from the ornament. Ellie and Kate took turns in tugging at it, but its tendrils would not release their grip and, making the job even more difficult, its tiny leaves seemed to melt on contact, turning the women's gloves green and slimy. Nor could they lift the thing, or even knock it to the ground. It seemed to be fixed in place, as if it had put down its own roots.

"I surrender," Kate said finally. "I give up." They had established a routine by which they broke for tea a half-hour before Kate had to embark on the school run, and it had gotten to that time. She seemed let down by their failure to remove the last of the weed, more than Ellie felt was appropriate. The two of them went inside and Kate sat at the kitchen table with her hands hanging by either side of the chair. While Ellie took the teabags down from the kitchen cabinet, Kate said, "I've been hitting the girls."

There was a din from the boiling kettle, and Ellie realized that she could convincingly act as if she had not heard what her neighbor had said. She was not in any case sure what she had heard or what it meant, or why Kate had chosen to say it to her. She had not thought that they were friends, at least not the sort of friends who confessed their sins to one another. She did not want any of that.

"We could try a weedkiller," she said. Kate nodded vigorously. Ellie poured the tea, sensing that the moment had passed. When she sat down, they only talked about the garden and the weeds.

Ellie watched from the window of her living room while Kate got into her car and backed out of the neighboring driveway. As much as she wanted to forget what Kate had muttered before tea, it would not stop coming back to her. *I've been hitting the girls.* Every time, the impact of the words was undiminished, the ashamed, despairing tone.

Ellie returned to the garden and, for the first time since the move, went to work alone. She set to the weed-enshrouded ornament in the middle of the lawn, tearing at the weeds with the open blades of a pair of pruning shears. It was hard but she made progress. Pieces of the weed—small strands at first, but soon thick clumps—fell away. Before long it became clear that the growth was thicker here than it had been on the ground. She had forgotten to put on her gloves, her hands were scratched and smeared with the residue from the disintegrating leaves, and beneath every layer of green was another. She tore through where she had expected to find the head of the statue, but there was only more and more weed. She started to suspect, and then to believe, that there was nothing underneath. Instead of hacking away at the last of the weed, she started to feel that she was at the source of it, and that everything she had removed from the lawn and thrown on the heap was just overspill from this central structure.

She had taken six inches off the top of the mound when she started to find things that were not of the plant, but buried within it. The first was a carved wooden toy or trinket the size of her thumb, in the shape of a fox standing on its hind legs, that recalled the bizarre mural on the bedroom wall. There were other things: a milk bottle top, shiny and blue, of a kind she hadn't seen for years; clumps of what looked like fur, still attached to something that might have been skin. And three human teeth: tiny, baby teeth, still bloodstained at the root. She recoiled at this last find, stopped to fetch her gloves, finished the job of cutting the green mound to the ground, and put everything in a plastic bag.

When she dropped the bag into the bin at the front of her house, Kate had returned and was herding her children inside. The youngest daughter was in tears, not in a tantrum, but sobbing quietly, her head hung low as if embarrassed. Kate stopped to acknowledge Ellie, rolled her eyes theatrically and chirped, "Drama!"

Ellie went back to the garden to finish the job on her own.

KATE DID NOT visit again for a few weeks. Two days after she and Ellie tackled the weeds together, her husband came home from wherever he had been and then she seemed to disappear into the house. At around the same time, there was a series of violent thunderstorms and Ellie's nascent lawn was swamped. Ellie focused on painting the hall and sorting out her family photographs on the computer.

It was a humid day, late in the afternoon with another storm threatening to break, when Kate came to the door with a bottle of wine.

"Mike's taken the girls to his mum's," she said. "I'm free!" And she waved her left hand around in a contrived show of jubilation.

Ellie was not much of a drinker but she invited Kate into the kitchen, opened the wine, and poured two glasses. She had the patio door open and they sat at the table while the garden outside grew darker under the building cloud. They talked about the lawn and the house. They both drank quickly. The conversation was awkward at first, faltering. After the first glass of wine, Kate brought up the subject of the Jacksons. She said how relieved she was that they were gone, how she had never liked them, had never known how to speak to them. The more she revealed, the more candid she seemed to become, as if she were building momentum, gathering courage as she did. She told Ellie how the old couple would get up in the night and clatter about the house with the radio on, and how she might be playing in the garden with her daughters and glance up and see one or other of the Jacksons watching them from their bedroom window.

Then she stopped, coughed. Ellie filled her glass.

Kate said, "You know, I did see a child once, a boy." Kate reached for her glass, and Ellie noticed that her hand was shaking. "I mean, they didn't have children of their own—I know that—so it couldn't have been a grandchild. It was summer, and it was dark, so it must have been late, and they were in the garden. I was up in the bedroom—I'd been in the bath—and there was all this noise outside. This noise, this fuss. I went to the window, and the Jacksons were in the garden." She paused, giggled, though there was no joy in it, and looked past Ellie, out the patio door. "You remember how overgrown it all was. She was there on the patio, and her husband was on the lawn. And he was sort of . . . crawling."

Kate gulped her wine and Ellie felt suddenly desperate, trapped. She felt an almost physical compulsion to get up and walk out of the room. Instead, she sat on her hands and laughed. It sounded feeble.

Kate continued: "He had his top off. He was on all fours and my first thought was that he was looking for something in the weeds but for some reason he had his top off, and he wasn't looking for anything. He was just sort of crawling around, an old man with his top off. But her—she was hysterical. That was what brought me to the window in the first place. The amount of noise she was making. Tears and snot, the works. And she kept saying, 'Stop it. Please, stop it.' I felt like I ought not to look. But then I saw the boy. He was in the back corner by the wall, sort of, half-standing, half-crouching, completely naked. God, he was an ugly thing. And it occurred to me that it wasn't her husband she was screaming at, that it was the boy . . . "

She sat for a moment, stroking the stem of her glass with her finger and thumb. Ellie poured more wine into her own glass and then into Kate's. Kate giggled again.

She said, "He smiled at me. The boy. He looked straight up, right at me and smiled. Isn't that the oddest thing?" She rolled her eyes and shook her head. "It must have been close to midnight. Mad!"

"Was that the only time you saw him?"

Kate nodded, then said again, "Mad."

A few streaks of rain appeared on the patio door and there was a rush of cool, moist air from outside and it started to pour. Ellie got up to close the door. Standing on the threshold, she looked across the garden, now more brown than green. An image came into her mind, clear and fully-formed, of a boy, standing in the corner by the back wall. The image was so bright, so intrusive, that it felt like it was not her own, like it had forced its way into her mind from somewhere else: the boy, eleven or twelve years old with dirty black hair coming down over his neck and back, an overbite and a wispy mustache, grinning. She shivered, shut the door and drew the curtains.

Kate had stood up. She said, "So when are we going to deal with that wisteria?"

"I might keep the wisteria," Ellie said. Kate pulled a scowl. Ellie could not tell if it was an expression of genuine disapproval, but she chose to ignore it anyway. "When are the kids back?"

"I don't know," Kate said, distant. "Tuesday, I think."

Kate was gathering her things—her keys and hat—making a show of departure. Ellie let her. She didn't like the way the wine had made her feel and the unpleasant image of the boy in the garden was now driving other thoughts from her mind, making her feel tired and sick.

She saw Kate to the door. She did not expect another visit, and did not receive one. Tuesday came and went with no sign of the family's return, and when they did return, over a week later, it was Kate who seemed to be absent.

In the meantime, the weather had turned warm and dry. Over a period of weeks, patches of green started to appear on the lawn.

SOMETIMES, ELLIE WOULD dream that she was back in London with Jack. They had owned a large flat overlooking the canal, which they had bought together, before regeneration and gentrification turned the area around the canal into somewhere other people wanted to live. In those dreams, things were always as they had been just before Jack died, with Thomas in his room, playing his guitar too loud, and Jack working on his computer in the sunshine on the balcony. When she woke, there would be a brief, but almost unendurable, sadness. Then, she would look to the wisteria that grew around her bedroom window, and she would find some comfort in it. In this way, she had fallen into a habit of turning her eyes to the window each morning, before doing anything else.

The first time she saw the boy, it was autumn. A "For Sale" sign had been in the Scott's front garden since August. On the day they were due to leave, she awoke late, to a commotion in the back garden: raised voices, screaming. She had been dreaming of London: Thomas in his room, Jack on the balcony. In the dream, she had been angry, though she did not know why, but violently angry, in tears and raging. Ellie went to her bedroom window and looked down over the fence. It was a moment before she understood what she was seeing.

The noise was coming from Kate and the children. Kate's husband, Mike, was there, and he was standing at the edge of their lawn, ripping plants out of the flower beds. There was something in the way he was going about it that suggested panic. He lurched forward, grasping indiscriminately at the flowers and shrubs, yanking them with his bare hands, throwing them across the lawn, or leaving them bent and stripped of leaves when they refused to lift their roots. Kate was crying. The children just yelled, "Dad! Dad! Dad!" as if he were too far away to hear them. And he carried on, pulling at the plants, flinging them behind him.

Ellie stepped away from the window. As she did, she saw, on her own side of the fence, a black-haired boy. He was pressed against the wooden slats, peering through a knothole at the scene unfolding next door, and banging the palms of his hands on the fence to either side of him, in what Ellie took to be a compulsive expression of glee. It was not only his being there, like an apparition, but the look of him: the pale skin, the proportions of his body—not quite right, not quite like a child, nor an adult—and his hair, long and ragged, hanging down his neck and back. A shudder went through her at the sight of him, and she fell back from the window as if from a strike of lightning.

Afterwards, she sat on the bed. She was afraid to look at the window. Instead, she found herself staring at her own feet.

The second time she saw the boy was in the winter. She woke early one morning and turned, as was her habit, to the window. It was not quite dawn. The boy was crouched on the windowsill outside, naked, one hand gripping a branch of the bare wisteria. His other hand was flat against the windowpane and his face was pressed against the glass, his dark eyes on her. She turned away, burying her face in her pillow. She stayed like that, frozen, for several minutes, even as she heard the rattling at the window, until there was silence, and she dared move again, and looked back and saw that the boy had gone.

She lay still until the room filled up with the light of the morning. Then, she got out of bed, took herself to the garage where she kept her tools, found a hand saw, and went to the garden, where she set about destroying the wisteria. She cut through its roots where they entered the earth through the shattered patio. She cut through its stem where it emerged from its broken pot. Where she could, she cut through its branches where they leaned on the wall of her house. It occurred to her through all of this how absurd she must have appeared, in her bare feet and nightie and frantic, with her saw, at eight in the morning. She looked to the upstairs windows of what had been the Scotts' house, but they were vacant and black. When it was done, she sat on the step with the wet saw on her lap.

She never saw the boy again, but neither did she dream of her old home in London, nor of an alternative suburban home, like the one she had always dreamed of before, a place of dappled sunlight and gentler air. Her sleeps were only ever dreamless, or vaguely troubled, and when she woke she turned her face to the wall, away from the bare window, and everything that was on the other side of it.

American House Spider

Shannon Scott

————— ♦ —————

"What are you looking at?" Marie calls from the kitchen where she can see her eight-year-old son, Thomas, tracking something on the floor.

"It's a spider. Can I step on it?" he says.

"No, you may not." Marie puts down a jar of mashed pear and plum, leaving Madeline in her highchair. She goes to Thomas and places a hand on his shoulder, surprised to find him sturdier, beefier, more like his father, than the last time she touched him. Hadn't he been her little chicken just last week? "It's bad luck to kill a spider," Marie tells Thomas, whose hunched body hides the arachnid from view.

"But Dad kills them."

Marie feels a wave of irritation. She and her husband are taking turns reading *Charlotte's Web* to Thomas.

"I'm sure you're wrong. Your father would only kill a poisonous spider. He was probably worried about Madeline. She's the only one small enough to die from the venom."

"She could die?" Thomas says.

"Yes, and it wouldn't be a pleasant death." Marie bends over Thomas and blows gently on the spider whose fangs twitch at the sudden gust of air before scuttling away to the corner of the room.

"What would happen to Madeline?" Thomas does not look up at his mother. The spider climbs the wall, heading for the ceiling.

"She would probably vomit, then become paralyzed as the poison worked its way through her body. She might experience massive hemorrhaging or significant tissue loss. That is, if the spider is necrotic."

"What is necrotic?" His voice is barely a whisper.

"It means the death of cells in living tissue," Marie says. "If Madeline had necrosis, she could lose her arms and legs."

As if on cue, Madeline squeals from her highchair, kicking out her chubby legs and raising a tiny fist in demand for more mashed fruit or else release from the chair.

Thomas stares down at the floor, not at a spider anymore but simply at the hardwood. Marie knows what he is seeing. One of Madeline's amputated baby legs lying next to the sofa. He is imagining his little sister trying to crawl without any limbs. A worm. A junkyard doll. He has lost interest in killing the spider completely.

THE PARENTS IN the spinning circle (Marie must always correct herself and think *parents* now that Doug has joined the rest of the mothers) are working on a blanket for Victims of Domestic Violence. Every week they gather in the faculty lounge of Anderson Elementary to knit while their kids are in school. As Thomas learns multiplication tables in a nearby classroom, Madeline sleeps in her stroller, cocooned snugly in a pink romper knitted by the spinners, who always gender their gifts. The spinners are given sugar cookies and stale coffee donated from the school cafeteria. They are hoping to knit a blanket large enough to enclose all Victims of Domestic Violence, all the black-eyed women and broken-toothed children and shaken-up babies, to wrap them tightly and securely inside protective threads woven by their own benevolent hands.

"Spaghetti today," Doug says. "The smell is unmistakable." Doug's attempts at conversation are his way of compensating for the fact that the mothers can no longer discuss their husbands' requests for anal sex or bondage.

The needles click, click, click. There are no follow-up comments about spaghetti.

A mother with a ferrety face, whose name Marie always forgets, announces her need to use the restroom. "Can someone please take my chair?"

Her child is attached to her chair by a leash. It is the only way she can keep him safe. If he wanders out into the hallway, he could be crushed by a sea of elementary school children. Or snatched by a pedophile drawn inexorably to the school as a fox is drawn to a henhouse. There would be no blanket large enough to protect him then.

Marie takes the chair. It's warm from the woman's backside. The toddler plays with oversized Legos that cannot be swallowed. He seems unconcerned that his mother has been replaced by a stranger.

Where are you going for your anniversary? Branson. How fun. Lots of places to swim.

Marie lets the conversation swirl around her. She feels a jerk on her chair leg. The child of the nameless mother strains his leash for a Lego kicked out of reach. It is bright red and Marie can understand why he wants it. But the leash is not just a safety device, it is also a lesson. The tug on the line is a signal of his captivity and entrapment. If he were clever prey, he would remain still and not draw attention to himself by creating disturbances on the line.

Gary likes to play the slots, but Las Vegas is terrible. Loud. Expensive. Strippers.

The blanket grows by several feet every week. Marie works on her pieces at home. She likes to knit with browns and grays, although the spinners insist that Victims of Domestic Violence prefer cheerful colors, like blue and yellow. But cheerful colors hurt Marie's eyes, which have always been weak. Her husband disapproves of the spinners. He worries that she will go blind. He says she will have to use a thread to find her way through their home, like the Minotaur in the labyrinth. She assures him she knows the house so well she could go anywhere in it blindfolded. She has offered to prove this to him. *All right*, he concedes, *you know the house. But what about reading Thomas and Madeline bedtime stories? Or knowing when it's time to clean the toilet?*

ELBOW MACARONI MADE from rice needs very little chewing. Marie watches Thomas shovel cheese-smothered spoonfuls into his mouth, scarcely hesitating for air, as if she has neglected to pack him a lunch or offer a nutritious afternoon snack. Thomas suffers from a gluten allergy that was diagnosed shortly after he stopped breastfeeding. Marie didn't take it seriously at first. She thought it was a passive aggressive attempt to get back to the teat. Then one evening she experimentally gave him a handful of Cheerio's and he turned to stone. Not really, but they spent the night in the ER. Now the whole family eats bread made from potatoes and pasta made from rice. There are no wheat-based cereals allowed past the threshold of Marie's home. When a commercial for any variation of Cheerio's—chocolate, peanut butter, or banana—comes on the television screen, Marie snaps it off like a snuff film.

After dinner, her husband insists they all go to the park and play Frisbee. He believes in exercise and fresh air after meals. He has been cooped up in his office all day finding ways to prevent sick and injured people from collecting insurance policies. Sometimes he shares the cases with Marie. One man lost his thumb in the rotating shaft of a milling machine. Another fell from a catwalk in a pet food warehouse and broke his pelvis. But mostly it's mesothelioma from asbestos exposure. His best days are when he must leave the office and take depositions from the wheezing, nearly-expired clients of opposing counsel. It allows him to speed away on the open highway, headed north to mining towns, his windows rolled down, his speakers blasting John Mellencamp. He can pull off the road anywhere to piss in fields of creeping foxtail and purple coneflower.

In the park, he throws the Frisbee like a Midwestern Olympian while Thomas and Marie scramble like dogs to catch it. Madeline looks on dispiritedly from her stroller. Someday she will be a dog, too.

LATER, WHEN THE children are tucked into bed, Marie goes back downstairs to wipe up the mud they tracked in from the park. She pauses in the living room, beneath the ceiling corner, where a messy web has been constructed since the spider crawled up this morning.

"Hello," Marie says, though it is too dark to see the spider. "It's nice to have company."

Then she squats down and inspects the ground. Sometimes, when house spiders are done with their meals, they neaten up their webs by dropping out the debris. With her hands, Marie scoops up a ball of dust and trots upstairs into the bedroom she shares with her husband. He has his laptop open, preparing a case for tomorrow. First degree burns from a fast food fryer. She examines her palm under the lamp: one desiccated ant and two black flies. She turns to show him.

IN THE MORNING, when Marie carries Madeline, heavy as a ship's anchor, down the creaking staircase, the web waits for her. The strands of silk glint in the morning sun that shines through the transom window, the whole web moving rhythmically in the quiet, steady draft from the front door. It's a chaotic web, unlike Charlotte's. Charlotte, the artistic barn spider, the talented orb weaver; she wove spiraled webs that were sure signs of nature's perfection, like a Nautilus shell or a newly hatched snapper turtle. Marie's house spider will not create a new web every night like Charlotte, who would eat the old web so that no spinning silk was wasted. Marie's spider doesn't have the time. There is nothing Fibonacci-like or Escher-esque about her web. But it serves its purpose. It is a home and a trap.

From the family room, there are explosions coming from the Xbox. Thomas reclines on the couch with a bowl of rice cereal, playing his father's video games. It sounds like the one where you pick a weapon—a blowtorch or a corkscrew or a gun—then tie up your hostage and question him until he gives you information that will save America. Marie should tell Thomas to turn it off or switch it to cartoons or spare the hostage, but she is exhausted. The night was long. Thomas had a nightmare and woke up screaming. Then Madeline woke up and started screaming too. It took several teaspoons of acetaminophen to get everyone back to sleep. And when Marie finally stumbled back to her bedroom, her husband was awake with an erection. Marie is supposed to be prepared anytime this occurs because her husband often loses his erections like a kid loses mittens. She is to be patient and supportive but also encouraging and vaginally ready as these speedy, arid triumphs are essential to the stability of their marriage.

At the bottom of the staircase, Marie stops suddenly and Madeline's head sags back against her arm like a top-heavy sunflower. From the family room, a man screams in agony. Marie ignores the screams and walks directly beneath the web, peering up. Her heart thuds hard once, then quickens until she can feel each walloping beat in the tips of her fingers. Madeline slides down her leg and plops onto the floor.

The web is a mess—the spider's meals have accumulated—mosquitoes, ants, flies, a millipede, and a moth, all tangled up in strands like her grandmother's hair, which was always rinsed clean with apple-cider vinegar to keep it extra white and shiny. But there is something else in the web. The pounding moves to her ears now, a rush of blood deafening her to the pleas for mercy that her son disregards.

Something is written in the web. It is a single word. An amazing word. A message. An affirmation. Maybe the beginning of a longer piece ... a haiku or even a novel? Certainly, it's a communication meant for Marie. Who else can the spider be writing to? There are no other pen pals around the house. Crouched behind her hinged and variegated legs, the house spider watches Marie from her web, seemingly unafraid of her pale, looming face.

Marie leaves Madeline leaning against the foyer wall and grabs her phone from the top of the entryway cabinet. Her husband has left the requisite morning-after text, something about a special night followed by a heart-eyed winking emoji, which Marie swipes away with a shaking thumb. Then she flips on the overhead light, aims the camera at the web, and snaps a picture. She sends it to her spinning circle before sending it to her husband.

She waits several minutes, but no one responds. Madeline looks up at Marie, a shoelace hanging from her teething mouth.

"Want to see a message for Mommy?" Marie says, then hoists Madeline into the air, where she hovers several inches below the web. "What do you think?"

Madeline reaches for the web, her pudgy fingers snatching recklessly at the delicate threads. Marie quickly drops Madeline back to her hip as the house spider races across her web to hide in the shadows. A gunshot is fired in the family room and a man wails. Has Thomas picked a foot or a kneecap?

"Thomas, come here," Marie calls. The agonized wails stop abruptly as Thomas pauses the game.

Her son wanders into the foyer, bleary-eyed despite the stimulation of torture. There is rice cereal clinging to his cheek and Marie leaves it there.

"What is it?" he says.

"Look," Marie points to the web. "The spider's written a word, just like Charlotte."

Thomas perks up a little at the mention of Charlotte, one of his favorite characters besides Paddington Bear, and he stares up at the web. He is silent for some time. Marie thinks maybe he is sounding out the word in his head, as she and his teacher have taught him to do with two-syllable words.

"I can't see anything," he says. "The cobweb's all clumpy."

"That's just it," Marie says. "She hasn't written with the threads, she's used the clumpy parts to spell out the word."

Marie once again marvels at how the dead insects form letters. The clever spider has consistently selected ants for all the vowels, flies for the consonants, and the wings of a moth for the voiced dental fricative.

Thomas makes a face. "That's disgusting."

"No, it's *terrific*," Marie says. "It's *radiant*."

"Stop it."

"She is *some* spider." Marie beams at the house spider, who is still hiding, probably exhausted from her nocturnal literary endeavors. Marie wishes her own exhaustion stemmed from such rigorous creative work.

"Can I go back to my game?"

Marie shakes her head. Charlotte wove her words to save Wilbur from the butcher's block, but hadn't the words also changed Wilbur on a psychological level? Charlotte's words, meant for others to read, had an even greater effect on Wilbur. They made him more confident and jovial. They convinced him that his contributions to the world had more to do with his character than his cracklin.

"First, tell me what you see." Marie's phone vibrates in her fist, but she ignores it, her attention riveted to her son.

"No," he says, rubbing his eyes. "I don't want to."

"Your father thinks it's cool." Marie glances at her phone. A big red question mark followed by a big red exclamation mark.

"He said that?"

"You bet. He can't wait to come home and see it in person. He might even drive home on his lunch break."

Thomas looks once again at the web, his eyes appearing even wider from the dark circles beneath. Madeline coos and puts a handful of Marie's hair into her mouth.

"I can't. It's too scary. All the dead things."

"It's not scary," Marie says. "The insects are long gone. They're just husks. They've been drained of their blood."

Thomas covers his ears.

"They can't hurt you," Marie says.

"But she can," he says.

"Her?" Marie laughs. "She wouldn't hurt a fly."

MARIE STANDS ON the front steps of her house. Behind her is red brick and ivy. The autumn air is crisp and patches of yellow glow inside the linden trees lining the parkway. She rolls up her sleeve. The fine hairs on her forearm stand on end. She can hear it before she sees it—the unmistakable high-pitched whine of a hungry female mosquito. Though the males are satisfied with nectar, the females demand blood. Marie closes her eyes. Like a kid getting her finger pricked at the doctor's office, she doesn't like to look. Instead, she feels the sting, the lubrication of saliva meant to keep the tiny wound open. She resists the urge to swat. Her reward will not be a lollipop but something much better.

Marie doesn't whack the mosquito too hard. She made that mistake the first time when she placed the smashed remains in the web and the spider rejected it. Marie had never seen disappointment reflected in all eight eyes of a house spider before. It didn't feel good. She already has problems with her self-esteem. So now she swats the mosquitoes lightly and sets them in the web, concussed and teeming with her own blood.

"What a beautiful day."

Marie's neighbor, who had been weeding her vegetable patch on the other side of the lawn, sidles over to Marie. She wears a neon pink visor and dirt-caked knee pads. In one hand she wields a zucchini like a caveman's club.

Marie sucks at the bite on her arm and holds the dazed mosquito deftly between her pointer finger and thumb. She's pretty sure the neighbor saw her lure and incapacitate the insect.

"How are things?" The neighbor lifts her visor, which leaves a deep indentation across her forehead like a do-it-yourself lobotomy.

In response, Marie holds up her kill, which she thinks of as both sustenance and supply for her artistic house spider, like providing oil paint for Van Gogh as well as a sandwich.

"I have zucchini for you. Damn things are taking over the garden." The neighbor edges closer, squinting at whatever hangs limply from Marie's tapered fingers. "But maybe I should wait until your husband comes home. He's the zucchini fan."

"Actually," Marie says, "he's not. It would upset him to handle such a perfect phallic specimen."

Already flushed from the exertion of pulling out dandelions and crab grass, the neighbor's face glows red as a beet, the one vegetable she doesn't grow in her showy garden patch. "Yes, well… how is Thomas?"

"We have a new pet."

"That's great!" The neighbor exclaims. "Did you finally get him a puppy? I know he's been wanting one for ages. Boys do better when they have pets."

"Do better?" Marie says. "In what way?"

"You know, it teaches them responsibility. Unconditional love. That sort of thing. And it's something to cuddle up with at night."

"There won't be any cuddling." Marie cringes at the thought of her petite arachnid tucked inside the increasingly robust arms of her budding son. "It's cold-blooded."

"You got him a lizard?"

Marie shakes her head.

"A fish tank?"

If Marie were a house spider, she would shoot sticky silk at her neighbor and scuttle back inside the house.

"Sounds like we're playing a game of twenty questions," says the neighbor.

"I'm not playing anything," Marie says.

The sun has dropped low on the horizon, reflecting off the bowls of beer her neighbor puts out to drown slugs. Synchronized sprinklers go off across the parkway, wetting decayed day lilies. On the sidewalk, families walk by with their warm-blooded pets on leashes, carrying colorful baggies filled with excrement.

"It doesn't have to be a dog or a cat," the neighbor says. "Joshua has an ant farm and he loves it."

Marie stares at the neighbor's freckled face, at her dimpled chin, at the dirt and sweat in her cavernous pores, and at the zucchini. She realizes that although she has been providing nutrition to her house spider, she has not provided variety, which is the spice of life.

"We got Thomas an ant farm," Marie says.

"Wow, really?" the neighbor says. "That's a coincidence."

"Yes, it is," Marie agrees. "But, you see, he doesn't have enough ants. Can I have some of Joshua's? Not his favorite ants, just the ones that don't have names."

AFTER DINNER, MARIE serves gluten-free zucchini bread for dessert. She has made enough to give to her neighbor as a thank you gift for what is now crawling inside a jar on her nightstand. Air holes punched in the top and a linden leaf tucked inside for munching.

It's storming outside, so Frisbee is not an option, and everyone heads to the family room. For two hours, they play board games. They charge each other rent, send each other to jail, and sink each other's battleships. Thomas goes bankrupt as Marie fishes a pewter thimble from under Madeline's tongue. Then the electricity goes out. They soldier on by candlelight, grinding their teeth hard on potato chips, counting pastel money under the table, and rolling dice so forcefully they bounce like bullets, glinting snake eyes in the candle flames. Thomas looks longingly at the Xbox while Marie thinks obsessively about the jar.

After her husband takes the children upstairs to bed, Marie puts away the games, hoovers up the crumbs, and blows out the candles. She hums to herself in the dark house as flashes of lightening illuminate the decor: a convincing but fake Tiffany lamp, velour throw-pillows, a framed Modigliani print, a black walnut coatrack. She hums because everything seems possible tonight, with the smell of electrical charges and beeswax in the air. She hums because she has the house to herself, because something impossible and wonderful has happened to her, and no one else needs to know about it or understand it to make it better.

Marie examines the web, galvanized by electricity, glowing with creative sparks thrown by two species connected through one word. But there is something else suspended in the illuminated silk, a new creation: a small white pouch. Marie cranes her neck. It is indeed an egg sac, filled with hundreds of possibilities and tucked safely behind the husks of finales. It's the reason the house spider's been so hungry, the reason she hasn't written another word besides the one that now defines them both. It isn't writer's block, it's impending motherhood. Marie wants to tell her, *I understand completely.* Instead, she sprints upstairs for the jar.

On the second floor, Madeline is asleep in her crib, tucked under her favorite blanket, covered with Beatrix Potter's rabbits. The bathroom is dark and empty, and when Marie slips into her room, so is her bed. Her husband's lumbering tread usually alerts her to his location in the house, but he has disappeared. Marie grows still, her feet slow, and she creeps silently back into the hallway.

Thomas' bedroom is at the far end of the hall. A light shines beneath the door. Perhaps her husband has put a battery in Thomas' G.I. Joe nightlight. Perhaps he is reading the end of *Charlotte's Web* to Thomas. Perhaps they are both snug inside a fort made from the freshly washed bedding that Marie put on this morning, t-rex and stegosaurus and pterodactyls smelling of lemon and lavender. Marie listens to the lowered voices, although they're hard to distinguish from the rain pattering on the shingled roof. She moves closer, sliding her sock feet over the floor, noiseless because she knows which boards creak, and which hold their breath. Marie presses her ear to the door and hears her husband's voice first.

"No one will miss her," he says.

"I don't want to get in trouble," Thomas whispers.

"You won't. No one will find out." Her husband's tone is confident. He must sound like this when he says the plaintiff is responsible for their own misfortunes, their burns and broken bones and ungainly, baleful tumors.

"How do you know?" Thomas says.

"Because it's our secret. I won't say anything. Will you say anything?"

There is a pause. Marie imagines Thomas shaking his head vigorously, earning his father's approval. Maybe a hug or a squeeze of the shoulders. Or maybe a handshake, the signifier of manhood, a transition to decision-making and picking the side most likely to win.

When she catches Thomas' voice again, it is muffled, as if pressed into a pillow. Is he sobbing? "She'll figure it out. I think she already knows."

Marie's toes are numb on the wooden floor, so numb they feel like the trapped ants have escaped and are crawling all over them.

"No, she doesn't."

"You'll have to be careful," Thomas says.

"I'm always careful."

There is a rustle of sheets and Marie pictures Thomas moving closer to her husband, tucking his head under his father's chin and leaning into his girth, into his Farnese Hercules in wrinkled khakis.

"Will it hurt?" Thomas asks.

"She won't feel a thing," he says. "I promise."

IN THE FOYER, propped inside a sleeping bag that reeks of wood smoke and bug spray, Marie wakes from a dream. She tilts her head back and looks up at the ceiling. The web is gone.

In the kitchen, her son and husband are clattering bowls and plates, laughing and singing while making their Saturday-morning special: gluten-free waffles with peanut butter. Madeline chatters nonsense words from her highchair.

Marie wonders if her children witnessed her husband removing the spider's web. It probably took no more than fifteen seconds to destroy the house spider, her home, and her egg sac. Sometimes spiders will attach their egg sacs to their spinnerets and flee to safety. Marie tries to suppress this hope as she climbs out of the warm bag and inspects the ceiling. She doesn't see the spider or the egg sac.

She worries that the spider, nearly domesticated, must have thought it was her at first, coming with more treats, as opposed to her husband starring in the most brutal horror film of all, a nature documentary. The house spider had become bolder with Marie lately, nearly snatching the prey from her fingertips, and not bothering to spin it up in silk before tucking in. Occasionally, Marie joined the spider. Her mouth salivates at the sweetness of her own blood.

The broom, the implement of demolition, rests in the corner. Marie picks it up, turns it over, and examines the silken shambles that trail across the bristles, the debris from the web strewn over the surface like a tornado hit: desiccated flies and moths, tacky pieces of dust, the egg sac now a pulpy brown, busted open. When something moves between the bristles, Marie's heart catches.

"You're up!" Her husband stands in the doorway wearing boxers and a T-shirt from a marathon he ran twenty years ago. He holds out a glass of orange juice. Thomas trails behind him, Brutus in penguin pajamas.

"I had to get rid of it," he says. "There would have been thousands of those creepy little things. We could have had an infestation."

"Why didn't you put her outside?" Marie asks Thomas.

Her husband raises his jowly head and sniffs the air. "I think the waffles are burning." He retreats to the kitchen.

Marie pulls apart the bristles, moving aside sticky bits of web, and reaches gently in between.

"What are you doing?" Thomas lingers in the doorway.

"Your father didn't quite kill her." Marie places the twisted body of the house spider in her palm, only two of the eight legs are left, and they rotate confusedly, crookedly in the air. "Look."

"She isn't dead?" Thomas takes a few tentative steps in the direction of his mother.

"She probably wishes she was." Marie waves her other hand in front of the house spider, who doesn't react, who couldn't if she wanted to.

"Can we fix her?"

"No," Marie says. "The only merciful thing to do now is to kill her. Can you do that?"

Thomas shakes his head.

"It's important to learn how to kill things," Marie says. "If you come over here, I can show you. I'm good at it."

"The waffles are ready," her husband calls from the kitchen, but Thomas doesn't move.

"Dad said the spider would have eaten her babies. He said spiders do that. Eat their babies."

Marie does not want to give into hysterics, but the thing that used to be her house spider is flexing its mangled body in her hand, and the pain is right there, right on her skin, as real and thick as her own blood. She feels it so strongly that it takes her breath away, and for a moment she can't bear it, the nearly dead but not dead thing, the wanting to be dead and not, all at the same time. That kind of pain. But then it comes to her, bubbling up from beneath, and she knows what must be done.

"It's a common misconception," Marie says, "that spiders eat their young. While spiders have cannibalistic tendencies, which means they sometimes eat each other, with their children, it's more often the reverse."

Thomas stares at the misshapen spider stirring slowly, inevitably in the palm of his mother's hand.

"After an egg sac hatches," Marie continues, "the baby spiders sometimes eat their mother. She's very nutritious, and even willing, though it can take a week for them to finish eating her."

She picks up the house spider and holds it out to Thomas.

"In cases of matriphagy, the young spiders do better than those who do not eat their mothers. The babies grow large and stout. They develop stronger immune systems."

Her husband emerges from the kitchen, a stack of waffles piled on a plate, and Thomas moves closer to Marie, mesmerized by the broken thing, by what it offers.

"They have higher self-esteem," Marie says. "They get into good colleges and find jobs that have health benefits and paid vacation."

Thomas stops directly in front of his mother. His eyes meet hers. He is no longer wary, no longer even curious, but resolved and ready.

"Open your mouth," she says.

The Plague Victim

Samuel M. Moss

———◆———

I WENT OUT for a walk today. The days have begun to warm noticeably but I have traveled so far north that a sort of innate cold persists
through the earth and the air. I passed some peasants on the way.
Conversation with them is, of course, impossible. I glance at them
and they avoid my gaze, hating me. There is no way I could see them
as people anymore, only as playthings, as pawns in this action. How
could I not? They are interchangeable. Every time I set eyes on them
I am amazed. It seems that no matter what village I am in, nor which
settlement I pass through, the same handful of bland bodies appear,
clothed in the same stinking sweat-soaked cloaks. Even the prisoners
I saw earlier, scarred by years of labor and confinement, retained that
beaten down look of the peasant's upbringing. And this is what I
would like to free them from.

I ended up at the drinking house.

The only topic of conversation there was the plague. The fear here has grown deep and I heard rumors pass around that are totally new to me.

Some men said it was now moving at great speed, passing through the prison camps to the east like a mad beast in toward the settlements. If it were to reach the settlements then it would be mere months before it penetrated the heart of the Empire itself.

One man, Artyem Gulevich of Politsovo, related to us the symptoms of the plague, which he claimed to have heard from a traveling merchant he met in Skirlinsk. This man—the merchant—claimed to have seen the plague's effects firsthand. Though Gulevich did not hear its name the Merchent said that this village was like any other: quiet, hardworking people grinding through the motions of existence, paying their part tax, praying to god and not drinking any more than they should. The plague swept in silently just as winter was breaking. There was no warning, no time to quarantine or set up herb fires to ward it off.

At first all of the children of the village fell silent. Many continued to go about their daily duties but did so in complete silence. Others kept to bed all day staring at the wall and not eating. The adults of the town whipped and yelled to get the children to speak but it was to no avail. One by one the children retreated to their beds or simply lay down in the fields or the streets: silent, staring, and unresponsive.

When more beatings failed to raise them they called in a doctor from a nearby settlement. The man looked at one child, measured the blood, the urine, the intake of breath, and prescribed a tea made from the local bark they call *kutysh* or horse-bane. After three days this doctor left the town, promising to return, but he did not and the villagers were unable to find him.

Some few days after the children of the town fell silent the livestock began to show a peculiar aberration of the skin. These were white spots that grew rapidly then remained a steady size, the width of a man's palm and mottled pink. The swine then developed these lesions as well. They were driven into a frenzy by the pain. Two men were trampled to death while trying to prevent some cattle from escaping their pens. The animals ran off into the Taiga and were lost to the wilderness. Perhaps all the better for them.

Once the livestock had fled the adults of the town fell ill. The first was an itinerant drunk who slept in the church barn. The man was well known to the people, and while his presence was rarely appreciated he was considered harmless, even given small tasks to complete in exchange for liquor. He rarely drank to the point of delirium and even when he did it was generally into a jovial state. In the general chaos following the fleeing of the livestock the man sank into a violent silence. He roamed about the town pulling over stacks of crates, banging on the windows of homes, running madly from door to door. All told he destroyed some five hundred kopecks worth of property. When arrested by the villagers the man said nothing and fought against them.

The villagers, so distraught over the silence of their children and the trouble with the livestock, never considered all these phenomena to be connected and attributed this man's madness to drink alone. The drunk was removed from town and shown off with blows.

Not long after this drunk fell ill the other adults in the town followed. There was no pattern to the illness. A whole house would fall ill while its neighbors showed no signs. The progression was uniformly ruthless. A man would go from planting rye in the morning to exhausted in the space of a few hours. Some set of symptoms would confine him to his bed, whether it was painful boils, aching bones, bleeding from the mouth and eyes, or any of a thousand other horrors and from there he would be brought to the point of immobility. Thus the village was swiftly rendered silent. Within a week the whole village was engulfed by the plague, fully taken up by it. Those few who could still walk left the village but the days were still short then and they surely perished on their way. From the first signs it was less than a month until five hundred souls had suffered utter destruction.

Gulevich finished relating the tale of the plague and took a drink. The others in the drinking house had sunk into a pensive mood.

One man—who had been listening with a look of deep concentration—spoke first. He pointed out that the plague, while it struck individuals, seemed more precisely to strike the village as a whole. That is, while the individual members of the village were infected, it struck with such rapidity and thoroughness, touching one part of the village, then *a far distant part,* as if it were attempting to kill the village as a single organism. Some nodded at this, others mumbled, skeptical.

"And what sins had the village committed in order to face these punishments?" a Circassian asked.

"Lechery surely!" cried out a man with a ruddy face.

"They had not been paying their tithes," offered Stemyovich, that red haired local Priest. "These sorts of plagues only strike when one has not been paying tithes. If it were only one or two who passed on their duty perhaps they would have survived but that it was the whole village that suffered? Surely they had lost the practice of tithing. One perfidious villager spoke softly to another behind the backs of the others, saying *Brother brother, why pay this money to the church? Spend it instead on this good meat that I have!* and thus each one convinced the other and so on until the whole village had ceased to pay. When it came out that each had ceased to pay they all felt emboldened and cursed god and so were struck down in this way for their insolence!"

The men all assented to this analysis, grunting and nodding.

By this point they had all become drunk and a piece of salt pork was pulled out and handed around. After some time had passed, where the only sound was the crackling of the stove, one man spoke up.

"And what are the chances that the plague will spread here? Skirlinsk is not far from here, only a two day's journey. If the merchant had been there he must not have had far to travel through."

"We don't know how the plague is spread. Surely the bad air of that place will not travel this far," the ruddy faced man said.

"Yes, but certainly if one of their villagers were to wander over here, perhaps to find food or cry for help, to find a doctor or priest, he would bring the sickness with him. It could spread here in no time at all."

One man—his face patched with beard, a hand raised with a finger crooked up toward the sky—stood slowly.

"And how are we to know that you are not a part of that hateful village?"

He was pointing at Gulevich, the storyteller, and soon the rest of the men in the drinking house turned to face him.

Gulevich's eyes grew wide for just a moment, then he became very calm.

"I am not from that village." His speech was slow and measured. "As I explained I simply passed through Skirlinsk. In that village these events were related to me by a man who heard them from a man who himself had passed through the afflicted village."

"Liar!" The man with the patchy beard turned to the others. "He is from that village that he will not name, he has come here to spread the plague, to pull us down with him. It is he who has seen the plague first hand, for how else could he have related the symptoms and progression in such detail?"

The accused man was speaking but the din of the other's voices blotted out his words.

I stood aside.

One man pulled the storyteller up from the bench on which he sat. Gulevich stood for a moment then sagged back down, knocking a mug and plate onto the floor. The clatter made the crowd cry louder, the unexpected action driving them into a deeper rage.

The crowd pulled him outside. Men took turns holding him, berating him to his face. There was no longer any question as to whether he was from the plague stricken village or not, whether he had seen the plague, or heard about it, or simply made it all up as a good story to pass the time.

I followed the crowd at a distance. As it passed through the village men would break off and explain the situation to passersby. These were then pulled into the mob. Some curious farmer carrying a bucket was converted into a hollering madman in the space of fifteen seconds.

They carried the storyteller a good distance away from the drinking house to outside the bounds of the village and there released him. He seemed unable to carry himself fully, his body slumped and sagged.

The crowd propelled him forward with kicks and blows. One man carried a spade and struck Gulevich with it once to great effect. This dance continued for some distance—perhaps a half verst—at which point the crowd was safely away from any in the village who might judge this action.

Even in my time in the army I had never seen a situation similar to this. True, I had seen men kill and be killed, though only a few times. Each time shook me but I grew accustomed to it, had accepted it as an inevitability in war and times of great desperation.

The villagers stood for a moment, a collective in breath. They all grew quiet, as if some outside force, some bereft spirit, was silently flowing into them. The air too grew terribly still, the whole stretch of farmland around us thrumming with a sound beyond sound. This man, the outsider, was then obscured for a moment from my view by the surrounding bodies. Though my curiosity was strong I dared not move closer.

They approached then. For a brief moment the crowd split through the middle and I caught a last glimpse of him. That moment-image has remained with great clarity: he was bloodied already, blood about his crown and flowing down his body and he had a fear about him that I had never seen in a man before. It was the look of a trapped animal, a prey animal, caught after a long chase and resigned to its station. Would I say that he was being sacrificed? A more charitable person might, but no, he had simply surrendered. This man, who by all possible accounts was absolutely innocent, who had done nothing but relate a story to the people of this village, had now been pinned with the disease itself, the fear of this village sublimated into his soul and was being sacrificed to some strange god of the Taiga for their repentance.

They fell on him silently, with a silence otherworldly and impossible, and the man himself—who had once held the name Artyem Gulevich but who now had no name—was silent too. No screams from the sacrifice, no shouts of anger or exertion. He shrank into them and I could only see vague movement, a rustling of cloth and flesh and then the crowd fell inwards as if some object there which had been supporting them suddenly gave way.

The crowd parted all too quickly. Surely it took longer than a few meagre seconds to render a man into a corpse? And yet when they parted there was no corpse. All that remained of the cursed man was a patch of disturbed earth, darkened slightly as if nothing more than a chamberpot had been poured there. The attackers themselves stepped away from the scene looking dazed, like men just awoken from a dream. Some wiped their hands—bloody, but only slightly—on the cloth of their tunics, or on some rushes nearby. Some others wiped the area around their mouths with their sleeves.

No one spoke.

Looking around me I found I had been joined by a handful of other villagers watching as I was. We stood in silence and it was very peaceful and as I looked at the others they all stood with looks of resignation or perhaps complacency. One lad walked up, glanced at the distant spot of blood on the earth and asked what had happened.

An old man turned to him and said quietly,

"They just dispatched a man who carried the plague."

The boy sneered and spat toward the cursed spot and turned back to the village.

And so this thing that started with a fevered rush, a hot panic into the countryside, dissipated like a summer stream run dry. The villagers dispersed slowly, saying nothing to each other, truly as if nothing had happened. Some seemed all of a sudden very tired and returned to the village with their eyes half closed.

I cannot explain to you my own feeling, the shock at witnessing this event, but even more so the distinct feeling of its impossibility, that is: *that it did not happen and could not have happened.* That those villagers fell back to reveal *so little*, that it was simply impossible for this man to, at one moment, have been standing directly before me, and in the next to have evaporated into this pile of rushing anger. And as these villagers walked away they seemed so far from how I would imagine a group who had just torn a man limb from limb or rather, *torn a body from the very world itself.*

I left the village this evening on foot to travel further east. On the road a cart came up behind me loaded with some goats. The driver offered to take me as far as the fork from which I could easily make my way to Skirlinsk. We spoke for a short while about forgettable things, fell into silence for some time, then he said,

"Did you witness the dispatch of the man with the plague today?"

Though the light was at our backs and fading, I thought I noticed the hint of a smile on his face.

I nodded and replied that I had.

He seemed disappointed at this and said nothing further. He was like me then, I thought, a dissenter from the crowd.

The fury of the events of the day released from me and I turned to him.

"And what if they were wrong? What if he did not carry plague with him? What if an innocent man has been murdered today?"

He scoffed at this, looked at me for some time in the half-light then assumed the demeanor of a teacher explaining an elementary fact to a lagging student,

"All the same, with the plague or without, we would have had to dispatch him. Surely you understand?"

I nodded at this. I had to assent. How could I not?

Thus I have discovered that I am eternally on the edge of death here and not only at the hands of nature, who would dispatch me at a moment with its storms or its wild beasts, and not at the will of law, which might force upon me its might, but of some other entity altogether, some other thing which lives in the hearts of men and which has lived there forever and for whom we have no name but of whose presence we are ever aware, if only in the space of our dreams. And so I have stepped into its lair and live now by its grace—or its ignorance—simply living in the shadow it casts. And perhaps at any moment I may slip by accident into the light and into its gaze and—like this poor traveler who meant no harm—fall prey to its unearthly urges.

I disembarked from his cart at the fork. I trod off into the evening and the mud of the lefthand path and turned to see the driver one last time as he made his way down the right. He waved at me as I went, a smudge of some dark material just visible on his palm. Perhaps this was blood from the plague bearer, perhaps blood from a goat he had slaughtered or perhaps just a bit of mud he had forgotten to wipe off in his haste.

Sometimes We're Cruel

J.A.W. McCarthy

———— ◆ ————

FOR MOST, THE story is secondhand: a classmate's cousin who didn't come home after school one day; a great-grandmother's sister who vanished while out in the fields; a family friend's husband who disappeared while fishing, presumed overboard and drowned. There have even been TV shows about it—an American one, a French one, an American remake of the French one—but they always get it wrong. The people who come back here days or months or years after they've vanished don't stay. They don't try to reintegrate into their old lives, refugees from another time who are just as bewildered by their presence as those they left behind. The ones who come back avoid, and they take, and sometimes they're cruel. And then, just as suddenly as before, they disappear again, like the man who was supposed to be my father.

THERE HASN'T BEEN one in a long time. Christine notes this as she steals a french fry from my plate.

"I know," I agree. "Makes me nervous, like there's going to be one soon, any minute now."

Christine talks through a big bite of grilled cheese from her own plate. "You afraid you're next?"

"Aren't you?"

She shrugs. "You can't live like that, Erika, always looking over your shoulder. Besides, didn't it happen to your mom's old boyfriend? I've never heard of it happening twice in the same family."

"He wasn't family."

I'm about to launch into my usual tirade about how my mother is obsessed with a man who wasn't "taken" as she claimed but left her because he couldn't stand to be around her anymore, when I see Marisa Kim getting out of a pristine white Prius at the far end of the diner parking lot. I know it's her before she even turns around; no one else in town has platinum blonde hair with pink tips and black roots that spider over the top of her head. She's wearing a leather jacket with silver hardware that glints and sparks in the afternoon sun like fireflies alighting all over her torso. I watch as another woman—her mother, I think—gets out of the driver's side, and they link arms when they meet behind the car. They stop to share a giggle, something I've never done with my own mother. Marisa's lightly tan like she got the perfect amount of sunshine between classes at Stanford, and she stands up nice and straight, boobs out and butt high like high heels are supposed to make you do. When I was little I used to think that doves braided her hair every morning and fairies polished her teeth while she slept. My mother said it was just good breeding, something I certainly hadn't gotten from my actual father's side of the family.

"Is that Marisa Kim? What's she doing back in this shithole?"

"Shush!" I admonish Christine, slumping down in the booth once I catch sight of Marisa pulling open the diner's heavy door.

"Seriously? You're still—? I swear, I don't know if you want to *be* her or fuck her."

I throw my jacket over my face, but the hostess leads Marisa and her mother to a table on the other side of the restaurant, their backs to us the whole time.

"She's just visiting before her new job starts," I say, pulling the jacket from my face. "Her not-shitty-retail-job, her actual publishing *career*."

"Still stalking her online, I see."

I take the last of Christine's grilled cheese to punish her, toss some crumpled bills onto the table. "I gotta get back to the shop."

"You're still coming over tonight, right?"

I stuff the sandwich in my mouth and shrug on my jacket, which is not leather but old brown canvas scarred with worn spots and frayed edges. "Of course. How else am I going to get away from my mother?"

CHRISTINE FALLS ASLEEP halfway through the movie like she always does. She stirs a little, kicking her feet out stiff like a stretching cat as I slide out from under her legs. The stairs of the old farmhouse don't creak any less when I move slowly, but I'm careful anyway as I go up, peering down at Christine on the couch the whole time, the pulsing glow of the TV lighting up her still, pallid face. She makes a little *huff* sound, an assurance that she's dreaming, that she doesn't hear me.

Upstairs, the door at the far end of the hall is open just enough to stick my head in. I do this sometimes, while Christine is asleep, after I use the bathroom. Even though she says her father can't hear or see anything, I'm still careful to avoid the floorboards that whine, and I slip through the crack in the door rather than bother the hinges. Tonight his eyes are closed, but I'm still tempted to pull the quilt all the way up over his face. Next to his bed is a little hospital monitor with rows of glowing dashes where numbers should be, and next to that an IV stand suspending clear liquid in a plastic bag coated in sticky dust. Christine's father has been like this as long as I've known her, this withered old man tucked away upstairs, always sick and always silent and blind even when his cloudy eyes suddenly fly open as if he hears me running my hands over his books and spritzing on his wife's perfume. When her mother was still alive she wouldn't let me follow Christine in here. I would sit out in the hallway and listen to the low murmur of her voice as she read to him. Sometimes she would sing, and I would sing along as quietly as I could so Mrs. Prentice wouldn't know that I was right outside the door. Christine said her mother believed that the sound of their voices kept her father alive, that it took more than just the machines. We still never talk about the fact that her father isn't actually hooked up to anything.

Mrs. Prentice's bed sits at the far end of the room, a large window and twin nightstands between the two single beds like in a 1950s sitcom. Christine stripped the bed after her mother died, but I don't know why she made it up again—it's not like any guest would want to stay in this room with her comatose father just a few feet away. Christine wants me to move in here with her since she can't move to the city with me. She doesn't know that I still intend to move as far away as I can, with or without her.

Before I leave the room, I try the closet door. The antique brass knob rattles in my grip like it might finally fall off this time, but it hangs on, the door locked as always. So I move on to the big oak dresser and admire all of the little things on its polished surface: a tarnished pocket watch with ornate engraving (*T.S. Love you more. J.L.*), a tortoise shell brush with yellowed bristles, various gold-plated compacts with bits of pink and tan and silvery dust winking like glitter in the light cast by the hospital monitor. I slip on a gold necklace dotted with tiny rubies and admire my reflection in the dresser's mirror. I hold pair after pair of gaudy, dangly earrings up to my ears, enjoying the way the stones throw light across the peeling wallpaper. I squeeze the atomizer balloon on a pink crystal perfume decanter then apologize to Christine's father as the overwhelming scent of magnolias fills the room. Sometimes I feel like I've stepped back in time when I'm in this house, like if I look out the window I'll see endless fields of corn and a 1940s farm truck sitting in the driveway. I'm afraid that if I move in with Christine I'll be stuck here forever, sunk deep into this town like the roots her family made generations ago.

As I'm turning towards the door, my eyes catch on a delicate gold ring jumbled among the other jewelry on the dresser. It's shaped like a branch with a couple of silver leaves on the front. I'm surprised I haven't noticed it before. I'm surprised it fits perfectly on my finger.

While I'm admiring the ring on my hand, Christine's father makes a disapproving little hiss, so I stand very still and wait, but his eyes never open. I keep my gaze on him anyway as I slip back out into the hallway.

When I get home my mother is five beers in. I can tell because she has one in her hand and two empty on the table; she always makes sure to put the first two bottles in the recycling bin as if that somehow tricks me into thinking she's had less.

"I was at Christine's," I say as she starts to open her mouth.

Shaking her head, she takes a big sloppy slug from the bottle in her hand. "Again, huh? You live under my roof, you eat my food, but you can't spend one evening with me?"

I take my jacket off and toss it over the back of the couch next to my mother. I know she will take the opportunity to complain that it smells like cigarettes, that Christine's house smells like a dirty ashtray because the Prentices are dirty trash, but I don't care. I can't let myself care tonight.

"Just once, Erika, I'd like you to sit down to dinner with me. Just one evening. You could even make dinner, do something nice for your old mom."

"I'm gonna go to bed," I tell her, heading towards the hall.

"Keep staying out late like this and you're gonna be next."

It's a mistake—I can't tonight, I promised myself I wouldn't—but I turn away from the hall and back to my mother staring at me from the couch, both her legs splayed across the top of the coffee table so that one wagging foot is dangerously close to knocking over the two beer bottles there. When I speak next, I focus on the shiny dribble of beer snaking over her bottom lip and down her chin.

"Maybe it would be a good thing," I say slowly, deliberately so her pickled brain can absorb every word. "Maybe wherever those people go is better than where I am now."

My mother's face turns hard and she slams her beer down on the coffee table, making the two empties drop and roll like a fire safety lesson. "Don't you say that! You think my Eric's in a better place now?

He was supposed to be here with me and you were supposed to be his. He would've stayed here with us because this is better. *This* place is better!"

"He left, Mom. He left just like my father left. They're scum, whatever, they abandoned you and moved on."

"He didn't abandon me! Someone took him! I know because when he came back—" She stops short here as if she might start to cry, and I regret more than ever not ignoring her and continuing down the hall to my room. "—when he came back, he wasn't right. What they did to him . . . they changed him. They made him act like that."

The thing is, I believe her. There were times—after I had to clean her vomit from the rug, or when I had to beg the bartender not to press charges, or when I got the call to pick her up from the side of the road at three in the morning—when I would yell that her precious Eric left on his own because he couldn't stand to be around her just like my father couldn't. She would burst into tears and fold in on herself like an old rag, but I wouldn't feel bad until I was rolling her into bed. That's when I would linger for a moment and I would look at my mother lying there like that with her long blonde lashes grazing her cheeks and the sun-worn freckles dusting her nose, and I would see myself in her features, just like I could so easily see my future right on her face.

I was five when Eric came back, two years after my father left and right before my mother's drinking got really bad. I remember because that was the night my mother threw the toaster at the wall then told me that the bad people made the resulting hole in the plaster when they were dragging Eric away again. She said it was the bad people's voices I heard telling her she was worthless and ugly and no one would ever love her again. "The way you take and you humiliate—you didn't think that would come back on you? I regret ever being with you, you spiteful bitch!" I heard as I pressed my ear to my bedroom door that night. There were doors slamming and my mother crying "Eric, please" over and over again until it sounded like she was calling for me. I snuck out of my room and slipped into the living room just as the toaster was hitting the wall, just as the man with the shaggy dark hair was storming out the front door with a six-pack in one hand and a fistful of my mother's jewelry in the other.

"They did something terrible to him, made him do that," my mother reminds me, swinging both feet off the coffee table.

She's wobbly as she stands, stumbling over the magazines and unopened mail that she accidentally swept onto the floor. When I approach her and reach out to steady her, she grabs my left hand and swings it out then back towards her face, squinting in the flickering light from the TV.

"What? What is this?"

"Let's get you to bed, Mom," I say, wrestling my hand from hers.

"No, this—" She catches my hand again and holds it so close to her face that her glassy eyes cross. "Erika, where did you get—"

Under my mother's thumb the knobby details of the ring I took from Christine's house rub uncomfortably between my fingers, pinching the skin there and making me cry out. I get my hand away again, but she keeps grabbing at me, tugging on my sleeve as I struggle to drag us both down the hall. "Where did you—" she starts up again once we reach her bedroom, but she vomits down the front of her bathrobe before she can finish.

I USED TO think Christine's father is the way he is because he was almost one of the taken, perhaps injured in the struggle, but she said he's like that because he fell off the roof shortly after she was born. My mother, even when sober, says he's that way because Mrs. Prentice abused her husband, liked to take shiny things and didn't know how to care for them. They went to high school together and she still brings up how nobody liked Christine's mother because she was always saying weird shit like she was spying on other people's conversations. Once, during senior year, my mother caught her stealing out of a friend's locker, so she pulled her pants down in front of everyone in the hall. I thought that was cruel at first, but I think I would do the same thing if I caught someone stealing from Christine.

Christine wishes she had a firsthand story. She wishes her mother had been one of the taken instead of tucking herself into bed with a plastic bag over her head, leaving her only daughter with a comatose father and a life insurance policy that won't pay out. That's why when Marisa Kim vanishes right after coming into my work, I wish Christine was there too so she'd finally have a firsthand story of her own.

MARISA KIM MAKES the local news: a picture of her at her Stanford graduation, sandwiched between her beaming parents; smiling self-consciously as she holds up her collection of essays at a book signing in San Francisco; surrounded by her gorgeous, shiny-haired friends at a restaurant. There was a time when I hated Marisa, or tried to. Once in fifth grade I snapped that I didn't need her charity when she offered to pay for me to attend the museum field trip after she over-heard me telling Christine my mother hadn't given me money. She backed off after that, but I knew the new colored pencils in my desk were from her, and I knew when I got bullied it was Marisa who came to my defense and made the mean girls back down. I nodded along when Christine said she was a rich show-off, though my grow-ing admiration was obvious. Marisa Kim becoming one of the taken feels worse than any firsthand story I could have, especially knowing that when she comes back she will be just like all the others.

This time I'm the one who falls asleep in front of the TV. Last thing I remember is watching Mr. Kim tearfully offer a $20,000 reward for information leading to the safe return of his daughter. I imagine myself taking a walk on a misty evening and hearing Marisa calling for help as she bangs on the cloudy basement window of a decrepit little house choked by weeds. I break the glass and get her out and we run to the police. The homeowner is arrested and I am lauded as a hero for rescuing Marisa and finding the man who has been kidnap-ping people all of these years. I use the Kims' reward money to move to San Francisco or Los Angeles. I write a bestselling book. I give a few interviews: talk shows, a magazine profile, a short college lecture tour. I mainly like to stay out of the spotlight.

Christine isn't next to me on the couch when I wake up. I watch a couple of soothing minutes of people using a small wand to shave the peach fuzz from their faces and arms, then head upstairs. The bathroom door and Christine's bedroom door are open, but her father's at the end of the hall is closed all the way, a dampened light leaking out from underneath, turning the floorboards there a sickly yellow that dissipates gradually like a water stain. I approach as closely as I can, careful to avoid the parts of the hall that squeak and whine. I have to stop six feet back, but I can still hear the low rounded sound of Christine's voice softly reading to her father through the door.

I didn't know she still does this, even after her mother died. We used to laugh about it; she once told me that she sometimes read the disclaimers on coupons to him when her mother wasn't in the room. Now I recognize *Watership Down*; she even reads the dialogue in different voices, like a radio play. I mouth the words along with her, think about the ring I took the other night, all the necklaces and earrings and watches before that, and the pocketknife that I swiped at age eight, the very first thing I ever took from this house.

"It's late," Christine says when she emerges from her father's room. She's careful to close the door right behind her so that I only see a sliver of the open window, the tea-stain colored curtain fluttering in the night breeze.

"I'm gonna head home," I say.

"No, I mean it's really late, so you should stay here." She parses the look I give her, the way my eyes move to the closed door just over her shoulder as if she knows I can see right through to her mother's empty bed, and she says, "No, not—I have a surprise for you."

The surprise is the room between hers and the bathroom, what used to be her mother's sewing room. Now instead of bolts of ditzy print fabric and a lopsided dressmaker's form that scared me as a child, there are new things, things that are supposed to be for me: a double bed fitted with sheets and a comforter in shades of my favorite green, a small bare desk under the window, and a chair serving as a nightstand already topped with books and a box of tissues. Christine shows me all of this with a great flourish, her eyes and teeth catching light from the overhead fixture as she points out how even the closet is completely empty.

"I got it ready so you can move in—before you go, I mean," she says a bit shyly, and I know she is picturing the city as a much darker place than we imagined as kids. "I just thought . . . I know you don't want to stay with your mom anymore. And if you stay here you can save up money just the same, maybe even faster because I won't ask you for anything. I don't need anything."

Though I can't imagine actually living in this stuck-in-time house where her mother died and her comatose father stares at the ceiling just a few yards away, I accept Christine's offer for tonight. The real reason I agree to stay is because I want my mother to think I've been taken. I want to hide here with Christine, then come back to my mother in a month and say all of the things I've been wanting to say to her before I take the cash from the shoebox in her closet and leave this town for good.

I WAKE UP abruptly in the middle of the night. As my eyes adjust to the darkness, they catch a spark of silver winking in the closet across from the bed. Then there are more little sparks lighting up the indiscernible hollow, swaying ever so slightly from the breeze coming in through the window. Once my eyes adjust, I get up and go to the closet and see that it is not empty like Christine said. Tentatively, my fingers reach inside and feel leather.

I imagine myself walking through a neighborhood like my own, hearing Marisa banging on the basement window of the little house from my dream. The zipper-pulls on her sleeves clink against the glass.

I listen at the bedroom door before stepping out into the hallway. Every door is closed—Christine's, her father's, the bathroom—making the darkness seem as thick and suffocating as animal fur. I feel my way along the wall until I come to Mr. Prentice's room. I try his door but find it locked.

In the morning the leather jacket is gone. At breakfast, when I mention it to Christine, she says, "God, Erika, now you're dreaming about Marisa?" Then she forces a little laugh, keeps her eyes on her toast. "So . . . did you finally get to be her?"

THE SHERIFF COMES into the shop the next afternoon to ask questions about Marisa. He asks when she came in and I tell him, but I don't tell him about how embarrassed I was for her to see me still working at the same retail job I've had since high school. He asks if she bought anything, so I tell him about the candle that was supposed to be a gift for her editor, but I don't tell him about how long she dug around in her purse before finally coming up with a crumpled twenty and how that made me like her even more. I do tell him about her coral blouse and leather jacket because on TV the cops always ask what the missing person was last wearing. I also tell him about how she suggested we catch up over a drink before she leaves town next week, and I realize I sound like a giddy teenager with a crush. Later, when I meet up with Christine for dinner, I don't tell her any of this.

I'M GLAD CHRISTINE'S not here. I think this when Marisa's mother walks into my shop two weeks later.

I know who she is, but I don't let on; I keep busy behind the counter affixing price stickers to a new shipment of perfume oils. Even though she takes a moment to stiffly run her hand over a rack of sun dresses by the front door, I know the gesture is only a technicality, muscle memory of what you're supposed to do when you first walk into a place like this.

"Excuse me. Were you working here on Wednesday the 30th?"

Mrs. Kim is right in front of me, her fingers anxiously working the purse strap over her shoulder. She's reedy and angular, her face made up of all these sharp lines that could be either severe or glamorous depending on the lighting and the lipstick. Today, though, she just looks crumpled like the paper bag weariness of her beige trench coat.

"Yes," I answer. "You're Marisa's mother."

She looks down at the counter between us, nods as her fingers twist and untwist the purse strap against her breast. "So you talked to her? How did she seem? Was she . . . okay?"

"Yeah, she seemed like she was in a good mood. She said she was glad to be back, to see you—her parents." I don't know why I say this. I guess I'm bolstered by the way her face starts to lift as I speak. "She bought a candle," I add, as if that will make her really believe me.

"So she wasn't acting strangely? She didn't seem angry or distraught?"

"No, not at all. We made plans for next week, to catch up."

At this Mrs. Kim looks stricken. I imagine Marisa and myself sitting in one of the peeling vinyl booths at the back of the Oak Tavern down the street, sipping gin and tonics (after she thanks me for pushing her to try something new) while she helps me decide if I should move to San Francisco or Los Angeles. I wonder if Mrs. Kim is having trouble picturing her daughter in this place, if all she can see is Marisa's empty Cole Valley apartment, her cat waiting for her to come home, her friends still saving a seat for her at brunch.

"Do the police have any leads?" I ask once her silence grows hooks.

Mrs. Kim shakes her head slowly, and when she drops her gaze down to the price sticker I've still got in my hand, I can see the tears bullying the edges of her eyes. "The case is closed. They say she's not a missing person anymore. She came back last night, but then she left again."

I want to ask what Marisa did and said, find a way to ask that won't seem so intrusive, won't make her mother burst into tears right in front of me. Really, I already know: the ones who come back avoid, and they take, and sometimes they're cruel. And then, just as suddenly as before, they vanish again.

I'm making my mother dinner tonight: steak with bourbon-glazed carrots and her favorite potatoes, the ones where you scoop out the insides, mix it with a bunch of stuff, then pipe it back into the skins with a fancy pastry tip. It's a goodbye dinner, but my mother doesn't know that yet. Because she won't take it well, I've got the rest of my things packed up in my room. Most of my clothes are already at Christine's house.

The route between the grocery store and my house doesn't take me past Christine's, but I often find myself driving up the old state route when I'm putting off going home. Tonight the dilapidated barn that marks the start of a long stretch of overgrown fields looks like an enormous menacing owl with the moon glowing bright through the two gaping holes in the front and the fractured wood around the edges loose like feathers. I like this part the best, one perfect mile of uninterrupted gold and green before the elevated bones of the new housing development rise up under the shadow of the Prentices' farm house. I wonder what Christine is doing tonight, if she's reading to her father, if I'll still find myself sneaking around and taking things even after I live there. I'm about to turn the car around and head back towards town when I see a woman with pink-tipped platinum blonde hair walking up the Prentices' driveway.

"Marisa!" I yell without thinking, before I've even got the car window rolled down. "Marisa!"

She doesn't stop. She doesn't turn around. Her pace never changes as she continues up the long dirt path to the farmhouse.

At first I drive alongside her, trying to get her to turn and look at me, but she moves with such unrelenting purpose that a hailstorm or my car couldn't stop her. It occurs to me to get out and confront her, but a part of me is afraid to talk to her, afraid to see her face. It's not that I imagine her as a grotesque monster, or fear the ugly things she might say to me. Unlike what my mother believes, I know that when the ones who vanished come back it's the same person, now just unburdened of previous proprieties. The real Eric. The real Marisa.

So I stop my car only a quarter of the way up the long driveway and watch her grow smaller and smaller until I see her disappear into Christine's house.

A light comes on in Christine's father's room; I half expect to see him standing at the window, but there are no figures anywhere in the light or the dark. I look at my phone before I start driving again, though I stop myself from dialing Christine. There's a text from my mother: *When's dinner?*

I park where the dirt turns to gravel and let myself into the house with the key Christine gave me. Even though it's not that late all of the lights are off downstairs except for the bluish glow of the TV. The sound is low enough that I can hear the creaking of floorboards overhead.

I don't know what I expect to find when I get upstairs. Christine and Marisa braiding each other's hair while having a good laugh on her bed? Marisa lying in the center of a pentagram while Christine lights candles and her father chants? The upstairs is dark too, the only light coming from underneath Mr. Prentice's closed door. I know that once I go in there, no matter what I encounter, it will be a secret I'll have to keep.

"Marisa!" I call, a hollow reflex as I push the door open.

Christine is in her bathrobe, standing in front of the open closet. She's hanging up a black garment bag, not at all startled by my presence. On her mother's bed I see a coral blouse, leather jacket and jeans all folded neatly on top of each other. Her father is in his bed, eyes closed and chin pointed to the ceiling.

Christine smiles at me. She steps aside as I approach.

Hanging in the closet are at least twenty identical black garment bags, each one with a white card pinned to the front like a name tag: *D.N.*, *T.S.*, *P.H.*, *E.J.* The tag on the last bag—the one Christine just hung up—says *M.K.*

"Go on," she says as my hand lingers on the bag. "That one's for you."

I can't open it slowly enough. I have to make myself pull the bag out, place it at the foot of the bed (her father doesn't move, doesn't even twitch), tug on the zipper, as if prolonging this moment will somehow deaden the shock of what is inside. Christine's face is encouraging, warm, a promise that doesn't slow my heart despite her efforts.

"It's okay," she assures me.

What's inside is not what I expect, though I'm not sure what I expected beyond a platinum blonde wig or bones even though I know Marisa hasn't been gone long enough to be just bones. Instead, what I see inside the garment bag marked *M.K.* is a pearlescent pinkish-brown substance in no discernible shape or form, this mass that looks like it would leak through or at least settle in the bottom of the bag but doesn't. It's disturbing and beautiful at the same time, and I want to touch it. Sensing my desire, Christine plunges her hand into the pearly pink-brown and we watch as the skin on her wrist then her arm slowly turns the cool almond of Marisa Kim's.

"We've been doing this for generations," Christine says, withdrawing her hand. The color drains from her skin and back into the mass as if being sucked out with a straw. "My dad taught my mom, then my mom taught me. It can be dangerous, though." At this her father's eyes flutter open then close again. "My mother said he couldn't stop—it was like an addiction. I guess he just liked being someone else. She used it mostly for petty stuff, like stealing and revenge, like when she came to your mother as Eric. I don't want to be like that, though. I know you won't be either."

Christine holds the garment bag up while I slowly push one hand then the other into the pearlescent mass inside. It feels like warm steam, not wet or sticky like I thought it would be. I watch my skin change as organically as blood into water, this substance that is the essence of a girl I always envied pulling me into her so gradually and gently that I don't even feel my limbs lift to crawl inside. I don't feel the engine of my heart or my eyelids blinking or the rise and fall of my chest. I don't know how long it takes for Marisa to absorb me—or am I absorbing her?—but I'm not aware of my body again until I feel Christine turning me towards the mirror atop the oak dresser.

I stare at my reflection, amazed at how wrong I was, amazed as the girl in the mirror touches what is now my face, the notch of my collarbone, a bare breast that feels so unexpectedly familiar. I tug on the pink tip of my platinum blonde hair. When I look at Christine again she is holding Marisa's coral blouse out towards me.

"I wasn't too mean to her parents," she says. "I said enough that I think they'll leave you alone for awhile, at least give you some time to get to San Francisco and get settled."

I pull the blouse on over my head and step into the jeans she holds out for me. I wonder if she'd wanted me to put on the leather jacket I found in the closet that night. Was it a test? Was I supposed to be ready then? If I hadn't come here tonight, would she have changed her mind?

"You did this for me?" I ask, watching Christine's reflection behind mine in the mirror as I smooth my hair down over my shoulders.

She nods, and I can see that this is hard for her. "Of course, Erika . . . You should be free."

THE ORCHARD

Sean Logan

————— ◆ —————

THE ODD GENTLEMAN with the square face watched them perform all afternoon. Elton thought of him as a gentleman because he wore a suit and a bow tie and he had a flower in his lapel. He sat on the bus bench with his fingers laced, a tight smile on his puckered pink lips. The features on his face seemed too small and crowded together. Or maybe the head around them was too large. He had a bulky jaw that was wide and low and his neck was very short.

The gentleman put a dollar in their banjo case after every third song and Father tipped his head in thanks. He asked the man once if he had any requests, but he did not. "On no," he said, "whatever you'd care to play would be delightful."

The cloudy gray sky was growing darker and oppressive, hovering low above them. They played "Mule Skinner Blues," their final song for the day. Father thanked the gentleman and the few others who had been observing.

Father knelt to retrieve their earnings. The man stood. "May I approach?" he said.

Elton thought this was a strange request, but Father affirmed that he may as if this was a perfectly normal question to ask.

The man crossed the sidewalk with small, precise steps. "I just wanted to say how much I enjoyed your performance. It was just lovely."

"I thank you kindly," Father said.

"And what sort of music was that?"

Father folded the bills and put them in the breast pocket of his denim coat. "Folks call it skiffle."

"Fascinating. And, if I may ask, what do you call yourselves?"

Father scooped up the change and returned his banjo to the case. "We're the Baumann family. I'm Arthur. This is Elton, my youngest. And this is Ben," he said of Elton's older brother, an acne-speckled tangle of long limbs and shaggy hair who was solemnly wiping down his guitar.

The gentleman extended his hand, fingers straight, thumb skyward at a ninety degree angle. "I am Jonathan Golden. So pleased to meet you."

Father shook the man's hand.

"So will I find you here again tomorrow, or are you just passing through?"

The Baumanns had packed their equipment and started for their truck, which was just around the corner. Mr. Golden paced along beside them. "We're moving on in the morning, just here for the weekend," Father said. "Never stay more than a day or two in any one place. We find that the generous folks such as yourself get their fill pretty quickly. We don't like to overstay our welcome."

"I assure you that would not have been the case with me, but I'm afraid I can't speak for the others in town. And where will you be staying tonight?"

They reached the truck, the old '64 Ford pickup. Father patted the wooden camper shell on the back, which he had made himself. "You're looking at it."

Mr. Golden looked mildly shocked. But he pulled himself together and stiffened with an air of formality. "Arthur, Ben, young Elton—it would be my great pleasure if you would stay with me at my home this evening."

Elton felt a shrinking discomfort with Mr. Golden, but it had been weeks since they had slept in a real bed. Father, however, was already raising his hands in protest.

"Please," Mr. Golden said, "I assure you I have plenty of room and it is the least I could do considering the afternoon of entertainment you've given me. I have a hearty warm stew on the stove as we speak. And, if I may be so bold, I'd venture to guess it has been some time since your last home-cooked meal."

This was true. They had been eating from an ice chest and gas station microwaves for as long as Elton could remember.

Father looked up at the darkening sky and down at his sons, silently pleading with him to not allow his pride to keep them from the warmth of a night indoors and not crammed shoulder to shoulder in the bed of the truck. "If you're certain we wouldn't be any bother," Father said, "my family and I would be very grateful."

"Your gratitude is appreciated and entirely unnecessary," Mr. Golden said, grinning as broadly as his little mouth would allow. "The pleasure will be all mine. I'm parked just up the way. Please follow me."

And so they did, away from town and onto the winding narrow roads that led them into the dark and desolate hills that loomed over the town below. The farther they drove, the darker the streets became, leaving streetlamps and passing headlights behind, the last of the crepuscular light occluded by the canopy of the spiny redwoods huddled along the road.

They followed Mr. Golden's beautifully restored Continental, from the same era but a different world than their truck. Night was fully upon them by the time they pulled into the gravel driveway of his house, and there were no exterior lights, so the house itself was nearly unseeable. There was, however, one interior light that illuminated a small, circular window in the center gable of three along the house's façade, like a dying moon in a starless night sky. Elton couldn't make out the details of the house, but he found the vague black shape of it unpleasant. It was large, probably four times the size of his childhood home, before Mother had withered of cancer and Father had uprooted the three of them. However, the angles of the house seemed off, as if it was leaning, but in no particular direction. Or several directions at once.

"Please watch your step," Mr. Golden said as he led them up the stone path. "I'm so used to navigating in the dark I didn't think to turn on the porchlight before leaving this afternoon."

After surviving the perilous journey to the front door, which was several feet taller than it needed to be, Mr. Golden ushered them inside and flicked on the lights to reveal the large overwrought livingroom. It was filled with stiff, formal antique furniture, but it all seemed a bit disused and decayed, a faded facsimile of its former glory. It didn't have quite the homey quality Elton was hoping for, but it was a house, and that was enough.

Mr. Golden extended his arms, offering three camelback sofas the color of curdled milk. "Please make yourselves at home. I'll see about our supper."

Father took a seat on the couch closest to him, propped an elbow up on one of the scrolled arms and looked out at nothing in particular. Elton found his ability to sit quietly and comfortably at any time with no distractions an amazing quality. And he didn't know if it was enviable or pitiable. For Elton, sitting idly was a type of torture. If he was playing music, he was fine. But otherwise he had to be engaging in something, anything.

Ben took a seat next to Father. He also sat still, but managed to make it look like a great deal of unpleasant work.

Elton was having none of this. He paced about the room, lifting the lids from small ceramic jars, rearranging a dusty bowl of wax fruit, examining little glass figurines, turning a Tiffany lamp on and off.

"Enough," Father said. "Stop being a pest and sit down."

Elton did as he was told, but couldn't stop his legs from bouncing. As he sat, he heard the floor creaking above him, wondering why Mr. Golden had gone upstairs when he was supposed to be tending to their dinner. He also heard scurrying across the floor and decided that Mr. Golden must have pets and he had gone upstairs to feed them. He also decided they were fairly large pets because that didn't sound like the tiny ticking of mouse feet up there.

Soon enough, Mr. Golden was downstairs again and calling them into the spacious kitchen and dining area, considerably more rustic than the living room. They were seated around a butcher block table and Mr. Golden proudly presented them with great heaping bowls of grayish brown stew.

Father held his hands out to either side and bowed his head for grace. Mr. Golden seemed at first surprised and then oddly touched by this. He took both of the hands that were offered to him and bowed his large, boxy head along with the others.

Father asked Mr. Golden if he would like to say grace. He deferred, so Father began, "Lord, thank you for the bounty we are about to receive. Please watch over us and keep us safe from harm. And thank you to our generous host who has been so kind to give us food and shelter for the night. Amen."

"Amen," was echoed by all, then all began scooping up their stew. All but Elton. As much as he'd been looking forward to a proper home-cooked meal, he just couldn't bring himself to eat this one. The mushy pile of stringy meat was a congealed blob in the center of his bowl. It looked like dog food. Or what dog food eventually becomes. And once Elton had that notion in his head he was able to think of nothing else. He could get the spoon to his mouth but couldn't get it past the threshold of his lips.

Mr. Golden smiled at each of them in turn, then addressed Father. "You have such a talented family. I noticed that you each played multiple instruments."

"We sure do," Father said, "three instruments apiece. I take the banjo, harp, and jug. Ben's on second banjo, guitar, and tin whistle. And Elton plays the washtub bass and washboard."

"He only has two," Ben said, an ugly smirk on his hot, spotted face. "And they're the two easiest."

"They're only easy if you play them badly," Father said, "and your brother doesn't. He keeps time for the rest of us. And besides, we all know my jug's the easiest instrument in the band."

Elton knew the only reason the jug wasn't one of his instruments was because he didn't have the lung power. He just didn't have the talent and dexterity for fancy finger picking that Father and Ben had. Or at least he didn't have their patience to learn. But still, Father's words of praise warmed him.

"You've got yourself a real nice house here, Mr. Golden," Father said.

"Jonathan, please."

"Jonathan. You live here alone?"

"Me and my sisters," Jonathan said.

"You have sisters, then?"

"Half sisters. We share a mother, but their father was not mine. That's why I'm not ill like they are. They're ill, you see. Their father was ill and his traits carried on to them. He was from the hills, these hills behind us. There is a lot of illness up in those hills." Jonathan seemed to drift off for a moment, but he came back to them. "Anyway, that's why they won't be joining us this evening. They keep to their room. It's just us here now, but there was a time when this was a thriving farmhouse with a full staff. We're sitting in the staff dining area, if you were wondering. There's a formal dining room, but I find it too stuffy. Have you heard of the McLellans?"

"The McLellans?" Father repeated.

"The McLellans. The McLellan family. McLellan cider."

"I'm afraid we're not from these parts."

"Of course, of course. McLellan cider was once very well known. The family business on our mother's side. We inherited the house, but the business had already seen its last days. The orchard out back, the soil . . . As I said, there is a lot of illness up in those hills. A few trees still survive, but just enough for personal consumption."

Elton spied a basket of apples on a high shelf in the kitchen. "Jonathan?"

"That's Mr. Golden to you," Father corrected.

"Mr. Golden? Are those apples from your orchard?"

"They are indeed."

Elton knew he was about to anger Father, but he was hungry and he saw his chance. "May I have one?"

"Elton!"

Elton didn't look at Father, but could feel the heat of his stare.

"I'm afraid those are for my sisters," Mr. Golden said. "They're on a restricted diet. Their illness gives them very specific needs."

"I'm sorry to have asked," Elton said. "I didn't realize."

"No, that's quite all right. I would have loved to share the bounty of the land with you, but the land is just not as bountiful as it once was. And that is a shame. This is no longer a place for work. And with my sisters in their state, it's not much a place for family either. So it's not much of a home at all, really. The three of you are very lucky that you take your work and your family wherever you go. Your home is always with you."

"Sometimes I miss having a real home," Elton said, feeling Father's anger burning brighter. "Sometimes I wish I could stay in one place."

"Elton," Father said in a low, hard voice. "That's enough talking. Finish your stew."

Elton lowered his head and pretended to eat. He pushed the food around to make it look like he had eaten, a skill he still retained from the days of home and Mother and vegetables.

It seemed to have worked and when the others had finished, Mr. Golden cleared their plates. "Shall I show you to your rooms?" he said.

Father leaned back in his chair, his eyelids drooping. "I'd sure appreciate it. It's been a long day and that was a good meal. I think I'm just about worn out."

It couldn't have been much past seven o'clock. Elton didn't feel so tired himself. Ben looked like he did, but he was often slouchy and listless.

Mr. Golden led them back into the front room and up a staircase that didn't feel entirely stable, the stairs creaking and the banister wobbling under Elton's hand.

"You can take these rooms here," Mr. Golden said with the wave of an upturned hand, indicating the first three doors on the south side of a long hallway. "The washroom is just across from you. I thank you again for the afternoon's entertainment and for your wonderful company this evening. And now I'll leave you to your privacy."

Elton thought he was about to be scolded for his ill manners earlier, but Father clearly didn't have the energy. He trudged into his room, shut the door behind him, and Elton heard the squeaking of bed-springs as he fell into bed. Ben followed suit, leaving Elton to sleep without them for the first time in probably more than a year.

Elton was disappointed to see his room had no television and no books, just an empty dresser and a tall, narrow bed with frilly pillows and ornate wooden posts. Elton got in and tried to convince himself he was tired and that he wasn't hungry. He didn't come up with a convincing argument for either.

He gave everyone sufficient time to fall asleep and headed down-stairs for one of those apples. They were for Mr. Golden's ill sisters, but surely they wouldn't miss one.

He was cautious on the stairs, moving slowly so they didn't creak. He crept to the kitchen but didn't turn on the light, navigating by the glow of the moon, which spilled swaths of silver across the room. He scooted a footstool up against the counter and was able to reach the bowl on the high shelf. But when he gripped one of the apples, he nearly dropped it. It was soft in a way he found revolting. It didn't feel spongy from overripeness; it felt unnaturally squishy.

Elton set the apple on a cutting board and slid a knife from a wooden block. He was not about to bite into it. He could accept a few bruises, but he didn't want a mouthful of rotten fruit. He cut into the apple. It required more carving than it should have, and a dark juice spilled from the cut. It oozed onto the cutting board and looked nearly black in the moonlight.

It was clearly rotten. Who knows how long it had been sitting on that shelf. Elton took a quick survey of the kitchen and found nothing quite edible. He was so hungry he was nearly ready to bite into a raw potato or eat a mouthful of flour.

Mr. Golden said there were a few trees in the orchard that still produced apples. Perhaps Elton could pick a fresh one.

His stomach growled, as if giving him a directive. He obeyed, slip-ping out the back door into the cool night air, the moon painting the hillside covered with endless rows of withered trees in frosty steel light. He crossed the gravel path and walked among the black, shriveled limbs reaching out in every direction like the knotted fingers of a thousand witches. He searched the trees for one that wasn't desiccated.

Up ahead, Elton saw the round dangling shapes of apples through the cross-hatch tangle of dead branches. As he moved toward it, he saw that the tree that held the apples looked no healthier than the others, just more thick and wet.

Elton passed around the last few dead trunks, and when the slick, plump apple tree came into full view, his stomach turned in disgust. There seemed to be a human form on the tree. It wasn't carved into the wood, the texture was too moist and fleshy. Perhaps it was clay that had been molded into this sickening shape. It was a tortured figure, the face drooping and ghoulish, mouth hanging open, teeth rotten and falling from the gums. The trunk seeming to grow up through the throat, visible behind the parted lips. The limbs of the tree sprouted through the top of the head. The limbs of the body were indistinct, split and stretched and tangled up with the branches.

It looked as though the clay or other material that had been used to create this image had been melting. The mouth drooped too low, the lower lip curled over, fat and glistening. The slits of the two swollen eyes had both slid down along one side of the face.

A scarecrow, Elton decided. That was it. It was a scarecrow to keep the birds away from one of the few remaining trees that still bore fruit. And it probably served to keep more than birds away. He had nearly turned to run when he saw it. But now he knew better, so he approached. When he was close, he reached up for one of the apples . . . but the eyes. The world seemed to slow and the thin strand that held the reality of the world in place broke as the eyelids on the tree pealed back and the virulent red and yellow orbs within turned slowly up to meet him.

Elton had a moment of horrified paralysis as he gazed into those infected eyes, then he pulled away and ran back to the house. He burst into the kitchen. He saw a lightswitch and flicked it on.

The apple Elton had cut into was still on the counter and he saw it now in full light. The juice that had run out of it was thick and red like blood. He stepped closer and saw that the flesh of the apple, which should have been crisp and brightly colored, was instead dark and stringy. It looked like meat.

Elton turned off the kitchen light. He didn't know what was going on here, but he had to get Father and Ben and convince them to leave. Something was terribly wrong and Mr. Golden was surely a part of it.

He sneaked back up the stairs and when he reached Father's room he saw that the door was cracked open and a faint light glowed inside. He peered in and saw Mr. Golden sitting on the edge of the bed. An old fashioned crank drill was lying on the bed beside him and he had something small and black, like a seed, pinched between his thumb and finger. Father was slumped on the ground between the man's legs, blood dripping down his face. With his thumb, Mr. Golden pushed the seed into a small round hole at the top of Father's head.

Elton backed away toward Ben's room, but when he reached it, he saw that it was already open. He was slouching limp on the floor as Father had been, his head lulled forward, the hole in the top of his scalp staring at Elton like the pupil of a blood red eye.

Elton's head was spinning and he didn't know where to turn. Before he could think to run, Mr. Golden stepped out of Father's room between Elton and the stairs, a smile on his little pink lips, a glint in his little black eyes.

Elton remembered that earlier Mr. Golden had gone upstairs through the kitchen. There must be another set of stairs at the back of the house. He ran down the hallway, but saw only closed doors. He had to choose one. He could hear Mr. Golden's footsteps behind him.

"I don't know where you think you're running off to, Master Baumann."

Elton grabbed a knob and opened a door on a dark room. He reached in for a lightswitch but paused when he heard skittering noises coming from within. He remembered hearing Mr. Golden's pets earlier . . . but no, maybe that wasn't right.

Elton backed out of the room, Mr. Golden marching slowly but steadily up behind him. Elton started for the next door, but didn't get far.

From the open door, a naked old woman on all fours crawled frantically out, a knobby spine protruding from her bare back, a wild mane of frizzy gray hair radiating from her scalp, black eyes wide and mad. She scrambled across the hallway toward Elton with unnatural speed. Another old woman crawled out after her, and then a third, and a fourth. They scurried frantically on hands and knees, climbing over each other to get at Elton.

Elton tried to run, but he was so numb with fright that he could barely move. The first old woman lunged toward him and grabbed him around the ankles with her long, bony hands, knocking him to the ground. She pulled back her lips and hissed, revealing a mouthful of toothless gums. She clamped her wet mouth down on the side of his neck and started gumming at him, sucking at his bare flesh. The other three shriveled old women climbed on top of him and sucked at his arms and the exposed skin of his belly.

Mr. Golden stepped up beside him and looked down at his panicked face. "I told you my sisters were ill," Mr. Golden said. "And they have a restricted diet." He removed the handkerchief from his breast pocket. "They have very specific needs."

Mr. Golden reached down and covered Elton's nose with the handkerchief, which had a strong but sweet alcohol smell.

As Elton stared up at Mr. Golden's smiling face, his vision grew blurry and all the fight seemed to bleed out of him.

ELTON OPENED HIS eyes with great effort. It felt as if he'd been asleep for a thousand years and had awoken suspended in amber. He felt an indistinct misery. It was neither sharp nor dull nor pain exactly, just a vague and unwanted sensation.

Through fat, sticky eyes he saw now that he was in the orchard on the hill at the back of Mr. Golden's estate. The terrible scarecrow was there before him. It was facing the other direction so Elton could only see the back its head, from which the branches of the tree grew. There were two other scarecrows as well, but the trees that grew through them were just saplings.

Elton tried to cry out, but something was obstructing his air, filling his throat. And he knew he couldn't run. Like the others, he was buried up to his waist. And even if he could move his arms to dig his legs free, it felt as if his feet had grown very long, his toes reaching deep into the earth. It told him that he wasn't going anywhere. This was home now.

MR. AND MRS. KETT

Sam Hicks

———◆———

YOU MIGHT SAY I couldn't have been dead. But I accepted that my fight was over as I drifted like a feather, down into the soft spread of darkness. Then the darkness jolted from my lungs. There came the growl of a dog and distant words:

"It's Catherine, isn't it? There, there—you fell into the water but you're fine now. You know who I am don't you, Catherine? From Saint Jude's?"

Life was burning back; I felt it scorch me. Something made of cloth was being rubbed against my skin.

"Careful does it," said a different voice. "Just look at her arms."

I could see the Reverend Wilfred Lowe more clearly now: his big, familiar face hovering somewhere over mine. "Time for that later, my love," he said to the woman. "Just making sure she's safe, that's the main thing."

I pushed myself up on my elbows.

"Now, don't be scared, Catherine," the reverend said. "We'll help you. Not to worry, my dear, not to worry."

But he spoke too late; I was on my feet by then, swaying in rhythm with a world swimming sideways. My two saviors edged towards me, but their kind faces and their soothing words filled me with sudden fear and I staggered back and half-fell, half-ran into the leaning gray reeds that spread out from the water's edge. If I can reach the hawthorn trees, I thought, they'll never catch me.

When I came to the road and was in sight of home, I still didn't understand I wasn't dead. I didn't see how I could be alive.

I'D BEEN SENT away to boarding school the year before, just after my fourteenth birthday. My father had been promoted to manager at the local bank and he'd asked me, what was money for, if not to give your only child the best? So that was that: out of the blue an exile, and expected to be grateful to leave my friends and everything I'd ever known, in exchange for extra Latin.

That Easter when I arrived at the railway station for the holidays, my parents weren't waiting with the car. Instead, a man approached and introduced himself as the taxi driver they'd sent to collect me: I asked him why they hadn't come themselves, but he couldn't say. They could at least have warned me, I thought. But maybe something had happened; was Granny ill again? There'd been a stroke a few years before and you couldn't help being afraid. Or could something have happened to them—my parents. What would I do then?

We drove past the floral display outside the church and the driver waved to Reverend Wilfred Lowe, who was standing by the gate like a guard. It was a small town, and so the reverend must have known he wouldn't be seeing my family for the Easter services. My father was an atheist, for one. He didn't advertise it for fear of offense, but he betrayed his lack of faith in the Deity by avoiding His institutions and His celebrations and by staying silent whenever He was praised. My mother's beliefs were a more movable feast: a mess of palmistry and tea-leaves and color-illustrated myths; she'd even been to a séance once. It was as though, for her, the spiritual realm fulfilled a need for outré entertainment. But I don't want to give the impression they were unconventional types; in fact, they went to great lengths to conform to their small society. They played tennis and golf and bridge, ran cake sales and charity events, and my mother was a keen gardener who'd won first prize for her flowers at the annual summer fete. Mummy didn't work—this was fifty years ago—but she looked after her mother-in-law, who lived with us, and she looked after me as well, in a slightly more careless way.

That afternoon, the taxi stopped outside our house and I looked out, searching for my mother's face. All the curtains were drawn, making me doubly sure that something had happened and so recently that no one had had time to tell me. At the best of times our house had an unapproachable look. It stood on its own a mile from town, backed by fields of fenced-in pasture, beyond which were woods and the many-forked paths that led up to Coldhill pond. The house's dark windows looked down beneath a gray tiled roof, which on overcast days seemed to slide straight out of the sky. Its brick walls were dingy and mottled and its door, with a knocker like a small clenched fist, was the grim, unshining black of iron dug from a grave. In summer, when the roses in the front garden lifted their bright heads, the look of the house would jolly up, but that day was one of those when it turned a cold shoulder to the outside world.

After the taxi driver had helped me with my luggage and left, the front door opened: it seemed like my mother had been standing there, waiting for him to go.

"Mummy! You made me jump," I said as I went to step inside, but she held me back with a hand on my arm.

"I didn't have time to tell you, Catherine," she said in a rush, "but we've got some guests. I know you'll be on your best behavior, won't you?" She turned her head. "Look—there they are."

I looked past her down the black and white tiled hallway. At first, I thought they might be medical people, or undertakers.

"Oh. Yes. I see them . . . Is Granny all right?"

"Yes, dear," she said. "Granny's fine. She's doing very well. Now go in and say hello to Mr. and Mrs. Kett."

The couple made no effort to approach me, so it was I who walked down the hallway to where they stood, beyond the last angle of the staircase. The only daylight entered from the glass above the door, and, that afternoon, theatrically steep white rays sloped down towards these strangers, Mr. and Mrs. Kett. Only someone who'd seen them would understand when I say that there was something undefined about their faces. The planes and contours seemed to sweep away, as if they couldn't really be contained. Their cheekbones, their foreheads, their eyes, pitched forward, whilst remaining at the same time still. They were tall and slim, their hair fair and long, and they wore pale, loose clothing; the woman a long dress, and the man a shirt and trousers, possibly silk. But this was only an impression: it would be hard to give details or to be definite. It was like looking at a pencil sketch with highlights and unfinished lines, where forms are hinted at as they blend into the background paper. I'd never seen anything like them. It was the 1960s, but where we lived, you'd never have known. No one stood out, no one had glamour: no one glowed like Mr. and Mrs. Kett. How on earth had my mother found them?

"I'm very pleased to meet you," I said and held out my hand for Mrs. Kett to shake. Her mouth was a small shadow in her unfixed face. She made no move to take my hand so I let it drop, but neither she nor Mr. Kett took their eyes from me as they silently, just perceptibly, shifted their heads. I didn't find it at all rude, this unwillingness to small talk. Instantly, it won my admiration. They were wonderful, completely captivating, and I was very, very impressed. Then my mother's voice broke the spell, calling to them from the kitchen, and they moved away, like beautiful wraiths. I wanted nothing more than to follow them, but I knew my grandmother would be expecting me; she'd be waiting in the living room, whose door stood open across the hallway. I'll find them afterwards, I thought, when this is out the way.

The living room ran the length of the house, and that afternoon, with the curtains drawn at the front and only partly open at the back, it wasn't much brighter than the hallway I'd just left. Despite its generous size, it was a room with a closed-up, shut-in feel, crammed with furniture and thick-shaded lamps and too many paintings in heavy, ornamental frames. Granny was sitting at the end in her usual chair, looking out at the back lawn. Although her speech hadn't fully recovered since the stroke, her mind had stayed keen, and I saw with some relief that she'd taken up knitting again: from her thinnest needles, a fine lace shawl was growing, falling in red filigrees across her lap. She looked at me eagerly as I leaned to kiss her, and kept her eyes fixed on me as she strained for speech. I knelt by her chair and waited, holding her hand, until she said: "Help me . . . with this."

"Oh, Granny," I said. "You know I can't knit like you can. I'd be no help, would I? Anyway, you're doing so well without me. You're so clever at things like that."

She looked at me with bemusement, and for a moment I wondered if she knew me, or if she thought I was someone from the past. Clearly frustrated, she felt around again for words.

"Catherine . . . undo . . . this."

I squeezed her hand. "Oh, Granny. It's so beautiful, I can't. I'd ruin it."

Her eyes grew wide, as though amazed. Why on earth was she talking to me about her knitting? She knew I was hopeless at it. Had she forgotten?

"Have you seen our guests?" I asked. She closed her eyes and shook her head. "The Ketts?" I tried again. But the change of subject didn't help; tears escaped from beneath the crinkled eyelids and slipped into the hollows of her face.

I didn't know what to say because I didn't know what I'd done to upset her, and I was thinking it would be best if I just left, when my mother came bustling into the room. She looked at me accusingly. "What's wrong with Granny? Catherine—what on earth have you said?" She fussed across and started stroking my grandmother's hair.

"I only asked her if she'd met the Ketts."

"Of course she has. She loves them just like we do. Don't you, Hilda?"

Granny's head had fallen forward. Somehow, within seconds, she was asleep.

"I'm sorry. I honestly don't know what I did to upset her," I said, and then, softly: "Mummy, I wanted to ask—how did you meet them, the Ketts?"

She didn't look at me as she absorbed my question. Her top lip thinned and then she said, in the voice she used to close inquiries down. "Through a friend. Now, why don't you go into the garden and say hello to Daddy?" She gave me a quick smile. "He's taken the week off, so we can all be together. Isn't that nice of him?"

I FOUND HIM at the end of the long walled garden, where the apple trees were. He was standing over a pile of junk, emptied from the tumbledown brick outbuildings which my mother used for potting seedlings and storing tools. She must be having a re-design, I'd thought as I walked down; there was bare earth in the borders where the perennials had been, and shallow trenches dug into the lawns and vegetable beds. She'd always liked to move things around from time to time, although I'd have expected to have heard about a major plan, as this one seemed to be.

My father kissed me and then slumped down on a packing crate. "Oh, it's a job, clearing all this," he said. He had a thin, bloodless sort of face, but he was very fit, what with all the tennis and golf he played, so it surprised me that this not very heavy work had left him hot and breathless.

Around the open doors of the two small buildings were heaps of flowerpots and trays, watering cans, baskets, coils of wire, battered tins of preparations.

"But doesn't Mummy need all this stuff?" I said, starting for the first door.

"No!" he shouted, as soon as I moved. "Leave it alone!"

I turned around, startled.

"Why's that?"

"We can't disturb them. Can't you see?" He nodded at the little building.

"What am I meant to be seeing?"

And then I did see something through the cobwebby window; a smudged movement, the sort you catch at the corner of your eye, the kind a small, fast animal makes.

"Is something in there?" I said.

"The Ketts. We really shouldn't interrupt them. They're cleaning that one up for more guests. They don't need us getting in their way. They have to do things how they like them."

"The Ketts?" I felt myself flush as I spoke their name. "But I thought they were inside the house? Why would guests want the shed?"

"Better ask your mother," he said. He shifted on his crate and looked up at me with shining eyes. "So you've seen them, have you? Aren't they wonderful?"

"Oh yes. I've never seen anyone like them. Where ever do they come from? I asked Mummy but she wouldn't say."

He gave a short laugh and raised his eyebrows. "You know, I didn't think to ask her that. But I'm just very glad they came, to tell you the truth. It's been such a pleasure having them around the place. Yes, last week, I think it was, they came. Such marvelous people. You know—there is such a thing as the perfect guests. People say there isn't, don't they, but there is."

I took another, newly curious look at the old building, at its missing roof tiles and mossy bricks, finding it hard to picture what the Ketts could hope to do in there. And then, behind the dirty glass, I glimpsed another movement, which could have been anything; the loose flutter of a dress, or a silky sleeve, or the turning of a face.

FOR THE REST of the afternoon I lay in my bedroom, getting up every now and then to fetch a glass of water. My parents were somewhere outside, working on the sheds, and so, I imagined, were the Ketts. I didn't want to interfere. I didn't want to upset them in any way, however small or unintended. Really, if I were such a considerate person, I should have spared some time for my grandmother that afternoon, instead of lazing around on my bed; I could even have tried to help her with her knitting if she liked. But her outburst earlier had scared me. How could I know what might make her cry? What was the right thing to say? I even convinced myself it would be kindest not to disturb her later by going in to say goodnight. So I lay there, thinking about the Ketts, trying to hold the image of them in my head.

At eight that evening, my mother called all of us except Granny into the dining room and, with some ceremony, lit candles in her best silver candlesticks in honor of our guests. The table was polished to a mirror sheen, and my father sat at its head, with my mother and I at either side. The Ketts sat at the other end, separated from us by empty chairs, which seemed to me to be a gesture of politeness, a shy reluctance to impose. The table made an island in the candlelight, framed by a fitful darkness from which our guests' faces arose, part-concealed and indistinct. Small reflected flames quivered in our cut crystal glasses as we drank, and we drank a lot (for the first time ever I was allowed wine) because we had no appetite for food. We spoke sometimes: we must have chatted away quite happily, because I have a memory of easiness, lightness, of feeling that we were basking in the fascinating company of the Ketts. I do remember asking my mother about the new guests that were coming and her telling me. "We'll always keep a welcome for friends of Mr. and Mrs. Kett." And we raised our glasses and drank toast after toast to lasting friendship.

I wasn't at all resistant to alcohol of course, and after dinner I went straight up to bed. The room spun when I lay down and then an annoying restlessness, a kind of twitching, nervous pain, built up inside me until I couldn't bear it any longer. I hopped up and bumped around my room, hoping movement might ease the horrible feeling, but after a few circuits came to rest at the window that looked down onto garden at the back. My parents and the Ketts were out there, standing on the soil where the grass had been. Our guests were making wide, languid gestures, like people turning in their sleep, and my parents, rooted to the spot, were watching and listening, caught in a kind of rapture. It was so predictable, normally, life at home, and my parents never seemed to know quite what to do with me, but now we were all coming together, all doing new and interesting things, due to the inspiring presence of the Ketts. It felt like the deepest honor anyone could ever receive had been bestowed upon us.

WHEN I GOT up the next morning, I went to the window again. They were out there already, at not even seven o'clock. My parents were marking out lines with sticks and string, while, with their backs to me, the Ketts might have been Roman emperors directing their slaves, as they sipped their wine, and watched. But that's not to say there was anything imperious about them, not at all. My parents' shining faces, their giddy, rushed actions, showed them to be as excited and willing as children on Christmas Eve.

A delicious thought occurred to me as I dressed: I could have a quick look in the spare room, where the Ketts were staying. Here was my chance, now the coast was clear, to see something of their secret selves. Just a look, just a peek at the little things they kept about them. I'll only be in there a few seconds, that's all, I thought, as I crept along the landing. They'll never know, I said to myself, as I pushed open the door. But there was nothing there, no sign of them, no clues; no socks, no scarves, no hairpins, no books, no magazines. They'd brought nothing with them, and didn't even seem to have slept in the bed.

I had no appetite for breakfast when I went downstairs, so I drank a cup of tea and more water, which I tinted pink with the dregs from an open bottle of wine. On my way out to the garden, I looked round the living room door: my grandmother turned her unsteady head and for a moment I thought the look in her eyes was not frustration at her efforts to speak, but hopelessness.

"Help . . . with this," she said.

I laughed an uncomfortable refusal and told I'd see her at lunchtime, but that now I had to go outside because we had guests. I knew how condescending I sounded, how weak my excuses seemed, but I really intended to make it up to her later, when I had more time.

It had rained during the night and the freshly dug earth smelled of rot and leaves and mushrooms. A grid of taut green string stretched out before me over the remains of the grass and as I looked, it seemed to levitate, rising and rolling into a slowly spinning maze. Of course, that's what it was—a maze: lines joining and dividing, dead ends, reversals.

"Why didn't you tell me what you'd got planned?" I said when I reached my parents, who were busy shoveling soil into a wheelbarrow. "What a wonderful idea! And you've got to let me help."

"Oh, darling, would you?" my father said. "You know, it's a big job with just us."

A few feet away, the Ketts seemed to be smiling. They leaned against each other, loose and relaxed, drowsily sipping their red wine. I didn't ask, but I knew this project must have been their idea. It was so adventurous, so daring.

"And then we'll have to get the stones to finish it. We'll need all our strength for that," my mother said. "There's going to be walls. Walls all around it, so you can get lost."

"That'll be even more incredible," I said and I jumped down into the trench they'd dug. As they handed me a shovel, I looked to check if the Ketts were watching, but they were drifting away, down towards the outbuildings at the back, behind the trees.

"Are the Ketts all right?" I asked. "Mightn't they get bored?"

My mother stopped digging for a moment. Her curled hair was bound up in a spotted scarf, and her chin was smeared with dirt. "Oh no," she said. "They've got lots to do today. They're getting things ready for the other guests."

"And when will they be here?"

"Oh, I don't know that yet," she said, and I knew, by the way her top lip tightened, that it would be futile to question her further.

At midday, or thereabouts, we stopped for lunch, but none of us were very hungry and we made do with a crust of bread left over from a previous day; but we had water and several glasses of wine, which was what we felt was needed. Then we went back to the garden, with me forgetting the promise to look in on Granny, although I'd made it only hours before.

It was hard to gauge our progress from ground level, but as we dug, Mr. and Mrs. Kett would appear from time to time and by the subtlest of signs, they let us know that we were doing well. I would see the blur of their flowing clothes, the slow expressive gestures of their hands, the eloquence of their hazy eyes, and understand how truly glad they were to see people so committed and hardworking. And we worked at a breathless rate, my father wheeling the earth we'd removed round to the front of the house, where he tipped it over the rose beds and the gravel path. We'd see to it later, my mother said, when we had more time. I reveled in the simple pleasures and discoveries of our task: the hair-like roots ripped from the turf, the round brown stones that tumbled from my digging blade and the fat worms that flipped about in panic when I lifted them away. We didn't really talk, so deeply were we focused on our work, so determined to complete it as quickly as we could, to impress the Ketts.

By the evening, we'd dug out half the former lawn, the borders and two of the vegetable beds. I went upstairs to change before dinner and was astounded when I looked down and saw the intricacy of what we'd created. It was going to be stupendous, like nothing I'd ever seen.

That evening, when we gathered in the candlelight around the smooth and shining table, I suppose we were all too tired to eat. Instead, we lifted the cut crystal glasses in shaking hands and drank toast after toast with our guests. To friendship, we said. To getting the job done, we said. To dreams, we said, again and again, as the exhilarating hours fled by. Sometimes our guests seemed to retreat into the dark, but then the candle flames would straighten and briefly reveal them, bathed in snowy, moving light. Eventually, so overcome by intense emotion that I could hardly speak or see, I left the table, embarrassed at myself, not wanting the Ketts to know how weak I really was.

I should've been exhausted, but my heart was beating so fast, and my limbs were aching and twitching in such an uncontrollable, internal way, that I passed the night in a fever of restlessness, my waking thoughts as unlikely and confused as the dreams which suddenly took me. It's possible I was genuinely ill, because in the morning I couldn't remember how I came to be standing outside the old brick outbuilding, my hands pressed against the misted glass, my eyes unblinking, fixed upon the dark interior. My mother found me and told me to come away, and soon, after forgoing breakfast, we started digging again.

What about Granny, I thought as we got near lunch. Did I see her last night? No—I'd forgotten. With everything going on, the usual routine had just fallen away. And what were the odds of finishing the maze anytime soon? Perhaps we had overestimated our abilities. I had the feeling that the Ketts, who had seemed so happy with us before, were starting to think the same way. I started to feel that they were disappointed with our progress, that they expected more. They came into sight less frequently, and there was a different quality to the movements they made, a touch of impatience in their graceful limbs, a reproach in their inscrutable gaze. They lit a fire at the end of the garden, presumably to burn the stuff from the sheds, and I could see the flames, intensely red, rising up from the pile of rubbish. Please don't let them leave, I thought, please never let them leave.

We drank water for lunch and at a quarter past four, my father fell forward into the trench, and lay there, panting, his eyes wide and trying to turn backwards in his head like a stricken beast. He brushed my mother and me away and pulled himself up.

"I'm sorry, girls," he said. "What an old fool. Overdone it a bit, that's all. I'll go and sit inside with Granny for a while, and leave you to it. What d'you say?"

An hour later, my knees gave way. My mother said she thought it was probably time to stop, and, mainly because I couldn't face the stairs, I went to join my father and Granny in the living room. They were sitting in their chairs by the window, staring out at the garden. They're as tired as me, I thought, as I dragged over a chair to sit beside them.

IT SEEMED THEY had forgotten about us, my mother and the Ketts. I could hear my mother talking to our guests as she moved around the house; sometimes her high-pitched laugh, sometimes murmured words, from the dining room, or the hallway, or moving upstairs.

"Help me with this," Granny had said when I'd taken my seat, and I'd answered: "How can I do that, Granny, when I can barely lift my head?"

Her hands trembled, white against the lacy red knitting that fell across her lap.

"Well, perhaps you'd like to help me instead, Catherine?" my father said. His voice was strange and I leaned forward, trying to read his face, but it was becoming as vague and unknowable as the Ketts'.

"Daddy, I'm not making excuses," I said. "I don't think I can move. I'm so exhausted."

He looked at me with the same bemusement as Granny. Was it his idea of a joke, a way of saying I was being selfish by not helping with her damned knitting? Was I supposed to say yes just to please her, and then make a mess of things? I would've gone up to my room, but I didn't have the strength to move.

The evening darkened, but not one of us rose to turn on a light. Outside, the sky was solid, black marble streaked with gray, but the house around us was fragile, whispering with breath. The whirr of a moth in another room, the slow drip of the kitchen tap, seemed as near as the echoing tick of the glass-cased clock that sat upon the mantelpiece. Every so often, I caught a glimpse of gossamer movement which barely registered on the air, and I would anticipate the appearance of the Ketts, but each moment of anticipation seemed to rob me of that wished-for possibility.

Moonlight gleamed on the carved wooden arms of our chairs, and fell across my grandmother's white hair and my father's open eyes. It glinted on something lying in the garden; the steel of some tool we'd left behind. The light fell across my feet, which I noticed were bare.

When the birds began chirruping at dawn, I seemed to hear them as through an illness; queasy, garbled caricatures. The thick pile carpet lapped wet against my feet: when I tried to move my toes, it released an odor of decay, and I closed my eyes in fear of filaments and spores and green clouds of dust. Help me, I thought, and something moved inside me. Was that a voice, or the sound of something walking, shuffling, through dead leaves?

"Get away from here," I heard.

It couldn't have been my father's voice, could it? No, it was the sound of something walking through dead leaves, imitating speech. They were still asleep in their chairs, my father and Granny, their faces in shadow, untouched yet by the faint morning light.

"Get away from here," I heard.

But I was only dressed in shorts and a T-shirt, summer clothes, and my cold arms and legs were covered with marks, like rust.

"Get away from here," I said out loud, but to move those limbs would be to dislocate them, to move them would mean excruciating pain. But I had to breathe; I had to breathe air beyond the boundaries of our house, if only for a short while, before the work started again.

I moved those screaming limbs; I left my chair and went into the hallway, where the black and white tiles tilted and the walls bubbled beneath their skin. The door swung open to reveal the earth mounds where the front garden had been.

I ran up the path that skirted the cattle pasture and onto the one which led up through the thickets of hawthorn and larch. At the banks of Coldhill pond, I stopped. I hadn't intended to run so far, but now that I had, I gulped the morning air like a person who'd been suffocating. The pond looked black, yet it glittered with light and suddenly, a breeze split its surface into a thousand freezing beads and I looked down and saw, in the deep, what I knew at once was the face of a corpse. Without a thought, I jumped.

Reverend Wilfred Lowe's wife bent down to where I knelt. She peeled my fingers from my grandmother's legs, which were deathly cold and streaked with dried blood; like her hands, they were tied to the chair. Mrs. Lowe put a blanket over my shoulders. I knew she didn't want me to look at the other chair by the window, the one where my father sat staring out with frozen eyes to where, I'm told, my mother lay.

"What about the Ketts?" I said to Mrs. Lowe as she led me away.

I asked everyone that. I told them all: you need to speak to the Ketts. They'll tell you how happy we were. They'll know what happened, and when they explain you'll see that it must have been someone else. Because how could they ever have done what all of them said they had? Only someone who'd never met them would think that. It made no sense. If they had, why not kill me too?

What do they look like, they said? Where did they go? How do we find them? Where do they live? They don't live anywhere, I should have said. They visit.

Yesterday, after fifty years, I saw them again. They haven't changed: why would they? I was on a train bound for the coast, when, just outside a town, we slowed to a stop behind an isolated house. I saw the pale circles of their faces, the mysterious luminance of their forms, and as we gathered speed again, I saw a hand rise as if to acknowledge me. I raised my own hand in answer, to let them know I'd seen them and was grateful, even now, to be remembered.

Jason's in the Garden

Simon Strantzas

———◆———

OF ALL THE kids in my middle-school, no-one ever claimed they'd
seen a ghost. No-one but Jason Keane. He was infamous among us,
our pudgy misshapen classmate with a perpetual red ring around his
mouth. It wasn't that we hated him—we were still too young to really
hate anyone—but his constant fibbing about what he'd said and done
grew frustrating. No matter how many times we called him out, he
continued to spin tales in an effort to impress us. And, when that
failed, he'd fall back on simply giving us the candy from his pockets.
That, unlike his stories, we ate up hungrily.

Maybe the problem was Jason lacked the finesse of a good liar,
that momentary conviction that every word out of his mouth was
true. Instead, his eyes shifted and his pitch rose, and it was instantly
clear that he could not be trusted. I often marveled at how terrible he
must have been to be so desperate for attention. But I learned young
that everyone was terrible in one way or another. It was just that most
hid it better.

But, the ghost. We were on the school grounds in those early morning minutes before the bell rang, challenging one another to inordinately complicated dares and games designed to test our limits, when Jason arrived. He did so silently, appearing on the periphery of our large group, his unwashed shirt the same stripped gray and red hand-me-down he always wore, his face raw from persistently licking his chapped lips. We would have ignored him had his eyes not been watery and swollen, and his pallor yellowed. He looked so unnerved, we reluctantly stopped our games to ask what was wrong.

"I saw something," he said, sniveling. "Something I wasn't supposed to see."

There were groans and eye rolls, and a chorus of mocking jokes at his expense, but Jason never faltered, never walked back what he said or tried to over-explain. It secretly unnerved us, and our ridicule bled dry abruptly when Eric stepped forward to ask Jason what he'd seen.

"I'd left the house and was going down the stairs to go to school. I didn't want to be late again, so was I running pretty quick, and you know how there's the garden in front of my house? The one my mom tells us to stay out of?" We nodded, though as far as I knew none of us had seen the garden or been at his house in years. "I opened the gate and ran through because I was late and as I was running I saw another kid in there, one I didn't recognize. I asked him who he was and if he went to school here and if he wanted some candy, but he didn't say anything. So I told him he had to get out of the garden before my mom found him. He just looked at me like he was angry."

It was the least interesting, least ambitious story Jason had ever told, and the lack of effort enraged some of us. Sean and Keith started shouting, wondering how any of that made the boy a ghost. Simply because he was trespassing?

"No," Jason said, licking his lips. "It was only afterward I realized he was a ghost. Because he wasn't wearing any shoes."

That stumped us. No-one knew what to say, and there was no time to figure it out before the morning bell interrupted.

After half a day in Mr. Hanson's class learning simple math and geography, we'd forgotten the story, as apparently had Jason, who retreated at lunch to the only group that would take him, that small cluster of outcasts from our circle. Frail Winston, Gangly Stephen, Sweaty Jim, and the rest who had no place among us so who stayed out of our way. Even among that crowd, however, Jason didn't truly belong. His lies and tale-telling repeatedly caught up with him, and those misfits who took him in found themselves as often casting him out. No pocket full of candy could prevent it. So Jason ended up bouncing between our two groups, neither wanting to lay claim to him, and during those times our two expulsions would overlap, with nowhere else to go he would end up walking the perimeter of the school yard fences, stooping occasionally to pick up a stone, a clod of earth, or a particularly interesting stick, and then lobbing it over into the narrow creek beyond.

We only remembered Jason's story the next day, and only because when he appeared, he was impossibly more ashen and unkempt than the day before. Dennis noticed his chapped lips were drawn thin.

"I saw him again today. I saw him again standing there, barefoot in the garden. As soon as I did I closed my eyes because maybe if you don't see a ghost it can't see you, so I closed my eyes and tried to walk through the garden. But I couldn't walk fast because I didn't know where I was going, and it felt like I was walking for a lot longer than there was garden to walk through, and I started worrying I wasn't in the garden anymore, like the ghost had taken me somewhere else and I didn't know it. And then I was afraid of where I was and I opened my eyes even though I told myself not to and when I did I was at the end of the garden—a step away from the gate—but beside me an inch away was the ghost. But now he had these big black eyes and was barefoot. His lips were moving like he was saying something but I couldn't hear anything."

Ben and Dennis laughed at him, incredulously. Donald simply turned and walked off, taking Jon and Brett with him. The rest of us stayed because the game of ball we'd been playing no longer held any of our interest, and because it was so close to the morning bell that starting another game would only frustrate us.

It was Mark who asked why it was so important the boy was barefoot, why that suggested he was a ghost not someone from a different school or a visiting neighbor? Jason shook his head and wiped his runny nose on his sleeve.

"You can't walk without shoes in that garden. Too many animals got in there and ate the flowers and vegetable my mom grows, and she got so angry my dad put broken glass in the dirt to keep them away. It's everywhere, and you can't walk through without shoes unless you want to bleed to death out of your feet. But this kid wasn't bleeding at all. He was just standing there, mouthing nothing."

We didn't believe him, of course. Why would you believe something like that? It was the kind of crazy story Jason would tell, something so outlandish you'd have to pay attention to him, and he got his wish; that's what we were doing. But we'd known Jason long enough by then not to fall for it for long.

I think it was Billy that shoved him, suddenly and violently, and you could see Jason's soft pudginess absorb most of the blow. But Billy was persistent, and continued shoving until Jason toppled over. It was some sort of punishment, I guess, for how he was treating us, and I don't know what would have happened next if the bell hadn't rung. I want to believe nothing, and that's probably the case, but I'm not convinced I'm right. It was a confusing time back then.

Jason spent most of the morning whimpering in the back of the classroom, quiet enough that Mr. Hanson didn't notice, but we all heard. None of us did anything about it, though. None of us grasped what was happening. Was Jason afraid that Billy would attack him again? Was he afraid of whatever he thought he saw in the garden? Or was he afraid he was making up another story he couldn't get out of? I remember passing a note to Spencer suggesting we had to do something, but Spencer didn't read it. He took it from me and creased his eyebrows before tearing it up and dropping it in his desk.

At lunch, I wanted to talk to Jason—more to straighten out my own head than anything else—but he'd already vanished from the school grounds before anyone knew he was gone. I wondered if we should go looking for him, but no-one seemed concerned. They just wanted to go home for lunch. Jason wasn't our problem, they said.

He was probably looking for his mom to cradle him. But I suspected in a way I couldn't articulate then that his mother was not the cradling sort. Nevertheless I gave in, and instead of searching for him, we all went our own ways, convinced he'd be back for the afternoon.

But he wasn't. Jason did not return to class. Not for the rest of that day, which I found surprising and irritating. Not the next day, which I found unusual and unsettling. And not on the day after that, which I found troubling and worrying. But, I still did nothing about it because what was there to do?

Jason finally returned on Friday. We were in front of the school, picking sides for a game of ball we wouldn't actually start until the midmorning break, when one by one we noticed the sickly odor of unbathed prepubescence and turned to find Jason behind us. But he was different this time. It wasn't that his pallor had become completely white and bloodless, though it had; and it wasn't that he stared at us wide-eyed and without blinking, though he did; it was that he was perfectly and utterly still, as though he were some soft lumpy statue carved of soapstone by the most undelightful of artists. Eric complained Jason was giving him the creeps, and though we all acted as though we agreed, I suspect it was something else. Something deeper, and more troubling on a primitive level. Something akin to how animals know a disaster is imminent. An early sense of oncoming danger. At least, I felt that way.

Jason's pale face and empty eyes watched us, and though it wasn't me who first noticed his feet, once I did I couldn't stop shouting. His feet. What was wrong with his feet? Darryl ran inside to fetch Mr. Hanson while the rest of us stood there dumbstruck. I remember the sound of the morning bell ringing, but none of us heeded it. None of us moved. Even when Mr. Hanson emerged, Darryl trailing behind, and yelled at us, we didn't respond. Jason had started to sway, eyes fluttering, and we watched as Mr. Hanson heaved Jason into his arms as he collapsed and dashed him back though the school doors while the rest of us were left behind to stare at the trail of bloody footprints that stretched back across the bridge over which Jason had apparently crossed.

We found our way to class shortly after, once the bellowing Mr. Gilroy, teacher of the third-grades, stepped through those same doors and shook us from our collective stupor. We filed up to our room silently and without protest, but once we took our seats the murmuring began. What had happened? What was wrong with Jason? Had he been in an accident? Had he hurt himself? Had someone else hurt him? It was Joey who brought up the garden, and the broken glass therein, but it made no sense. Why would Jason knowingly walk on broken glass?

Mr. Hanson eventually came to our home room, his face flushed. He announced that Jason had hurt himself and wouldn't be attending class, and that his parents, Mr. and Mrs. Keane, were on their way to retrieve him, but none of those facts eased our curiosity so Mr. Hanson eventually and begrudgingly took our questions. Where was Jason now? The school nurse was tending to him. Had Jason mentioned what happened? No. Was he going to die? Of course not; he just needs rest. Did he lose his shoes? We don't know. Then Eric asked the question I dreaded hearing. Do you think it was the ghost's fault? Everyone waited for the answer, but Mr. Hanson's response was so confused and irritated that it was clear Jason had not mentioned seeing the boy in the garden. Only we knew, and though it was clear we shouldn't believe it, that it was likely an attempt to garner attention, still some of us couldn't shake the feeling that there was something more happening than any of us wanted to admit, and that translated to a feeling of unease that never left us.

Or, at least, never left me, because I spent the rest of my day in class watching the window beside me as though I expected someone to walk up and peer in. Someone small and thin and translucent, with eyes like aching pits and feet stained black with dried blood. I never saw that, but I did see Jason's oversized father leading his hobbling son away from the school. His mother walked beside them, stopping periodically to say something I couldn't hear but could imagine from the strict way she bent to meet his eye and the sharp wagging of her bony finger. Each time she did, as soon as her attention shifted away, he'd reach into his pocket for a candy to slip between his chapped lips, only to have it knocked away by his incensed mother. In an instant Jason's entire life unfolded before me, and I saw what I never could before, what none of our classmates had seen. I saw a home life of neglect and punishment for the tiniest infractions; I saw Jason alone in his room, or his basement, or in his yard, without a friend to speak or laugh with or connect to in any way at all. He was alone and always had been, and every attempt he'd made to change that or correct his isolation had been met with a wall of disinterest and dismissal. His bribes for friends didn't work; his slow-wits prevented him from being a good student and impressing Mr. Hanson. Even the stories designed to impress others into wanting his company failed. I saw Jason as I'd seen him every afternoon at the end of class, slowly trudging home along the perimeter fences, his unclasped backpack hung haphazardly over his shoulder, and now instead of a slovenly kid I saw one that had exhausted himself trying to connect, and needed to steel himself before he reached home, where the most attention he could hope for would be a series of reprimands for being an inconvenience. I even saw Jason in the future, behind the wheel of a filthy pickup truck, heavy-set and balding, his face a relief map of the neighborhood. It was no wonder he saw ghosts in his garden. As a manifestation of his loneliness, it was clear that they at least would speak to him. As I said, I understood him then for the first time, and I didn't know if I liked it, nor if I was going to do something to help him.

I wanted to gather some classmates to visit Jason with me after the final bell. True, the nurse said he should rest, but I had to believe seeing us on his doorstep would help buoy his spirits. I was certain it would assuage some of my guilt. But despite multiple attempts, I could not find anyone willing to join me. They all expressed the same ambivalence or open hostility about Jason as ever, and yet there was also something more in each pair of eyes: an irrational fear Jason's latest stories might be true, and a worry that coming face to face with the impossible would change them, as though life weren't doing that already.

So, I made my way to Jason Keane's house alone. I crossed the hydro fields and over the creek bridge. I walked down curved suburban streets and fenced-in pathways, until I was let out onto the alcove where his two-story house stood, its fifty-year-old oak tree casting shadows across its front lawn. Along the side of the house ran the wooden staircase that Jason had often described; its plain, utilitarian appearance, coated in dull maroon paint, a surprising disappointment compared to the grand and ornate version featured in many of his implausible stories. But at least the staircase was there, as was the small garden positioned between me and its foot.

From a distance, the fenced-in plot was no different from any vegetable garden. Rows of leafy greens and tuberous roots took up the bulk of the space, but there were also vines and some ornamental flowers that must have been grown strictly for decorating the house. The entire garden was no more than eight feet long and nearly half that wide, surrounded by a few feet of wire-mesh—tall enough to keep out the rabbits, skunks, and squirrels, but not enough that a person might feel trapped. A gate on either end further lowered the risk.

I walked toward the house, intending to climb the staircase to Jason's door, but the straightest possible route ran through the garden. The sight of it unnerved me after Jason's stories, so I decided to circumvent it out of politeness, but a strange gleaming from within caught my eye, drawing me closer and insisting I take a look. I watched the house as I approached for a sign of Jason or his parents, but there was nothing. No evidence of life. By the time I reached the garden and peered in, most of the shimmering had faded, leaving behind scattered reflections from mirrored shards half-buried in the earth. But there was something else, too, something I could see between where the spinach rows ended and the geraniums began, something whose reflection wasn't quite right. It made me uneasy, as though someone were watching me despite no one else being visible. And yet . . . and yet something drew me onward into the garden. Even though my heart was beating faster than it ever had, even though my mind was screaming at me to turn and run, even though I questioned why I was unable to resist coming to Jason's house when our other classmates easily stayed away, still I found myself opening the garden gate without knowing I was going to, and stepping inside before I could stop myself.

Immediately, the world became quieter. The air felt slightly cooler as well, darkening as though a cloud had selected that particular moment to cross between me and the sun. As I took hesitant steps, I heard the creaks and stresses of glass cracking beneath my feet. Ahead was the garden's other gate, a mere eight feet away, but the fear calcifying my muscles slowed my progress, and those feet might as well been miles. I trudged them slowly, green leaves brushing my ankles, each step feeling as though it might be my last. I believed then with all my being in what Jason had told us, that the barefooted ghost was real, and that at any moment he would appear and frighten me, or worse drag me down with him into that sharp black earth.

But that's not what happened. Instead, my journey ended when I placed my hand on the opposite gate, and the clouds I had been so worried about parted, revealing the warming sun. I looked behind me to see the garden and only the garden, with its crop of vegetables and my footprints traveling along its length. If there was a ghost there, I did not see it, did not feel it any longer. The part of me I had gathered up tight against my chest was then released, and I felt all the tension drain from me in relief. The world once again made sense. Jason's stories were once again stories.

I looked ahead at the house whose long wooden staircase I was approaching, looked at the darkened windows of Jason's home, and was startled to see him there behind the glass, staring down at me and mouthing words I couldn't hear. His face was still pale from that morning, his eyes still sunken, but he had a queer expression as he watched me in the garden. Was it terror? Excitement? Anticipation? Was he even looking at me or something or someone else? I spun around and saw nothing else behind me, nothing but the shadows of the old oak tree.

I turned back but Jason had left the window, and for a moment I wondered if he had ever been there, if I hadn't imagined someone watching me from above. It then occurred to me that the someone watching might not have been Jason, which seemed an infinitely worse proposition.

But, no, it was Jason. It had to be. I knew because a moment later I saw him, spilling from the house and onto that wooden staircase landing above. I saw him look at me—reach out his hand and look directly at me, unflinchingly locking eyes—and then descend the stairs in a slow deliberate panic on bandaged feet bloodied and scabbed. He seemed excited, possessed, desperate to get to me, but I didn't understand why. Even though every step appeared to inflict a momentary grimace of pain, he did not stop, did not slow further. He just continued to make his way closer. He was yelling something I couldn't make out, but it was clear he wanted to reach me before it was too late. But too late for what? Without thinking, I took a step back.

The Parchment Thief

M.K. Anderson

———◆———

HUMAN SKIN MAKES a very poor parchment. It is far too brittle—crackly and yellow with fat—to stand on its own. To be used as parchment, it must be backed with a more supple cowhide core, but even then it tends to flake and peel away with normal use over the centuries. Thus, only five ever existed. Two were stunts by doctors who stole cadavers of ignominious men. Proofs of concept. The last three claimed to be occult texts (though that, of course, is nonsense). One, the one I am holding, is the only one that survives.

It is perfect. It was made for a 16th-century Neapolitan count who was rumored to have murdered his six wives. This is a trophy of Maria Louisa, his final wife and victim. It is rare. It is valuable. But that is not why I'm planning to steal it.

My colleague, Eunice, adjusts her glasses. She is a historian. I am primarily a chemist who recreates historical methods of parchment making to investigate the implications in preservation. I am currently seated in a back room full of shelves and repair materials at a small table, alone with the book and her. She's standing over me, watching me. I don't think she suspects what I intend.

I should not communicate indifference here. That would be strange. I place my hand on the binding, linger there. It is a rich, pleasant chestnut at the edges, fading into a color like marzipan or the head of a drum in the center. I am not very interested in bindings, but this one is beautiful. I think it is pig leather, but then remember—

"Is the binding also human?"

"Yeah."

"Same source?"

She shakes her head. "It was re-bound in the 1670s."

I open it.

Manuscripts are arranged in *quires*. A quire is folded sheets of parchment nested, and several are stitched together, side-by-side, to form the manuscript. They are then placed in a binding. There are a total of 60 quires in this manuscript, and only two toward the back are from a human source.

I am uncomfortable with how Eunice is watching me. She recently embarrassed me at dinner, after a flight of ciders, by introducing me as "Teddy" (I am Theodore) and complimenting my presentation that afternoon. "I wonder about this guy. He's way into parchment as skin!"

All parchment is skin. How else would I describe it? But Eunice has intuited I would find this experience pleasurable and is watching me to leech a little of that pleasure herself. Her gaze pushes me to an awareness of myself, my body, I find uncomfortable. Therefore I do not stroke the pages as I turn them. Those white gloves sometimes seen on television are an affectation we archivists hate. A gloved hand cannot feel the give of the skin, where it is weak, where it could be damaged. Parchment is made to be touched.

Disappointed with my hesitancy, Eunice places her hand over mine. "You don't need to be so gentle!"

She guides my fingers to the center of the page, to stroke under a line of text. I cannot read Renaissance-era Neapolitan. It is Latinate, so I catch snatches here and there. *"Ensnare." "Command."*

Eunice still has hold of my hand. I can feel her body heat on my back, where her breasts are pressed against me.

I wish she would not. I tense, preparing to peel myself away from her.

"Need any help?" she asks. I gather she's offering to translate for me and I quickly, enthusiastically, agree.

Count de Silva's first wife, Francesca de Merlo it was discovered, was in the good confidence of the dõnas de fuera [the fair folk]. She believed her husband would intervene to spare her the questions of the Inquisition. But it was a marriage of convenience, though she, being a woman, had formed an unnatural passion for him.

I frown. Eunice notices.

"Fifteen fifties," she says. "Falling for your husband would be like … falling for your colleagues. Kinda icky." She picks at a hair on my collar. I tilt my head away. Something about that seems to hurt her feelings, though I don't know why. She says, "Uh, romantic love as part of noble marriages wasn't a thing until like, seventeen something?"

"Ah." I'm not much of a historian. I must be to some extent, but the anthropological details are tedious. Even dead people are needy. Parchment only yields.

Eunice reads more, but I don't listen. I know the story. The first wife admitted to the Inquisition her spirit left her body in her sleep (witchcraft), and she was sentenced to death. While burning, she cursed her husband to love many wives as he did not love her, to resort to witchcraft to keep them, and be damned. This book, supposedly, is the culmination of that curse.

Maria Louisa was married to the Count de Silva at sixteen. He was already infamous. She must have been terrified. Despite him, she was an accomplished poet and a minor mathematician by her mid-twenties. Who knows what she might have been if she'd lived beyond that? After her, the count took no more (known) victims. Possessing Maria Louisa in this fashion had slaked his bloodlust.

Truth be told, I've never understood why people are so preoccupied with one another. Eunice, for instance—*still* reading, oblivious—has asked me to eat dinner with her twice, which I declined. I am aware she eats. I don't need to see it. Upon reflection I realize perhaps she is . . . interested. I grimace. She does lovely preservation work. Really, a deft hand. That I can appreciate. All of her best qualities in a clean, tidy object. But the idea of that bag of flesh touching me, smearing me with fluids, *demanding* things of me, I—I—

I scoot my chair in to pull away from Eunice.

That stops her reading. She asks if I'm all right, and I pretend the fairy tale had gotten too gruesome. We flip through the remaining pages. There are strange illustrations in miniature of little creatures, small, naked men with lidless eyes and webbed hands, pawing at a fully dressed lady's knees. What appear to be ingredients lists. Something in the format of the Lord's Prayer, but the only words I can pick out are obscenities.

I don't like the idea of these images in my house, even confined within a book. Manuscript thieves typically disassemble and sell manuscripts piecemeal to collectors. I considered, fleetingly, of dismembering the manuscript and disposing of those sections before recoiling from the thought. I am horrified with myself. That would be a desecration.

"Ready for the real deal?" Eunice said.

I wet my lips and carefully part the final pages.

They are yellow and mottled, yes, but they are supple. Immaculate. They, unlike any other specimens of human parchment, are palimpsests. They have been written on, repeatedly, then the words washed off and re-used. I knew they were palimpsests but what leaves me suddenly breathless—

"They're blank!"

Eunice breaks out smiling. I have seen hundreds of palimpsests, but never *blank* ones bound in a manuscript. Why would someone do that? I gingerly reach out, this time unguided by Eunice. Shy, but I know what I am doing.

It is soft. My God, it is soft. There are pores and fine, soft vellus hairs, what little had not been shaved away. Shadows of a slanted script are still, faintly, visible here and there. A quill has left shallow grooves. I wish I could have felt the skin unmarred. As it should have been. This would have been her back or belly. I choose to imagine it's her back.

"H-have you any idea what was here?" I ask.

"Love letters. A few of them."

"To whom?"

"Maria Louisa."

"*To* her?"

Eunice smiles as if to say *Cool, huh?* but I am horrified. From whom? Her husband? No, his pattern was to turn immediately cold after a murder. So these were other men. Subsequent owners of the manuscript.

Oh, I didn't like that.

"Do you think removing the ink helped preservation? Maybe they did something unusual?" Eunice asks.

"Hm? Oh, no." I say. I am irritated to be pulled out of thought. "Anything effective at removing ink would speed deterioration."

"*What* deterioration?"

She lifts a corner to show where a very thin, pale strip of cow parchment is sandwiched between two yellowing layers. No sign of separation. I have no idea how to reproduce it, which means nobody does. This was someone's lifework. But more than that, it would have required inspiration.

I am euphoric.

I've only ever felt kinship with things. When I found out *this* manuscript existed, in *this* condition, I set out to find anything at all on how to reproduce it. How would I take, say, Eunice and make a sheet of parchment? Beyond the obvious, beyond flaying her corpse. Others had tried using a corpse and failed. So something about Maria Louisa herself and her circumstance was special. What I think, if I really put myself into her husband's mind—she was alive when he flayed her. I'm sure of it. That is why she is so well preserved. He flayed her alive because of who she was and what her betrayal meant to him. Who she was *made* this manuscript. It could not have been anyone else. I understand this manuscript, and therefore her. She's my very first love.

Eunice could never inspire a man to make her into a masterpiece.

There *was* something I didn't understand, though.

"Why risk infidelity?"

"Hm?" says Eunice.

"She knew what he was like. Why cheat?"

Eunice gives me a funny look. "You think she cheated?"

"That's what the story says."

The story is actually more interesting. Maria Louisa's husband found strange stains between her shoulder blades, which she dismissed as mere dirt. But through investigation, he discovered the lady frequently, urgently, begged for a basin of water many mornings, but would not allow anyone to attend to her. She would use it herself. He burst in on her one morning, rent off her smallclothes, and found a note—*I love you*—written on her wrist. Still fresh, welts still raised from the quill on her skin.

I am too transparent. Eunice sees something about my expression she doesn't like. Across her face, a quick flash of what I think may be disgust or fear. She smooths it over with a smile.

"I mean . . . the man let his first wife die and killed the next five. He made the girl into parchment. He *wrote* her story. You think he wouldn't lie?"

"I . . . I don't see what else but passion would motivate this kind of . . . " I run my hand over the page. "Craftsmanship. I suppose."

Eunice straightens her back, reaches down, and closes the book. I daren't object. We discuss the binding a little more and its condition. I am relieved she is far more businesslike.

Here, I must take a risk.

"Would . . . would you mind if I have a few minutes to take notes?"

"Hm?"

I pull a notebook out of my back pocket. It is a little smaller than the manuscript I place it beside. "I know I should have while we were talking. I just don't concentrate well."

She sighs and checks her watch. "Fine. Just ... I'll be in the little girl's room. I can give you ten, and then I gotta check it back in."

My heart throbs. She checked the manuscript out of inventory for this. That would mean it'd be inspected upon check-in. The plan had been to cut the quires free and swap in my notebook, glued in, quick and dirty. It wouldn't pass a close inspection, but without a record of me being here and with enough time, the theft would be difficult to pin on me.

That was now infeasible. There was a record.

She would not be mine. I feel first anger, and then this sweet, awful chest pain.

Eunice leaves me. I open my notebook.

Do I risk it? It's not even a risk; I *would* be caught. My career would be over, and I'd be a felon.

I open to the final pages. Men—other men besides me—had wanted to do the same thing. I am ashamed of being so conventional in my fantasies. But isn't it also evidence of her allure?

I pull out the razor blade I'd hidden between the leaves of my notebook. Here I hesitate. I might cry. If I take the whole thing I *will* be caught, and well, it might be worth it. A few short hours with her, all that's left of her, and a lifetime to remember it. But how would I explain myself? And how could I deprive myself of my preservation work? While my work does pale in comparison to this strange new pleasure of joy in another person, it *is* worthwhile. There are hundreds of manuscripts that will survive because of me.

Surely I can desecrate just one.

I hope she'll forgive me.

With one deft stroke, I run the blade along the base of one of the inner pages to free a single sheet and tuck it onto my notebook. It fits, perfectly hidden. This theft *will* be noticed someday, and I will be among the suspects. But I will never be caught.

I HAVE SET the mood appropriately. I am by a window at twilight and am making use of the last of the natural light and a candle. I am no poet, and less of one in Latin, but as an educated woman she would understand the language. The draft I have composed (on cow vellum) I have laid at my left hand. I have cut a fresh quill and honed its nib. And I have, in front of me, the palimpsest. I have taken care to wash it clean one last time and let it dry. I have noticed some very minor delamination between the layers on the edge where I cut it. I have repaired that. I think the repair will hold.

My hands are still clean. I tend to get ink stains when I write. So, I take a moment to touch the parchment and be present. To breathe the sweet, heavy candle smoke. I cannot do this many times, perhaps four or five ever, and then I must spend the rest of my life remembering.

I spent all my practice run in anticipation. There is a rhythm to writing, a loop between heartbeats, the lift and re-wetting as the nib begins to scratch. It focuses the mind on only the feeling of the moment.

It will be perfect.

I dip my quill into my inkwell, and, in a cramped and heavy hand, impose myself upon the page.

THERE IS A CASTLE, modest and square, upon the Mediterranean Sea. Blue as her eyes. She is in her personal bedchamber in a four-poster bed, walled in by heavy silk. She is half-asleep in the rosy dawn, dressed in her smallclothes, which are rough-woven by our standards and the finest on earth in her time. If she was once terrified to live here, once stifled by the gold and the silk and the furs her husband piles upon her, perhaps she is complacent. Perhaps it is not yet day, and she only dons fear with the rest of her garments.

She stirs, brow furrowing, then, awake suddenly, sits up, thrown out of a nightmare. She clutches her back, paws at her smallclothes, yanks them with increasing panic, swatting at her rib as if stung by wasps, twisting in vain to see what is on her back. She pulls away her hand and finds it covered in ink and blood.

She begins to scream.

THE BORDER

Dan Stintzi

———— ◆ ————

MY CONTACT ON the other side of the border was a woman my superiors called Violet. She had information, they said, that could end the war. Which war though, they did not specify. The time and location of our meeting came to me by hidden message in the newspaper that I found by circling every third letter in a phony article about an artist who had killed himself using a hammer. The border crossing itself was uneventful; the soldiers on the far side of the bridge did not question my forged papers, they found no fault in my accent. I met Violet at a café and we sat on metal chairs on the sidewalk, drinking tea the flavor of grass while the sun set. We spoke confidently of things that did not exist, and events that had never happened. There were listeners everywhere. She whispered to me in code words. She told me secrets that only she knew. *There is something growing inside of me*, she said. *There's a face inside my face.*

I was well-versed in the more subtle, subterranean elements of trade-craft, and I understood that while her words were not immediately clear, their meaning would reveal itself to me as time went on. She slid a scrap of paper—folded over and into itself repeatedly—across the table, and when I had unfolded it completely, I read the contents once, then a second time, then swallowed the paper with a drink of my tea and stood from my metal chair. She made a scene of kissing me, right there in the street, and I tasted on her lips something just beyond the tea, something like cigarette smoke only harsher like the exhaust pumped out of trains. Our superiors had concocted a narrative to justify the meeting. We were lovers caught up in an impossible affair: her husband a diplomat, my second child on the way, but now our time had run out, the diplomat was on to us, this was to be our last meeting. She said goodbye and disappeared in the haze that rose up from the hidden tunnels beneath the city.

The light had faded and the gas lamps glowed over the heads of soldiers playing cards and smoking long cigarettes, their rifles leaned against the brick walls. The streets wound in spirals and I followed the growing shadows until I reached a tavern, the windows of which glowed a color I liked, so I found a seat at the bar and ordered a local delicacy, a dish I had never heard of with a name that, even after my careful practice, I managed to mispronounce. The tavern was nearly empty; there were shadows in the booths that may have been people. The lights were hung such that the edges of the room faded away, gave the impression of endlessness. I ordered a beer, which on this side of the border was blacker than coffee and served at room temperature. The texture was something like gravy and it tasted like its color; it was strong though, and after my first glass, the room seemed to grow brighter, open up a bit, and I found myself concerned with some of the bartenders more metaphysical postulations.

"Buildings have souls too," he told me. "People, we're like the souls of buildings. When we leave, they're just shells, just bricks and wood."

"Interesting," I said, even though it was not. I was only partially listening, my other half repeating the address Violet had passed to me at the café, trying to burn the numbers and letters into my brain, deep enough that another of the black beers couldn't find and erase them.

The dish I had ordered arrived. It was the size and shape of a sandwich only made of a pastry crust and sealed somehow, little indentations rounding the browned edges. Past the crust, submerged in a wine sauce, were various red and purple meats. I hadn't eaten since before I crossed the border. After my first bite, the crust broke apart and began to drain, a red fluid collecting in the corner of my plate. The meats were rich and flavorful, but the specific taste was unfamiliar.

"You know what you've got there?" The bartender was smiling. People on this side of the border were very proud of the cuisine.

"It's delicious," I said.

"It's all organs," he said.

I stuck to the crust after that and allowed the meats to slump together in a mound at the plate's center. A woman sat on the stool beside me. She was striking, the far side of her face obscured by shadow, a cigarette hanging from the corner of her lip, the smoke drifted over her face, making her eyes go gray.

"You're not going to eat your organs?" she asked. The bartender shook his tumbler and poured her a cocktail. The drink was the color of carnival lights. She kept the cigarette in her mouth as she sipped her drink, the smoke rolling over the liquid like a predawn haze.

"I find the texture too," I searched for the word, "gamey."

"Many foreigners do," she said. "May I?" She gestured toward the plate and I slid it down the bar top.

"Is it so obvious?" I asked.

"It is not your fault. I was born with an extra sense," she said as she scooped a small pile of meat onto her spoon, ladling the wine sauce carefully up to her lips. She removed the cigarette, popped a piece of meat with her molars and took a drag. The sauce had spilled over her bottom lip, now hung from her chin like a tear. "I can read thoughts. It's a gift and a burden. You were thinking that you are lonely in this strange country and that you could use some company."

"What am I thinking now?"

"That's not how it works. I can only see inside of those who are unaware that they are being observed."

"Do you always lie to strangers?"

"See him?" She pointed at the bartender, his back turned to us. "He is thinking of his cousin who was taken. He is thinking of the hidden places. Where they take you when your time is up."

"What do you know of those places?" I asked. She looked away, blew smoke from her nostrils. The cigarette was only a stub now.

"Only rumors."

"Have you been sent here by someone?"

"I don't know what you mean." She scooped more meat, slurped up sauce. Music started in the corner of the room, dark figures draped in red light played long-bodied wooden instruments. The sound of it was odd, had the rhythm of rain falling.

"Can you see what I'm thinking now?" I pulled back the side of my jacket and showed her the butt of my revolver. "Who sent you?"

"Oh my, a gun. How terrifying," she said and lit another cigarette. "Do you have an apartment in the city?"

I did. My superiors had it rented through the month. I nodded.

"I'd very much like to see it," she said.

WE LOST OUR way somewhere between the bar and my apartment. The streets all looked the same, and the black beer had put a laxness in my step. We passed a group of soldiers. They peered at us from under their helmets, laughing loudly when we turned the corner.

"Put your arm around me," she said, and I did. She felt slight beneath her jacket, as if were I to unbutton those buttons, remove the jacket and what was beneath, I would find only bones, moon-colored, the texture of chalk. I held her closely and heard something creak under her skin.

"What is your name?" I asked, caring less and less where the apartment was.

"Elina," she said, and I repeated it.

We found the apartment by chance, the white numbers appearing like an apparition on the side of a building that looked like all the other buildings. The key was hidden where my superiors said it would be. The gas lamps had been extinguished and the streets had been overtaken by shadows. I had the feeling of being observed from far away.

The apartment's furnishings were spartan. There was a reading chair, a desk, and a bed with only one pillow. I followed Elina to the bedroom, she stuttered between steps, lilted side-to-side. I reached for her but my hand only brushed her jacket, and she moved to the far side of the bed, where she perched and removed a silver case—the size of a pack of cigarettes—from her purse. From the case, she removed a slender glass pipe and a clear container filled with a lavender colored powder.

"What is that?" I asked claiming the bed's single pillow, spreading myself over the thick quilt that smelled of cat urine.

"The locals call it Oneiro."

"Are you not local?"

"I am local to somewhere, just not this place." She began the elaborate preparation of the powder. There were several steps and as many utensils necessary to make the substance glow green and turn to smoke. It held there in the pipe's chamber until Elina drew it to her lips and pulled. When she exhaled, there was nothing, the smoke remained inside her.

"Those same locals say that if you're lucky, or maybe if your spirit is suitably quieted, it lets you speak to the dead." She again prepared the pipe, filled it with smoke that smelled of fresh cement. "Mostly, it helps me sleep." She handed me the pipe and I inhaled the smoke, felt it crack like fire in my lungs. I exhaled and Elina turned off the lights, and we lay in the bed together, her smoking her cigarette, blowing rings toward the ceiling, me forgetting what I wanted from her, unsure why I was where I was, or why I was who I was. This room is not my home, I thought. In the distance, very far away, the sound of explosions carried across the night.

"Are those real?" I asked her.

"Yes," she said. "In this country, bombs are not make-believe."

I thought it strange, that just the hearing of bombs made them more frightening. They could not be heard on my side of the border. They were just as dangerous to me here though, which is to say, not at all. This city was protected. Treaties had been signed. But to hear them was to imagine their damage, the homes and heads on which they fell. I saw them clearly, the victims. Their images came to me freely and without warning, like memories of people I had known in a past life. I saw soldiers half-melted and missing limbs. I saw sexless bodies smoldering in the ruins. The melted soldiers spoke to me, they told me things that I had never heard; they spoke in a new language, in molten rock and fire. Their skin burned away as they spoke, it evaporated, left them only muscle and bone, but that too faded, as did their words, the secrets they shared.

"Hold me," Elina said, and I wrapped my arms around her listening again for the sound of the bombs, but they had stopped and the night was still.

I AWOKE STILL wearing my shoes and tie, and Elina was gone. She left no mark on the bed. Instead, after I had showered and shaved, I found Violet standing in the kitchen, blowing steam off the top of her tea. She had on a rain jacket. I could see the shape of her pistol beneath the fabric.

"I've made coffee too," she said.

"Thank you," I said, feeling mixed-up, replaying the night before in my mind. I felt as though a trick was being played on me, a sort of sleight-of-hand but with bodies.

"Last night was wonderful," she said.

"Why is that?"

"Don't be silly," she said, "because of you. Because of us. Have your coffee, darling."

Maybe coffee would help, the powder from the night before had left me in a fog. There was an index card on the counter in front of the coffee pot. On it a handwritten note.

Change of plans. Play along. They're listening.

But who was listening, I wondered. My superiors? Was the apartment bugged? I would not put it past them. But what would it matter to them how Violet conducted her business. She had her own superiors, her own orders and objectives. I had missed some piece of vital information. The world had changed while I slept.

"Of course," I said. "Last night was wonderful." I tore the index card into tiny pieces and poured myself a cup of coffee. It was cold and tasted like dust. "Did you sleep through the bombs?"

"I don't understand the question," she said, standing very still, the teacup held only by her fingertips. She would not look at me, and she stared out the window, her eyes trapping the blue-gray reflection of the sky. I was reminded of the men I'd know as a soldier, those who had trained themselves to sleep with their eyes open. I pretended as if I had not spoken and waited for her direction.

"Would you like to take a walk?" she asked.

I agreed and poured my coffee down the drain, and then we were out in the damp haze of morning, walking past the city as it awoke. On this side of the border, the butchers hung meat from hooks in the windows of their shops. There were skinless animals that I did not recognize suspended from thin ropes, twirling in circles like trapeze artists. Beside the animals were fat tubes of red sausage curled up in rattlesnake piles between baskets overflowing with apples and pears.

I wiped rain off the wooden slats of a bench on the edge of a long, pond-pocked garden park, and we sat together as the birds made sounds so sharp and clear as to sound unnatural, as if prerecorded and played on a loop. In the distance, beyond the buildings and the trees on the far side of the park, smoke could be seen rising from some unknown fire. I was made to think again of Elina and her lavender powder.

Violet put her head in her hands and began to cry, her shoulder blades pressed against her jacket, rising up and down as she let out little heaves.

"It was a trap," she said and came up wiping her thumb beneath her eyelids. "The address I gave you, it was a setup. I'm so sorry. I had no choice. They made me watch, said it would happen to me. They are not men, not really. They're something else. They're black inside."

"Who?" I considered the revolver in its holster, the thought gave it shape and I could feel its weight against my body.

"Who else? My superiors. Your superiors. There is no difference.

They all want the same things. They want bodies. They want to see who can stack the dead the highest."

"I don't understand. I have a directive. I'm going to bring back information that could end the war."

"Do you really think such as thing exists?"

I had no satisfactory answer. A woman pushing a stroller weaved along the garden paths. She had on a hat that sagged shadows down her face, and I could not see her eyes. Violet hid her tears by carving shapes into the bench with her fingernail.

"Why did you come back?" I asked.

"They took me inside, and now I've begun to change. I cannot begin to describe it. I couldn't be responsible for it happening to you."

"What about the clues? The things you said at the café?"

"You're confusing me with someone else."

The smoke on the horizon was thicker now. It had in it a shade of red. The stroller woman had laid out a blanket in the grass. She set her child down on the blanket and let it roll around while she read a book. The child began to cry but she ignored it, turned the page, tried to capture the light on the print.

"Soon they'll know I've told you."

"What can I do?"

"I have contacts inside the counter-insurgency, men who will help you, but their aid does not come without a cost."

Unconsciously, she scraped at a scab on her ring finger, just below the knuckle, and said, "There's a man named Rötenbach. He's wrapped up in all this. He has information that you need. Take that information to my contacts and they will get you out of the country. This is where you will find him." She wrote an address in the dirt with a twig. "Do you have it?"

I nodded and she wiped away the words with the tip of her boots. She told me where her counter-insurgency contacts could be found. They were hiding in a farmhouse outside of the city.

"You cannot go back to your apartment."

The stroller woman's child had rolled off the blanket and was crawling, like a soldier through mud, toward a small patch of daisies.

The woman continued reading, did not seem to notice.

"Will I see you again?"

"It is possible," she said. "But I may not be who I am now."

I went to kiss her but she turned her face. On her hand, the scab had been fully picked, the wound appeared infected, the blood more black than red.

"Goodbye," she said.

I left the bench and retrieved the stroller woman's child from a plot of dirt and mulch. When I came back to her with the baby in my outstretched arms, she dropped the book and stood, speaking rapidly in a language I did not know. She snatched the baby and returned it to the stroller, and then returned to me, nearly yelling, her eyebrows squeezed down toward the bridge of her nose, wetness piling up at the edges of her eyes. Her tone told me that I had made a mistake, crossed some cultural boundary I did not know existed. There was nothing I could do so I turned back to the bench and saw that Violet was gone. The smoke on the horizon filled the sky. It muddied the blue and made the light over the garden turn steel-colored. Whatever was burning had been fed, piled higher with more wood or trash or people, and I could see, just above the treetops, something like a face inside the billowing smog.

RÖTENBACH CARRIED A briefcase, and I knew that the information I needed was inside. More than a suspicion, I had an unusual sensation, a feeling that what was inside the briefcase wanted me to see it, as if the information was an agent in its own right. I found him at the address Violet had written in the dirt, through a process of waiting and watching. I sat at a café across the street from the address and stared for hours at the front door. When it finally swung open, I saw that Rötenbach was a short man made slightly taller by thickly heeled boots, and he wore a black trench coat and spectacles that gave his eyes an insectile warp. He held the briefcase in his left hand, kept the right hidden in his coat pocket.

Following him from afar, I pretended to inspect shops and vendors, trying on hats, inquiring about additional sizes and colors. It went on like this for several miles and we worked our way out toward the city's edge where the buildings grew further and further apart and the sound of gunfire could be heard clearly. The city deteriorated as we progressed. The buildings themselves began to crumble, some were boarded-up or charred black by long ago fires. It was as if we were walking through time, in the direction of the future, a future in which the wars continue and spread.

Rötenbach walked in an odd way. His stride was too long and his knees did not bend when he stepped. I was grateful when he turned sharply down an alley, disappeared through an unseen doorway. The building he had entered was windowless and made up of bricks the color of sand. I found a bench a block down the street and waited, watching the clouds drift, listening to an argument between a man and a woman who had left their window open. The woman believed the man was having an affair.

"No, no, no. You have no idea who I am, do you?" the man said. "I am not your husband."

"Who are you? What are you doing in my home?" The woman was crying, near hysterics.

"I'm a nurse," he said. "I've been hired by your children to provide care. You've become confused again."

"Oh," the woman said and then the window closed and their voices became unintelligible.

Rötenbach emerged from the alleyway without his briefcase. He stepped into the street. Our eyes caught and he approached.

"Excuse me," he said. His voice was sharper than I expected, and he paused very briefly between each word. "Do you have the time?"

I withdrew my hand from my jacket and examined my watch. Either I had not wound the watch properly, or some mechanism inside the machine had come loose. The face showed ten fifty, when above us, the sun had begun to set.

"I'm afraid I need a new watch."

"Not a problem," he said. "Let us assume that it is seven o'clock on the dot."

"Surely it's not that late."

"If we agree, then it is."

"I don't think I can agree."

"Oh well," he said and left me there looking at my broken watch.

He was gone soon after, fading into a crowd. Had it been a warning? It was only chance, I told myself. I waited to see if anyone else would enter the building. The sun set and the little flames inside the gas lamps began to burn.

To my surprise, the door was already unlocked. I leaned in slowly, looking for light, for Rötenbach's co-conspirators, but there was no one inside. The room was shadows and concrete. The only light source was a desk lamp across the room. The lamp was on a stool, directed at some vague shape on the floor. Moving to the light, I saw the briefcase clearly. This was a drop point, the briefcase's recipient would arrive soon.

I hurried, fiddled with the metal clasps that help the briefcase shut, but they too were unlocked. What was Rötenbach? Certainly not intelligence. This was all too sloppy. A politician maybe. Inside the case were several documents. I held them up to the light.

The first document was titled in a form of the language spoken on this side of the border, only it was an older form, a historical dialect taught in universities but rarely, if ever, used by anyone other than professors of ancient literature. The documents themselves did not appear old, but I had reason to believe that they were reproductions, possibly photographic copies. I had difficulty with the translation. The titles came out to something like: *Builders of the Flesh Home.* Or maybe a better translation was *Skin House.*

It was a sort of code, I was sure, and meant something other than what it said. The contents of the document were stranger than the title. The language here was different as well, it was completely foreign to me. I had never seen words like these. Beside the text were illustrated diagrams of human arms and legs cross-sectioned and highly detailed. The rest of the body was accounted for in the later pages. The images were elaborate, similar to those in medical textbooks, but the intention did not appear to be the identification of the body's contents, but rather instruction for application and repair, like the manual for a car or radio. There were many more drawings: ear canals, intestinal tracts, the brainstem, male and female genitalia, and the last page put them all together, showed the body as a whole, only there was a gap that ran down the middle, from the forehead to the groin. A zipper down the length of a jacket. Beyond the gap was nothing, only black shadow. There were handwritten annotations in the margins done in blue ink, in the same unreadable characters as the rest. The body was the last page. Nothing else.

Violet was insane, I thought. She'd been broken by someone or something and had set about getting me killed. If there were secrets hidden in these drawings, I could not decipher them. She had risked my life for nothing.

Beneath my feet, vibrations, then a crash like thunder. The bombs had begun and I was closer here than I had ever been. I stacked the documents back in the briefcase and fled, leaving the door as I'd found it, raising my collar to the wind as I wound my way back across the city in search of something, anything to hold on to.

I FOUND ELINA again after that, or maybe it was the other way around, maybe she had found me. She was standing beneath the arched entryway of the apartment where we had spent the night together. She was lit from behind, the light from inside the building glowing white, giving her an outline that radiated like divinity. She was wearing what she'd worn before. Her rain jacket was wet and I tried to remember the last rainfall but could not. She remained still, did not move her head, but even from a distance, I could see her eyes flit back and forth across the avenue, looking, I was sure, for me.

I stepped beneath the light of a gas lamp and our eyes met. She seemed shocked, disappointed maybe, as if she had been certain I would not return. She approached, her shoes against the street sounding like hammered nails, and pressed her mouth to my ear.

"Change of plans," she whispered. "Play along. They're listening."

She took me by the hand and pulled, and we huddled together like drunk lovers working our way down the same streets I had walked that morning with Violet. It was as I suspected on the night we met.

Elina had a role in this too. But a role in what exactly? You're here to end the war, I remembered. No, that wasn't right. You're here for the documents, the counter-insurgency, for Rötenbach and the builders of the Skin House.

Was that it? I couldn't remember.

I pressed the tips of my fingers to the place just below Elina's ribs, applying pressure, I pushed up and inside, and said, "Tell me who you work for." She flinched and twisted her body trying to relieve the pain.

"Who do you think?" She pulled my hand away. "Did you think they would leave it up to you alone?"

Of course, I thought, a backup. A contingency. My superiors were nothing if not thorough.

"Where are we going?"

"Someplace quiet," she said.

The quiet place, I discovered, was the same garden I had visited with Violet only a few hours earlier. It was empty now and lit with dull lamps that produced small pools of light and color. The rest was black. Empty space. We followed a gravel path deeper into the park, into a forested area where the tree branches cast shadows like the veins I had seen in Rötenbach's diagrams. They made me think of my contents, the things I was made up of, the tubes that carried fluids up and down the length of me. It was all a fragile balance. Remove one piece and the whole thing falls apart. I could smell the flowers of the garden but I could not see them.

"And what of Violet?" I said when we were near the park's center, the city lights only barely visible through the trees. "She seemed to think she was in danger. She believed she'd been set up."

"I do not know who you are talking about."

"My contact. The woman my superiors called Violet."

"Contact?" she said.

"It doesn't matter," I said. "What're we doing out here? What the hell is going on? Rötenbach's documents, did you see them? It's gibberish. Pictures of body parts and the scrawling of a madman. If that's what you're after, go home. Don't waste your time."

Even in the dark, I could see her smile. "Can I tell you a story?" she asked and spoke before I could answer. "When I was a girl, my family lived on a farm in the mountains. We raised goats and pigs and chickens. I learned at a young age about sex and birth. I saw that the process of creation was a messy business. Violent. Many of the mothers did not survive childbirth. There was one that I'll never forget: a doe had grown so large that she could not walk. My father had to help with the birth. He had to use a knife. The mother was dead before the child was born. I was there for all of it. I was six years old, I think. The goat came out wrong, it had gotten jumbled up inside the womb. I remember my mother screamed when she saw it. The goat had several heads that had all fused together. It had too many eyes and ears too, but somehow it was still deaf and dumb. It had the right amount of legs and its body was fine, only the heads were wrong. It made a noise I had never heard another goat make. It had three tongues all in the same mouth. I found something about it lovely, and I asked my father if I could keep it as a pet. My father was a man who lacked imagination. He saw beauty only in obviously beautiful things. He took the goat behind the barn and slits its throat." She paused. I was unsure if the story was over.

"Why are you telling me this?"

She had slowed her steps, was behind me now. "You remind me very much of my father," she said, and when I turned to see if her face, her body might tell me more of what she meant, I saw she was holding a small blade. Before I could react, she sank the knife into my shoulder up to the hilt. I fell to the ground, the blade still stuck inside of me, and searched with my hands through the gravel for something I could use to protect myself. I found a stone the size of a baseball. I clutched the stone, stood, and swung the rock in Elina's direction. There was a sound like a bird colliding with a window, only wetter, and I felt the force of the impact reverberate back through the bones in my arm. I thought I heard a tap open somewhere, water falling, but when the static in my vision cleared, I saw that it was the black blood falling from the dent in Elina's forehead. She stood still for a moment, blinking and bleeding.

"Oh," she said, and then the blinking ceased and she collapsed.

I removed the knife from my shoulder in three tugs, felt the blade tear unseen things beneath my skin. I used my good arm and dragged the body to a nearby pond. There was yelling in the distance, but it was joyous, drunken. It was followed by singing or maybe a sort of chant. I kicked Elina's body as deep into the pond as I could. Her face was the last thing to sink. The wound was still leaking. Her eyes had yet to lose the appearance of life, but those too melted into the water and all that remained were the weak ripples and lamplight.

The only place left to go was back, I thought, back across the border. I had returned to the apartment despite Violet's warning. I stitched shut the wound in my shoulder as best I could and slept, waking to the sunrise, my sheets and pillow bloodied, the images of Elina's face behind my eyes.

On the doorstep, I found a newspaper. The wars still raged. Soldiers on every side continued to die, as did civilians. A school bus had been targeted. There was a picture of its burned-out husk. Below that was an article about a dead woman. The body had been found near the train station. The picture that accompanied the article showed Violet splayed out on the concrete. The image was gray and white, her blood looked black. A suspect had been brought in for questioning. There was a hole in her head.

The article, I realized, was a plant, a clue. It had been placed there by my superiors. Contained within was a secret message. I circled the second letter of every word and copied the letters into my notebook.

The secret message was this: You can never leave the Skin House.

I took a train back to the border. Having disguised myself as best I could, I went through the process of solidifying, in my mind, the reason for my travel, the necessity of my return. Many of the passengers on the train were soldiers. They carried their rifles with them, standing the guns upright between their legs, as one might a parasol. I kept my head down and tried not to think about the pain in my shoulder. I had been defending myself, I thought repeatedly.

At the checkpoint, standing in line, I could see my country on the other side of the bridge. From where I stood, it looked very much like the place I was leaving. The sun was hidden and the afternoon air carried a heaviness. The line inched forward. Past the other border crossers, I saw soldiers carefully examining the contents of bags and purses, studying—like scholars over ancient manuscripts—each and every document necessary for passage across. I was two people back from the barrier when a young soldier with an invisible mustache approached and put his hand on my shoulder.

"Come with me please," he said.

"It's nearly my turn. I've been waiting for a very long time."

"Come with me please."

"I'm to meet my family. I can't be late."

He did not say anything more, only gestured toward a large tent marked with the twin-sword insignia of the military police. I followed him and entered the tent. Inside was a table, behind which sat another solder, higher ranking by the look of the medals on his uniform. He pointed to the chair in front of the table. The young soldier took my suitcase and emptied the contents onto the floor. He tore into the lining with a small knife and found nothing. I sat in the chair and faced the other soldier whose eyes were heavy, bagged, and ringed with purple. I could smell that he had been drinking. His hairline had receded and he had a gold tooth.

"Papers," he said and I handed them across the table. He glanced at them and threw them back. "This job is terribly boring," he said. "My brother is stationed in the south. He sends me pictures of the beaches. He tells me about the women he has slept with. And here I am." He held his hands over the table like it was a sacrament to be blessed. "Digging through the undergarments of strangers. Trying to find smugglers and *spies*." His eyes went wider when he hit the last word.

"My family is waiting for me," I told him.

"Please," he said, "please, please, please do not speak while I am speaking."

I did not respond. The young soldier had not searched me. I imagined the resistance I would feel in my finger if I pulled the revolver's trigger.

"My colleague has demonstrated that you are not a smuggler, now we must determine whether or not you are a spy." He pulled a black bound notebook from somewhere beneath the desk. He flipped the pages and said, "There are a few ways to go about this. There's the old way: I ask you what you are doing in this country, where you have gone, with whom you have met, etcetera, etcetera." He sighed. "And we will decide if we believe you or not. My colleague and I have done it this way many, many times. If we're honest, it's grown a bit dull."

The younger soldier did not speak, only nodded in agreement.

"But!" He held his index finger toward the tent's peak. "There is another way. My colleague and I believe in the value of invention. We believe that just because things have been done one way for ages does not mean there is no room for improvement. Therefore, I propose that we utilize our new and experimental method. Surely, you are a curious man, like my colleague and I, and certainly, your interest is already piqued." He took a metal flask from a drawer and drank from it. "Are you a believer in psychoanalytic theory? Do you credit the unconscious mind as the true source of man's will? Do you also believe in man's ability to see the true nature of another man's soul through careful questioning and hypnotic suggestion?" He paused and waited.

I knew what he expected of me so I said, yes I did.

"Wonderful! Let's begin. Question one." He flipped several pages in his notebook and said, "Suppose an antique fighter plane is to be moved from a hangar to an aviation museum. Suppose the only way to transport the plane is to disassemble it completely and then when the pieces arrive at the museum, to build it back up again from scratch. The question is this: is the airplane in the museum the same airplane as the one in the hangar?"

It was clear to me then that I was dealing with a madman. The correct answer would be whatever he wanted. "No," I said. "The plane is a different plane." I did not elaborate.

"Interesting." He made a mark in the notebook. "Question two. And this one will require a bit of imagination. Suppose there is a man, let's call him A, and another man who we'll call B. At the exact same moment that B is killed by a clot in the brain, A steps on a landmine and loses his lower half. Before he is truly dead, doctors are able to place A's brain inside B's body. The question is this, is the living man A or B?"

I thought for a moment. "A is the living man," I said.

"Very interesting," the soldier said and made another mark in his notebook. "Final question. Suppose you wake up tomorrow and realize that, while your whole life you believed yourself to be person B, in reality, you are actually person A living inside the body of person B." That was it. He was finished.

"I don't understand the question."

"That's an answer in itself, isn't it?" He made a show of flipping back to examine the other notes he had taken. I heard the young soldier shift his weight behind me.

"Well, we're in uncharted territory here. I've never seen answers like these. I'm unsure—" Before he could finish I drew my revolver from its holster and shot the young soldier through the eye, he buckled and sagged into the floor. And then I shot the question asker, only the shot was low and I hit him in the chin. He was still alive, and at first, did not seem to notice that he had been shot. The blood rushed out of his mouth and neck and he made a noise that sounded like someone trying to speak underwater. I shot him again and the noise stopped. I took his notebook from the desk and found it filled only with scribbles and the same spirals traced over and over again, so much so that the paper had begun to tear.

From outside the tent, I heard shouting and hurried footsteps. My choice was made. I would cross the border or die. I left the tent and ran, pushing through the line, barging past the men and women waiting to cross. I stumbled, dropped the revolver and felt the stitches in my shoulder tear. All I had to do was cross an invisible line, break a barrier conjured up by men who had been dead for centuries, and I could go back to my life. What that was I could not remember.

The soldiers had mobilized. I caught the glint of a riflescope in the watchtower. They were behind me now, dozens of them. I broke through the crowd, hurdled the barrier, and found myself running in the empty space on the bridge, the nationless gap between the two countries. I could see my home, could see the soldiers in our watchtowers, our civilians waiting to cross over. I would be among them soon. I would stop pretending. I would become the person I had once been.

Then the sound like a tree split by lighting, the echo thrown out across the river, then the bullet through my shoulder blade, the sensation of a hole in a dam coming unplugged, my spirit, my soul, whatever it was that made me who I was, slipping out of the twin holes in my back and chest, draining out onto the concrete, leaving behind a collapsing shell, now only skin piled in a heap.

I AWOKE IN a room with no doors. The room's size was difficult to determine, the light did not reach the corners. The holes in my body had been patched. My shirt was bloodstained and torn. I had a vague sense of relief at being alive. But I had heard of rooms like this, and I knew what they were used for. This is where wars were truly fought, in these hidden places that no one could see. There were no laws to govern what went on in rooms like this, no sanctions for those who disobeyed.

I was sitting on a wooden chair, an extended blink away from slipping back into darkness. There were noises on the other side of the room's walls, muffled voices, the hollow tap of footsteps. I could not gauge the passage of time. Sometimes it felt as if the origins of those muted voices was inside of me, the tapping was my own foot, and I would listen harder and become convinced that I had made a mistake, those sound existed separate from myself.

I tried to stand but could not find the strength. There was a leaky faucet hidden somewhere and a fluid was pooling at my feet. Had my superiors been informed of my failure? And what of Violet? Elina? I prayed that they were safe, and then I remembered that no, of course they weren't. The ghost vibrations, that old shock, still lingered deep inside my arm, and I could still feel the sensation of rock striking bone.

I closed my eyes and saw the night sky, the stars blinking in and out of existence, and when I opened them again, I was no longer alone.

Sitting across from me on his own wooden chair was Rötenbach, and standing on his left I saw Elina, but she was complete, the hole in her head filled somehow. Behind them, indistinct shadows in the shape of men lingered beyond the light. Guards or soldiers, I thought, but could not be sure. Rötenbach wore his thick-lensed spectacles, and I sensed, inside his pupils, a slight oscillation. His lips were dry and cracked, and he licked them often in a very slow and obvious way. Elina did not move, only stared at the wall behind me.

"Good evening," Rötenbach said, finally. I had no idea what time it was. "My contacts on the other side say that you have been disavowed. As far as your government is concerned, you no longer exist." He crossed his legs, pulled dry skin from his bottom lip. "That must be an unpleasant feeling, to know with certainty that you are real, that you exist, and yet, the state, the world at large, says otherwise."

I could not find the will to speak. He would kill me soon regardless. What good were my protests?

"Did you find my documents fascinating?"

I said nothing.

"They were very hard to find. It was worth it though. They've allowed us to do many beautiful things." The skin of his hand, I saw, was almost entirely black, as if he'd held it too long over a flame. I thought of rotten fruit, spoiled meat.

"How about this. I don't want to prattle on all night, and I'm sure there are things you'd like to know, so before our work begins, I'll allow you two questions."

Elina had not moved. I watched her eyes to see if she might blink. After some time, she did.

"I was under the impression she had died," I said.

"That's more of a statement, really," he said.

"Is Elina dead?" I tried again.

"Yes," he said. "And your second question?"

How was it that the dead could stand and breathe? I had been misled somewhere. Things were not what I thought them to be.

"The second question, please."

"What is the Skin House?" I asked.

"You're very close," he said, standing. "But not exactly there. Elina, have a seat."

She sat on the chair across from me. Rötenbach put his hands on her shoulders. I tried to catch her eyes but she would not look at me.

"The Skin House is not one thing. But maybe the best way to think about it is as like a body. Like Elina here." Slowly Rötenbach slid his hands up Elina's shoulders, around the curve of her neck.

"The Skin House can be a vessel or a tool. It can be a passageway." He pushed his hands through Elina's hair until his fingertips, the nails on the rotten hand purple and blue, rested on the peak of her head. He tapped her skull slowly. "The real question though is not what the Skin House *is*." The muscles in his jaw clenched as he dug his fingers into her skin. "The real question is what's inside. Here, let me show you."

His fingers sank into the skin up to the first knuckle. Elina's expression did not change as he pulled apart the flesh of her forehead. The skin made a sound like the tearing of damp fabric. There was no blood that I could see. Rötenbach worked his way down her face, pulling the sides apart, separating her into two halves. Strings of clear fluid draped between the halved parts of her face, growing thinner and thinner as he pulled, becoming infinitesimally thin. His bruised hand began to leak from the fingernails and the liquid left faint trails running down Elina's cheeks. When he reached the nose, he gripped each side tightly, and tugged, tugged until, with a snap, the face tore open and I could see into her depths, and what was inside became visible to me.

Sin Deep

Tracy Fahey

———— ◆ ————

THIS SKIN I'M IN. *It's a scaly hide of cracks and fissures; of pink patches and rusty blood. It's an old carpet, gummy and well-trodden. It's an ancient wooden building, rotten and frail.*

The words dance insistently in Eva's head. In bed at night her fingers splay flat on her torso, stroking the scaly skin beneath with careful fingers. Under her fingertips she traces a complex tapestry of scratches and patches; a legacy of a life of constant itching. She touches one arm, delicately, feeling the bumpy, cracked skin of her elbow. *Under my clothes I'm an alligator.*

She can't bear to look at her body in a mirror. Even in the dullest light her body is mapped in a tissue of scars and abraded skin. She is flushed and mottled with splotches of color, a spectrum of reds from palest pink to an ugly burgundy. Her body is a secret mesh of layered skin, bumpy and grainy where she's grated herself frantically in her sleep.

IT'S ALMOST TIME for another gallery tour. Eva walks through the dark rooms of Baroque martyrdoms, a tapestry of livid, contorted bodies splayed against dramatic, dark backgrounds. As she passes she silently tabulates them: *St. Lucy, blinded, with her eyeballs on a platter, St. Laurence roasting on the gridiron, St. Erasmus, disemboweled.* Everywhere is a stark reminder of death, the intense faces of the torturers, the saints' bodies split open like ripe fruit, the livid light illuminating all.

She passes into the next wing. Here the walls shimmer with the soft colors of Renaissance nudes. There it is, milky and cool, the silk-smooth Venus. She drinks it in, imagining running a hand down her marble flank, pearly and perfect as the moon.

This skin I'm in. It holds me within it, but barely. It leaks and flakes and itches. It's a secret sore.

EVENINGS MEAN VISITING time. Eva sits by her sister Sal's bed in the twilight gloom of intensive care. Her sister sleeps, her twisted face unknotted, dreaming. Eva feels her stomach clench in a twist of sorrow. She's only thirty. She shouldn't be here. But she is.

"It's the best place in the hospital to be," says the friendly nurse who comes by to check on her sister once an hour.

She nods mutely. "I know." Her book lies in her lap, unread. She jigs her knee up and down, tapping her foot lightly against the floor, once, twice, three times. It's her old ritual, the protective one, the one that wards off disaster.

"Maybe you might want to take a break. You look done in." The nurse's voice is kind, but Eva feels a flush of mortification. Since she's taken up her vigil in the hospital she experiences constant waves of emotion, everything from sorrow to anger. Her nerve ends are exposed and raw.

"That's fine," she says brusquely, and her voice spells an end to the conversation.

THE NEAREST AMENITY to the hospital is, oddly enough, the zoo. Eva has a season ticket, so she's been to it several times over the last month, just passing the time between the visitor slots in the afternoon and evening. It's winter time, so it's quiet in there. Most of the animals are in hibernation, retreated into the back of their enclosures; just the odd, suspicious flash of eyes from the bushes signaling their presence. The outside areas are too cold to linger in for long, but the monkey house stinks of feces and unwashed fur, and the aviary is too noisy. Her favorite place has become the reptile house; it's a bonus that it's almost always empty. Here the air smells of swamp, a wet heat that warms her. Somewhere in the building are the quiet sounds of water dropping, *plink, plink, plink*, onto a hard surface.

She sits on a wooden bench in the main hall and watches the snakes slither in the glass cases. They coil and uncoil, muscles undulating as they do so. She stares at them, hypnotized by their slow, deliberate movements. There's one in particular that fascinates her, a huge boa constrictor, its body a dappled mass of browns and grays as it slides slowly over its own rippling coils. As it does she leans forward and taps her fingers lightly against the glass. Once, twice, three times. But lightly. She doesn't want to disturb the enormous snake. The tapping is just her ritual, her protection.

Some days she just sits and watches the snakes for hours; their sinuous, heavy bodies moving like greased pistons behind the thick glass.

DEGOS DISEASE. SHE'D never heard of it before Sal was diagnosed. They've both lived with eczema since they were children. It was only when Sal got sicker, when she started developing a dappling of white dots on her arms and legs, that they began to realize this was something else. But by then it was too late.

Eva sits by her sister's bed and holds her hand. It feels dry and hard; the back of it livid with pure white spots. For the last week, Sal's been almost immobile. She has aphasia, the doctor tells Eva; so when she's awake, she can't speak, she just rolls her eyes and mouths silent words. Every time she does that, Eva feels her stomach twist in a sharp pang of sorrow. Abstractly she taps her fingers against her knees, once, twice, three times.

She reads a little of her book, and then stares out the window. Outside it has begun to rain.

That night she goes home and dreams of snakes, their bodies twining and writhing endlessly over each other.

It's almost a relief to go to work. She has to show her ID at the door, even though the porter knows exactly who she is as the main wing is closed to visitors. There's a new exhibition setting up, one of Venetian sixteenth century painting, and the place is a flurry of art handlers and crates and shouted instructions. Eva's glad to sink into the background. She turns into a quiet corridor off the café block towards the office. The Education wing of the gallery is stuffy, but it smells of books and dust instead of the pervading hospital odor of urine and disinfectant. As she sits down at the desk she shares with the other guides she realizes how weary she is. Slowly, over the course of the morning, her body starts to hum back into life; for days she's been running on a power-saving mode, oblivious to herself. Now she can start to feel again; maddeningly, the main sensation is the slow burn of itching skin under her clothes.

The day ticks by; a tour of Impressionist paintings, the teenage students bored and openly playing with their phones, a retirement group, happy to be entertained with stories about the Irish collection. And all the time the itch, the incessant itch burns at her.

It's afternoon when she finishes. She scratches her skin, but it brings no relief. Blood crusts under her fingernails, staining the white crescents with burgundy.

That night she dreams she is a snake again. This time she is the boa constrictor, muscular coils sliding and rippling as she moves. In her dreams, she feels the old familiar itch consume her like dull fire, but she flexes her muscles and rubs against the branches in her cage until her skin sloughs off in long, peeling strips.

She sits by her sister's bed. It's been a peaceful evening; Sal's barely stirred in the bed. One mottled arm is visible over the white sheets. Eva sighs and scratches absentmindedly at her own arm. The skin beneath her fingers is cracked and rough, and when she withdraws her hand it's speckled with red. She studies the bloody drops on her fingertips and thinks of her country childhood: skinned rabbits, like wet red lumps, pitifully small. Sad little bundles in stained plastic bags. The sounds of the ward drone on around her, the hum of machines, the brisk sound of steps on linoleum, the buzzing of the fluorescent light.

If her mother were still alive, she'd be lighting candles for Sal in front of the side altars in the dark, incense-scented church. Eva remembers the sputtering wicks, the steady little flames in front of bloodstained statues. She shrugs helplessly. All she can do is mouth the same mantra, over and over: *Please get better. Please let her get better.*

She crosses her arms tightly across her chest. It's cold in here, but she can't go home. If she goes home, there'll be no-one there for Sal. At the thought of it, she feels her agitation bloom; the red itch flares all along her legs. She scrubs at them through the fabric of her jeans. It's just eczema. Such a tiny thing in the face of her sister's sickness. She taps her hands on her burning knees; once, twice, three times.

My dis-ease. Her disease. She bargains silently in her head. *My skin for hers.*

EVA STANDS IN the gallery. The Venetian exhibition opens tomorrow, so although her eyes are grainy and dry with lack of sleep, she's walking the rooms, making sure she has the tour sequence in her head, so she can move through the show with her groups without having to think or plan, just follow the logical sequence of her script, like an actor in a play.

It's then that she sees it. Titian's *The Flaying of Marsyas*; huge and cluttered, a mass of frenetic brushstrokes. She stands in the early evening gloom of the gallery, looking steadfastly at the painting. She's familiar with it through classes in art history, but this is the first time she's seen it up close in all its fleshy horror. She looks at Marsus' beautiful, resigned face as he hangs upside down, surrounded by figures who hack at his skin, peeling it off in vengeful strips. Beside it, on a wall-mounted placard is a quotation from Ovid.

The Satyr Marsyas, when he played the flute in rivalry against Apollo's lyre, lost that audacious contest and, alas! His life was forfeit; for, they had agreed the one who lost should be the victor's prey. And, as Apollo punished him, he cried, "Ah-h-h! why are you now tearing me apart? A flute has not the value of my life!" Even as he shrieked out in his agony, his living skin was ripped off from his limbs, till his whole body was a flaming wound, with nerves and veins and viscera exposed.

She stands transfixed. Her arms prickle and itch under her long sleeves.

Marsyas, she thinks darkly. *Marsyas knew.*

SITTING BESIDE THE bed in the cool of a dull afternoon, she looks at her sleeping sister. Sal shifts in the bed; the white sheets ripple, her head turns from side to side. Her eyes flicker open and, for one slow agonizing moment, her gaze fastens on her sister. Eva reaches forward and holds Sal's cold hand in hers. Her sister stares at her unblinkingly, like a snake, her dark eyes wet and sad.

Eva shivers. She looks at Sal and remembers those long, hot summers they spent playing in the long grass. If she closes her eyes, she can recall the feeling of heat on her arms, the green warm scent of the crushed grass. She remembers those days of lying on their tummies studying the ants as they ran, busy and purposeful over the baked ground. On those long days it felt summer would last forever.

"Look Evie." Sal grabs her arm with a plump hand. "A baby dinosaur!"

Eva, startled, looks down and sees a tiny lizard, crouched and motionless. They stare at him, he looks back, frozen. His skin is rough and scaly. She extends her arm slowly.

"See Sal," she says. "Like me." Her forearm is mottled and cracked, a tracery of white fissures on pink skin.

"Like me too, Evie." Sal's chubby face breaks out in a wide, happy smile. "Like me too."

"TIME TO GO." The nurse's face looms up, shockingly close to hers. She jumps, she can't help it. The ward is dark, the afternoon visits are over; she must have fallen asleep. She gets up and walks out to the car park. Her feet keep on walking past her car, back to the zoo entrance, back to the reptile house.

She stands in front of the snakes and watches her face mirrored in the dark glass, the scalding tears coursing down her face.

LATER THAT NIGHT, in her bed Eva winds herself into a tight cocoon, swaddled by the heavy duvet. The weight of it feels good, but she aches inside and outside. *My skin for hers.* She weeps silently, tears soaking hot and wet into the cotton. There's no sense of release. She presses her sore, swollen face hard into the pillows.

IT'S DARK. IT'S night-time. Where is she? She realizes that she's in the zoo enclosure, lying in the tall, wet grass. It feels so real; the dampness beneath her soaks into her clothes. *Is it a dream? Am I awake?* She's so tired, she can't tell. She simply lies there, the reptile house silhouetted blackly against the navy sky. As she does, she feels the hot itch rise within her like a tide. It overwhelms her. It maddens her.

She rubs at her arms. The itch just grows and grows, red hot and insistent. She rubs her arms against the wet grass, feeling the coldness send goosebumps down her body. She starts to scratch now, lightly, then harder, but it brings no relief.

A hiss rises from deep inside her. She thinks of the snakes, of the smooth litheness of their bodies, intertwined and sinuous. She claws at herself, dragging her fingernails savagely under her hot skin. It peels away, the flawed and cracked epidermis. Her muscles and tendons appear, a symphony of beautiful reds exposed down to the white bone. Her body is marvelously cool in the night air.

I am the lizard in the long grass.

I am the boa constrictor in the reptile house.

I am Marsyas.

PARADISE POINT

M.R. Cosby

———— ◆ ————

"Do we have to do this? It's not my kind of thing at all."

"It's really not that scary, you know," Lisa said, trying to keep the impatience from her voice. "It's not even a very big one."

"It's big enough for me," said Josh. "It's also ancient. How can we be sure it's safe?"

"Silly. It wouldn't be open if it was dangerous—I know the place is old, but it's all being rebuilt. You can tell by how impressive it looks." She glanced up at the night sky, against which the spindly arms of the Ferris Wheel and its multicolored carriages shone in the garish light from the rest of the funfair.

Josh shook his head as they shuffled forward in the slow-moving queue. "If it wasn't for your precious job . . . "

"I know, I know. You wouldn't be here—and I wouldn't expect you to be. But remember, we're doing this for my career, which in the long term will be good for both of us."

"Yeah, great. We only have a week before you start work—full time—and we're spending a precious evening mingling with all these suits who, soon enough, you won't be able to stand the sight of anyway."

Lisa smiled despite her embarrassment. "Keep your voice down," she whispered, fingering the name tag pinned to the lapel of her best blouse and glancing around to see if he'd been overheard. "Like you say, I'll be working with these people soon!"

The summer was nearly over and so were the lazy months they had spent together since finishing university. Josh wanted the holiday mood to carry on indefinitely, but Lisa was impatient to make use of her newly acquired qualifications. She had lost no time in applying to all the larger law firms in the city and was delighted to have received several job offers. Her final choice, Heinneke, Prose & Split, was holding its annual induction for all the graduate recruits to meet and socialize with their future colleagues, including their families, so she was expected to attend. The venue this year was Paradise Point Amusement Park, which had been partially renovated and was not yet open to the general public.

"This is all very well," Josh said as they inched ever closer to their turn on the Ferris Wheel, "but it feels to me like we're being used as some kind of collective guinea pigs."

"Hmm? What kind of pigs are you collecting?" Lisa was barely listening. She was too busy scanning the crowd, trying to locate Carol, one of the company's partners, to whom she had been introduced when they had arrived—she was determined to impress the right people from the very beginning. Lisa slipped her hands beneath her blouse to feel the shape of her belly. It was too early for her pregnancy to be noticeable, surely, but she could not help but feel self-conscious the whole time. She looked at Josh. So far, only her doctor knew. Her plan was to give Josh the news at the end of this very evening, but something was nagging at the back of her mind, asking her if it was the best thing to do. *Still*, she thought, *doubts at this time must be pretty common, right?*

"No, I said *guinea* pigs. These rides haven't been used since they were fixed up—and now they've hired the place out privately, so that if there's a disaster it can be covered up." Lisa recognized the danger lurking in the tone of Josh's voice. She stopped peering into the crowd, then turned to study his face: she was presented with a familiar scowl which, if not addressed, she knew would linger for the rest of the day. Being dour and introspective were attractive traits in a student, but she was beginning to realize what a drawback they could be in real life. It was most important to Lisa that they came across to her employers as a happy couple and that she would not be held back by his reserved personality.

"Don't be silly, darling, just think of the bad publicity they'd get if something went wrong. Besides, I'm sure they wouldn't risk any-thing, especially after all that trouble from years back—" As soon as the words left her mouth, she wished she had not said anything. Did he know the history of the place? She supposed if anyone could be blissfully unaware of Paradise Point's checkered past, then that person could be Josh. After all, she'd never known him to take much interest in anything beyond himself—and, of course, it had all happened so long ago.

"Trouble?" his scowl deepened.

"Just a fire, that's all, but it's ancient history—actually, it happened when I was very young. I know all about it because my old man was a reporter back in those days and he tells us how the story of the fire was his big break at the newspaper. He was first on the scene." *And he still hasn't got over it*, she thought, but this was something which would have to remain unspoken between them. She was reluctant to tell him the truth about the tragedy which unfolded that evening. Lisa had to admit to herself that Josh was turning out to be more emotionally fragile than she had realized—or, perhaps, than she could handle. Not for the first time, she wondered how he would cope with the pressures of family life.

Josh had widened his eyes at the mention of a fire, but his response was cut short by a surge in the crowd as they finally reached the head of the queue. One of the cars of the Ferris Wheel hit the ground in front of them and its flimsy automated door popped open with a hiss. Several members of the staff appeared from the crowd as the chattering passengers spilled forth from the ride. Clearly, Lisa thought, no expense had been spared for this special event: the staff, dressed in jeans and black T-shirts emblazoned with "Heinneke, Prose & Split," seemed to be lurking everywhere she looked. For a moment, Josh's panicked expression told her that he might refuse to get on board. Then one of the staff members glanced in her direction and, briefly, their eyes met. Did she register some kind of approval as he took Josh's arm to guide him firmly into the cabin? She shook the idea from her head.

Once inside, they found themselves pressed closely together on a slippery wooden bench. A small, waif-like child, with wild blonde hair and an earnest expression, moved along politely. There was very little room to spare, so they were pushed closely together. Josh was clinging to her but she could not pull her arm free to fend him off.

"Are you sure this thing's meant to carry so many people?" His voice sounded unfamiliar.

"Of course it is," she said, but she was far from positive. "They built these things to last, back in the day." Nonetheless, by the time the door was slammed shut and the car shuddered into motion, Lisa was convinced that far too many people had perched themselves on the varnished benches, including some noisy, over-excited children. *I can imagine having a baby*, she thought, *but I just can't picture how I would cope with a child; an independent person.* And perhaps it was just her own situation which made her notice, but she became aware that some of the women in the carriage were noticeably pregnant.

She felt drained. The din was so overwhelming in the small space that she had to fight the desire to cover her ears. To begin with, the windows stared back at them blankly: all Lisa could see were the pinpoint reflections of the lantern suspended from a chain in the center of the ceiling. As the car continued its journey into the night sky, lurching from side to side, it caused the lantern to swing, then to oscillate wildly. Inky shadows were thrown all around, giving her the impression that the occupants were in a constant state of motion, jerking in and out of focus. She tried to relax, but as she scanned the passengers, she noticed something odd. She and Josh had been given black name tags with their names printed in white: however, nearly everyone else at the event had white ones with black lettering. In fact, on the ground she had only seen one other person—a bizarre figure dressed only in a loincloth and rudimentary headdress, complete with horns, presumably some kind of entertainer—with one similar to theirs. Yet in their gently swaying carriage, every single passenger's name tag was black.

Lisa felt the skin crawl on her scalp. She closed her eyes and forced herself to breathe deeply, waiting for the feeling of panic to pass. Then a sudden silence, followed by a general intake of breath among the passengers, jerked her back to the here and now. Everyone was staring out through the windows, apart from the small blonde child pressed close to her side, whose pale blue eyes were, disconcertingly, fixed on Lisa's face.

Even Josh had twisted around in his seat. "It's spectacular," he said in a whisper. Lisa was shocked by the wonder in his voice. It was the first positive comment he had made so far that evening.

The car had paused in its journey through the night sky and was swinging gently, providing a view which was more impressive than she had anticipated. Directly below them the river, sparkling in the light reflected from the fairground, faded into a grid of streetlights, then into the light pollution of the city which stretched to the horizon. The sky was not yet completely dark but a rich, obsidian blue, which morphed into the oblivion of the stars above. Lisa pressed her face against the window beside her to take in the uninterrupted view of Paradise Point, almost directly below them. But how far below? It was such a long way down. She remembered looking up at the Ferris Wheel from the safety of the ground, thinking that it was a fairly modest size and that the view, even from the very top, would be unimpressive. However, the panorama afforded from their vantage point was more akin to the view of the city Lisa remembered from the aircraft window as it came in to land at the end of her recent overseas trip. *At least it's not too windy*, she thought as she looked down, gripped by a spasm of vertigo. Her head spun, then she lost her sense of equilibrium and became very hot. She tried to wipe the sweat from her burning forehead, but a black curtain descended, obscuring her vision and turning her limbs to rubber. She felt the sweat begin to trickle down her neck just before she lost consciousness.

Lisa woke with a start as her head lolled, almost striking Josh's shoulder. Straight away she was aware of a different atmosphere in the car; the other occupants seemed more relaxed, chatting easily. She turned to look out of the window and was presented with a much more conventional view, from a lower perspective than before. They must have descended most of the way without her knowledge.

"Must be the bit of Paradise Point that was burnt down . . . " The voice penetrated her consciousness. Josh had twisted around in his seat and was peering intently through the window. How long had he been talking to her? She hoped he had not been fretting too much.

"Yes, it's that building across there," she said, trying to focus on what Josh was saying. Viewed from above, the fire-damaged buildings looked like the remnants of a battle scene.

"It looks like a lot of damage was done—I wonder why it was never repaired."

"I imagine it's something to do with the insurance," Lisa said. She was distracted by Josh, who was turning an item over and over in his hands. It was a small figurine which glinted despite the half-light in the carriage. Lisa reached out and he handed it to her. It was surprisingly heavy and much warmer than it should have been. "Damn! That's hot," she said, quickly passing it back to him. "What the hell is it, Josh?"

"When we arrived at the fair, we got separated in the crowd, remember? You went off with that woman Carol and I had nothing to do. Well, I was bored, so I had a go on one of the rifle ranges. I've never ever won anything before— but, first go, I hit the bullseye and this was my prize." He held the object up close to her, then pointed at its base, on which some words were engraved: *Passing the children through the fire.*

"Ugh! That's awful, Josh. It's got horns, and why is it so hot? I think you should get rid of it."

He looked hurt. "The guy on the stand said it was a Moloch.

Whatever that is." Josh wrapped the thing up in his handkerchief, then put it in his trouser pocket. Lisa had been repelled by the strange object, but she was not sure why. The hot and close confines of the carriage were making it impossible for her to think. She was relieved when the Ferris wheel jerked into movement once more, inching its way at last towards the ground.

ONCE THEY TOUCHED down, it was Lisa's turn to cling to Josh. She'd been so desperate to get outside, yet as the others huddled in front of the carriage doors, her limbs felt as heavy as lead despite the claustrophobia which was keeping her on the edge of panic. There was some confusion among the passengers when the door which opened was the one behind them, on the opposite side of the carriage. As the grumbling crowd and giggling children turned around, Josh disentangled himself from her arm, then stood up. He was smiling, seemingly amused by her reticence. She could not remember the last time she had seen him smile. "Come on, slow coach," he said. "Let's get going before we get stuck on this thing and it goes up in the air again!"

Slowly and stiffly, she unfolded herself from the unforgiving wooden bench. Josh skipped out through the gaping doors and for a moment she was alone. She had to force some intangible doubts from her mind before she was able to follow him. By the time her feet touched solid ground, the passengers from the carriage had dispersed and she could see Josh in the distance. How had he managed to get so far away? She squinted into the gloom. After the harsh lights of the funfair before they had boarded the Ferris Wheel, the darkness came as a surprise. Presumably they were further from the main attractions, having disembarked from the opposite side of the carriage.

"Josh!" There was something in the air which caught in her throat so that her voice was nothing more than a croak. In the distance, the figure turned and for a moment Lisa thought he was laughing.

She looked around. To her surprise, the Ferris Wheel had not continued on its journey. It towered above her, creaking as it swayed gently in the warm breeze, all of its carriages dark and empty. Somehow, theirs must have been the last group let on the ride, despite the rest of the lengthy queue which had been behind them. Their door was still open, and through the carriage she could make out blurred images of light and movement from the other side of the funfair.

It was simple. They had been let off the Ferris Wheel from the wrong door so that all they had to do was to make their way back around the structure to return to the main part of Paradise Point, to the event which was so important to her, to her career and to their joint success in the future. She looked to either side of the ride to see the best route back, but a tall chainlink fence stretched as far as she could see in both directions. To her right the fence stopped at the promontory which led down the the dark waters of the harbor, and to her left it joined up with the edge of a charred brick building. Through the fence all she could see were the same abstract shapes and movement as had been visible through the carriage windows. *So, maybe we go back to the carriage and see if we can get the other door open—the one we should have used in the first place. Why hasn't anyone else thought of that?* Lisa set off towards the ride but, as though it sensed her approach, the door slammed shut with a wheeze from its ancient hydraulics.

She jumped at a touch on her shoulder.

"Lise, what's up?" Josh had approached her soundlessly.

"Josh, there's been a mistake! We have to get back to the others, but I can't see a way around the Ferris Wheel. They must have let us off the wrong way, there's nothing for us here—"

"Hey, hey, take it easy. It seems that some of the guests have been given the opportunity to experience the rest of Paradise Point. That's why we were given black name tags rather than white ones. All we have to do is to follow the boardwalk to Funny Land . . . " He pointed away from the Ferris Wheel, indicating an imposing building which Lisa had not noticed before. The words "Funny Land" and "Asbury Park, N.J." were arranged above a grand porticoed entrance, surrounded by uneven shapes which cast bizarre shadows in the gloom. It did not look too funny to Lisa: she thought it must have been designed to look appealing in the midday sun, rather than barely lit in the moonlight as it was now.

"So how do you know all this, Josh? There's no one here." But as she looked, she saw that she was wrong: there were staff members all around, lurking in the shadows, only visible by their unnaturally pale faces and the white lettering on their T-shirts. She was about to ask him more when she realized he had started off along the boardwalk. As she followed on, she felt a hundred pairs of eyes watching her.

Lisa caught up to him as they reached the foot of the steps leading to the entrance of Funny Land. She reached out to him, but her hand only brushed his shoulder before he took the steps two at a time. At that moment, she realized what seemed so wrong since they had been on the Ferris Wheel. The quiet and introverted Josh had become inexplicably more animated, speaking and moving in different, more decisive ways.

He leaned his weight against the double doors but they did not give. Lisa let out a sigh of relief. "Come on Josh, we need to get back to the event, before we're missed. We haven't got time to look around; the welcoming speech is at ten o'clock."

"You don't understand," he said, breathless. "There's only one way back and it's through Funny Land. Let's see if we can get inside."

"But Josh, it's locked—" She reached out to take his hand, but once again he avoided her touch. He ran back down the steps then along the periphery of the building. Lisa followed on, bewildered at the turn of events, hoping against hope that he would be unsuccessful in his search for an alternative entrance, but she was to be disappointed. She watched from a distance as Josh approached several of the members of staff who were standing around, smoking, beside a small door set into the otherwise featureless side wall of the building. *The tradesman's entrance?* Josh said something to them that Lisa could not hear, a key was produced, then the door was pulled open, spilling out warm, flickering light. She noticed that there was no handle on the outside of the door, just the keyhole. Lisa glanced quizzically at the members of staff, but they were reluctant to meet her gaze. Nonetheless, they were nodding and inclining their heads towards the open door, signaling encouragement, so what could be the harm?

Inside, Josh turned left along a narrow passageway. "Follow me,

Lise," he said over his shoulder, but she wondered how he was so sure it was the right thing to do. The floor was made from narrow planks of varnished wood. The pungent odor reminded Lisa of the school gym which she had hated so much. The soles of their shoes squeaked on its glossy surface and as they walked, the floor flexed rhythmically under their weight. Lisa touched the wall to steady herself, but pulled her hand back as she felt a sharp pain: the wall was wooden too, but roughly finished beneath a perfunctory coat of paint. She swore under her breath as she picked the splinter from her knuckle. She was almost running now, her breathing ragged, but she could not quite catch up with him.

"Slow up, Josh! Should we even be in here? It doesn't feel safe."

"Just a bit further, Lise. The entrance must be here somewhere." *The entrance to what?* But then he stopped abruptly. She collided with him, losing her footing, almost sprawling to the floor. He spun around, took her by the waist, then steadied her. She felt embarrassed and indignant. She wanted to shout, to swear at him and to ask him what he was playing at, but all she could do was catch her breath.

"Are you all right, darling? I was forgetting—" The concern in his eyes and his glance down her body spoke volumes to her. Did he know? Surely he could not have guessed, but maybe it was obvious now. "You've been rushing," he added. "Let's stop for a moment." Lisa leant against the rough corridor wall and took a deep breath. She watched in silence as he examined a set of double doors to their right. He began to struggle with the ancient bolt which held the doors closed.

"It'll just take me a moment, Lise. This lock is rusted."

"What the hell?" She felt tears of frustration welling from her eyes. "We need to go back right now. This isn't funny any more, Josh."

"Don't worry—it's coming loose," he said, as if she cared, using all his leverage on the ancient bolt. It gave, showering flakes of rust into the air, getting in her eyes and making her cough. Josh pushed at the doors, which dragged and flexed, proving to be as flimsy as the roughly-finished walls of the corridor. She barely recognized his face as he turned back to look at her. His eyes were wide and his features were lit by a golden, flickering light.

"This is what we're meant to witness," he said. Confused, she tried to object, but once again her voice, at the crucial moment, was no more than a croak.

IT TOOK LISA some time to gather enough courage to follow him through the doorway. She found herself in a cavernous indoor space, on a balcony at the top of an enormous wooden structure. They must have gained access to one of Luna Point's historic rides, through a back entrance. She stood, dizzy, at the head of a row of slides which angled down endlessly into the gloom below, each one more vertiginous than the next, undulating at different stages of their descent. Piles of hessian sacks were scattered around the balcony, waiting to be used by the next thrill-seeker willing to risk the plummet. There were two staircases, one at each side of the structure. They must have been at least a hundred steps long—she struggled to believe that small children would manage them then still have energy left for playing. Nonetheless, as she watched, several tiny figures slid off the ends of the wooden chutes. They were being watched from the sidelines by a group of women Lisa took to be their mothers.

At the foot of the slides, however, stood the main attraction: a giant bronze statue of a human torso, with the head and the horns of a bull. Its arms were spread, palms forward, reaching for the sky. There was an arched opening in its abdomen, at ground level, which exposed a roaring furnace within. The intense heat, which she could feel on her face even from such a great distance, made the figure glow and provided the only source of light. She could only imagine how hot it would be on the surface of the statue. Lisa picked her way carefully across the untidy balcony and leaned against the railing to have a closer look at the barely believable scene far below. In the shadows beside the statue workers, dressed in black, shoveled coal to feed the furnace. She was too far away to read, but she imagined that their shirts bore the name, "Heinneke, Prose & Split."

The strange figure, dressed in loincloth and headdress, was making its way up the steps the right of the slides. Lisa shuddered at the prospect of being exposed on that rickety ledge when it got to the top of the steps. She rushed back to the doors, but they had been closed. She rattled their makeshift handles, but they did not give. As Lisa wrestled with the doors, she began to shake. She'd seen no sign of Josh and she had no idea why he would leave her all alone. Quickly she gave up on the doors, then forced herself back towards the precipice. A wave of vertigo threatened to overwhelm her as she got near the edge, so that she had to stop, paralyzed with indecision. Something small and hot crept into her left hand. She looked down to see the tiny blonde girl who had sat next to her on the Ferris Wheel, staring up at her with a concerned expression in her clear blue eyes.

"Will you go down the slippery-dip with me?" The child's voice was as cold as her hand was warm. Lisa was not sure if the girl was afraid for herself, or if she had picked up on Lisa's own trepidation and wanted to help her take the plunge. She decided not to think about it too deeply—and certainly not to ask.

"Of course I will, darling," she said, trying her best to look brave and encouraging for the youngster and giving her clammy hand a squeeze. Before Lisa could change her mind, she grasped the nearest sack, then sat down on the edge of the slide. She looked across to see that the horned figure had almost reached the top of the stairs, so there was no time to lose. She tucked her legs inside the rough material of the sack, then took the girl by the waist, lifting her onto her lap. She seemed to weigh almost nothing at all. "Are you ready—" But Lisa's question went unanswered as the girl's tiny palms found purchase on the side of the slide, propelling them past the point of no return.

At first, they were in free fall. Lisa's grip tightened involuntarily on the sparrow-like form nestled in her lap as her stomach was left behind. All was a blur, until the angle of the slide lessened at its first undulation. She took a breath for the first time, then realized she was almost enjoying the ride. The girl was making squealing noises, whether from excitement or fear, Lisa could not tell. After they crested the undulation, the drop became even steeper so they picked up speed. The girl squealed louder and wriggled in Lisa's arms, making them move from side to side, at first almost imperceptibly, then becoming a wild oscillation over which Lisa had no control. From then on, she was aware of their progress only through a series of details. The girl's bared teeth and the glint in her eye as she twisted around to look up at her. A glimpse of stars above where the ceiling should be. Josh, standing with the women at the foot of the slide, watching her disaster unfold without expression on his face. The hessian sack ripping on what must have been a loose plank, or perhaps the exposed head of a nail, pulling her violently to one side. The smell of varnish just before her head struck the railing on the side of the chute.

"LISE, WE WERE so worried." The sound of Josh's voice, combined with the discomfort caused by the hard, flat surface she was lying on, brought Lisa back to her senses. She opened her eyes to see his concerned face, far too close to hers. The smell of cigarettes lingered on his breath—but he'd never smoked, it was a pet hate of his. Everything was wrong. She struggled to sit up until he pressed her shoulder back down firmly. She tried to object, but her throat felt dry and her voice would not work.

"Whoa there, tiger! You've got to stay put," he said, with a smile. He stepped away from her, then looked to his side, beyond her field of vision. Lisa's neck was so stiff that she found it difficult to turn her head, and there was a fluttering in her abdomen which worsened when she tried to move. "I think she wants another go on the slide!" She felt indignant at the ensuing sound of mocking laughter. She wondered why Josh was being so cruel; ever since they had left the Ferris Wheel, he had been like a different person. She forced herself to look around despite the pain. She was in a cramped, brightly-lit but windowless box room. At the foot of her bed was an open door and a narrow white cupboard with a red cross painted on it. It must be some kind of sick bay, for the children who feel ill after too many goes on one of Paradise Point's gravity-defying rides. Her feet dangling off the end of the bed confirmed that thought.

Lisa hauled herself to a sitting position, this time unhindered by Josh, who was leaning on the wall whispering to someone outside the door. Her head pounded and she felt like she might be sick, so she sat still on the edge of the bed until her head cleared. As they so often did, her hands strayed beneath her clothes to linger over her stomach. She breathed in sharply. Her belly felt far larger than it should—and her blouse, her best blouse which was now filthy and ragged, was much too tight. She was thirsty. *How long have I been unconscious? None of this makes sense.*

"Josh!" At last she found her voice. He was at her side in a single step. "I've completely lost track of what's going on. How long was I out of it? I can't even remember why I'm here—"

"Shush, darling, everything's okay," he said. He placed his hand on her forehead. "Your temperature feels like it's back to normal now, so that's good. Don't you remember? For some reason, you went down the slide and had an accident. Banged your head. I don't know what you were thinking, Lise. You have to remember to look after yourself. Especially now." He looked at her distended belly.

She thought—but of course Josh knew. Now, Lisa realized that he had known all along. She must have been kidding herself, thinking that no one had noticed. She tried to add up the days, weeks, months in her mind, but she could not make sense of it. When was it she had seen her doctor? Time meant nothing. *Somehow, I have to take control of the situation.*

"You need to listen to me, Josh." She spoke slowly, with deliberation. "We need to get back to the others. Right now. This job is my dream come true—you must know how important it is to me. It'll set us up for the future." She slid herself off the edge of the bed, onto her feet. A cramp racked her body, doubling her up, taking her breath away. She hugged herself until her breathing returned to normal. Then, for the first time, she felt it: something for which she could not be prepared—*at least, not so soon, surely?*—which meant that her life had changed already and that things were beyond both her control and her understanding.

The fluttering in her stomach had transformed into a slow and rhythmic kicking.

"I know, darling, I know," Josh said, seemingly unaware of her revelation. "I wasn't sure about it at first, as you must have known, but it's all changed. Now, I understand that the most important thing in the world is our life together." This jolted Lisa back to her present situation. She had never heard him speak this way before. In fact, since they had met at university, he had barely acknowledged anything beyond his need to get through his studies without bombing out.

"Well yes, Josh, but—"

"Come on Lise, if you're up to it I want to show you something." He took her by the arm, then guided her through the door. Lisa was very conscious of her flat-footed stance, and of how she had to lean backwards to keep her balance. They made their way along a short corridor, then back out to the slides. The wave of heat coming from the giant statue was overwhelming; she clung to Josh, trying to shield herself from the onslaught, but it was no good. Close up, the bronze figure looked like it was melting, but the strange effect must have been caused by the sweat trickling into her eyes so that she felt like she was viewing the world through a shifting prism. Did that also explain how she could see the giant figure breathing? Lisa was shocked to realize that the rhythm of its breath matched that of the kicking within her own body. She shook her head. *Get a grip of yourself, girl.*

By now she was following Josh obediently, without a thought about the reason why. She watched in silence as he reached into his trouser pocket, then withdrew the small bronze figurine he had won at the rifle range. He kissed it, then threw it into the open furnace. It made a dull popping sound as it was consumed by the flames and it seemed to intensify the heat. Her mind was sluggish. There was something she should be doing, but what was it? In her fugue state, she barely noticed as they were surrounded by the group of women. Faces peered at her: shiny faces, dripping with sweat, suffering in the heat just like she was. Lisa saw that every one of them of them was extremely pregnant. "Cutie, how far along are you?" "So glad you've become one of us, sweetheart!" "You've made the best decision, darling." "All of us want the same thing, you know . . . " A hand rested firmly on her arm and Lisa found herself looking into the dark brown eyes of Carol, the partner from Heinneke, Prose & Split, whom she had been so eager to impress. She had not noticed earlier on that she had been pregnant, too—but how long ago was that? Time meant nothing. "We'll look after you, Lisa," Carol said, in the lisping tones that were familiar to her as though from a previous life. "There's no need to worry any more."

What were they talking about? Lisa didn't have the strength to resist as they propelled her towards the foot of the slides, skirting the very edge of an enormous pile of coal. Sparks flew from the open belly of the statue as T-shirted figures shoveled laboriously. Lisa watched as some of the sparks faded into black on the wooden floorboards at her feet. *This whole place is made of wood*, she thought. Alarm bells began to sound somewhere deep within her mind, yet she was unable to resist. *Have I been drugged?*

The others turned as one, to gaze upon the giant statue. Lisa took the opportunity to study the women around her. In the softly flickering light of the flames, all of their faces wore the same expression and their eyes were wide with the same kind of religious awe. They were standing back on their heels, feeling the curve of their bellies with their hands—*just like me*, she thought. Then, Lisa looked at the statue and gasped. Its giant arms, which had previously been reaching for the sky, palms forward, had changed position. Now they were down in front of its torso, forearms outstretched, forming a kind of ramp to the furnace raging within its abdomen. She looked to Josh for an explanation, but all she could see on his face was a beatific smile. He sensed her gaze upon him, then looked back at her with an open, earnest expression she had never seen before.

Lisa found her voice at last. "What is it you want from me?"

"It's what we want *for* you that you have to think about, darling, not what we want *from* you."

She stared, unable to think of a response. The frequency and strength of the pounding within her stomach rose to fever pitch.

"You'll have other children, Lise—remember, this is your firstborn. You're young, healthy, and fertile. Whatever else happens, we will always have each other." He stared into her eyes. "In any case, I know for a fact that you haven't even given it a name. Have you thought about that?"

Her scream was muffled by the hands and flight was made impossible by the sheer number and weight of the rotund bodies pressing at her from all around. She tried thrashing her arms and kicking, but it was no use. Soon she became tired and breathless and all she could do was listen to the fragments of conversation. "I thought this one looked like trouble," one of the women said. "You should have prepared her, Josh," said another. "Doesn't she want the best for her family?" "I thought you said that her old man—"

What was that about my old man? Lisa twisted her head, then managed to bite the hand which covered her mouth. She no longer cared if it belonged to Carol or not. "What the hell, Josh—tell these hags to let me go!" But soon other hands covered her face, silencing her once again and making it difficult for her to breathe.

"Lise . . . I owe you some kind of an explanation." *You sure do*, she thought, still thinking desperately that this must be some kind of mistake, or at the very least a gruesome practical joke. Josh moved closer to her and inclined his head so their faces almost touched. The hands which had been silencing her fell away, but she could not summon the strength to shout. What was the point? Once more, she noticed the smoke on Josh's breath, but now she understood—it was the reek of burnt flesh she could smell, rather than that of cigarettes.

"Do you know why your father was first on the scene at the fire, Lise? Of course you do, but you've never trusted me enough to tell me. He was on the ride with your sister when the fire started. Yes, I know you had a twin sister, born just before you were—the sister you never got the chance to know. You can't even remember her name, so it was like she never existed. Since then, your whole family has been in denial, but now the time has come to pay the next installment of the debt."

By now the women had stepped away from her, but Lisa was no longer capable of any kind of resistance. She covered her eyes with the palms of her hands; they came away dripping as she was wracked by silent tears. Her stomach cramped, forcing her to bend double. She had the sudden desire to sit down, to take the increased weight from her aching feet. In the altercation, her blouse, her best blouse, had been torn, exposing her huge belly, but she was beyond caring. She lowered herself to the ground, surrounded by thick ankles. Perhaps it was true that she had been in denial about her pregnancy. Maybe everything had progressed in a normal way, but she had blocked the reality of it from her mind.

Josh is right, she thought. *Why haven't I named my child?*

She stared blankly up at him, through her tears. "Not that I care, but how do you know all this?" Her voice was no more than a mumble.

"What do you think I talked about with your father on all those tedious evenings when you were up in your room, cramming endlessly for your precious exams?"

So you were resentful of that, Lisa thought. *How could I not have realized? I was so selfish.* "Josh, I'm so sorry. I didn't know you felt that way."

"And you thought you were studying so hard for a prosperous future, when all along it was too late. Our life together was already mapped out—and by the look of you, it's nearly time to carry out the next transaction."

"What? Josh, listen to what you're saying! It doesn't sound like you at all. I don't understand what you mean."

"Your father understood well enough."

"So he was on the ride when the fire started. What does that prove? It was just a coincidence. I never told you, because I didn't know how you'd take it." Yet even as she spoke, Lisa wondered if that was entirely true. The heat was making it difficult for her to think clearly. A wave of nausea engulfed her, and she thought she might be sick, but all she could do was to hold her stomach and dry-retch. She took a deep breath, then blinked away the sweat which was running into her eyes. For a moment, she thought that her vision was failing her, but then she understood the sudden darkness was caused by the shadow of a figure which had moved between her and the glare from the bronze statue. The women had all stepped back, in what she took to be a show of respect to the newcomer. Before she dared look, Lisa was sure that it would be the figure in loincloth and horns.

Close up, she could see that the clothes the figure wore looked ancient, filthy, and tattered, as though rarely used and badly stored. The headpiece was misshapen and made of discolored animal skin, with holes torn out for the eyes of the wearer, above which its horns twisted obscenely from a clump of matted hair. Around its waist was twisted the ragged leopardskin loincloth. Lisa gagged as she smelt its animal stink, but through her revulsion she could not help but wonder what the figure would look like without its bizarre outfit. She frowned. There was something familiar about the way it stood, arms loose by its side, head bent almost apologetically.

Why doesn't it say anything?

Instead, Josh spoke. "The cult of Moloch," he began, in a rehearsed voice, as though addressing some kind of congregation, "is carried on from generation to generation. What is most precious must be freely given, in order to appease the lust for blood which is harbored by the jealous gods. The true believer must understand that if the following generation refuses to acknowledge that the gods deserve such adulation, their own good fortune will end in agonizing pain—both mental and physical."

There was a murmuring of assent, followed by a heavy silence punctuated only by the crackling sounds of the coal burning ever more fiercely within the bronze statue. All the pregnant women still gazed at Josh, as though expecting his bizarre speech to continue. Lisa tried to stand, but her stomach cramped again. This time, she was sick, forcing her to give up the unequal struggle; yet even this did not ease the shooting pains in her stomach. *How can I have been so stupid? This is not just cramp—I must be having contractions!* She could do no more than to curl into a fetal position on the warm wooden floorboards, powerless to resist as she became surrounded by the others. The hands, which had so recently silenced her, now combined to lift her effortlessly. They placed her, with great care, onto the outstretched hands of Moloch.

The smooth bronze surface of the statue scorched her body through what was left of her ruined clothes, but she could do no more than squirm as the frequency of the contractions increased. Even this, however, became impossible once the women had reached up and grasped her limbs firmly. By now, the sweat was pouring from her prone body and the heat, so near the roaring furnace of Moloch, was becoming too much for her to bear. Through the haze, at the edge of her field of vision, she saw that the horned figure was removing its headgear. Lisa was not at all surprised to see the emergence of her father's concerned yet resolute features—and she knew why his guilt would not allow him to meet her tortured gaze. She tried to shout, but the roaring of the furnace drowned out her voice. When she reached out towards her father, Josh's hand closed around her wrist like a band of steel.

Lisa's contractions were constant now, and she accepted that it would not be long before she would give birth for the first time. Her screams came, too little and too late, but she understood at last why she had not given her unborn child a name.

The Surgeon

Mary Portser

———— ♦ ————

THE SURGEON STOOD in the doorway, his liquid eyes on Dani, stretched on a gurney in the narrow little room. Still high on anesthesia, she heard him say something about "time" and "reattached ends" and "not to worry." She lifted her head, confused.

"You see, you can talk," he said in his low voice.

Had she said anything? Her tongue felt woven. She licked her lips.

"Sing? Can I still sing?"

She wondered if she'd asked it out loud and thought maybe she hadn't as he only gave her the faintest of smiles.

"I will see you Monday."

DANI SPENT THE weekend closeted in her dark, north-facing apartment, curled on her camelback couch. The street outside, normally active with the goings on of singles in search of brunch or hook-ups, was strangely quiet. She went to the window. The only sign of life was a stray dog, his leg cocked against a pepper tree. Maybe a plague had ravaged the city, sparing the animals, and the survivors were holed up indoors. Maybe, like her, they were listening to the ragged whistle of their breath, the hollow ring of the phone. Or maybe they were dead. She wandered to the kitchen and pressed a bag of frozen peas against her throat. The cold burned her skin. It was good to feel something. She returned to the couch, recurled herself and envisioned the Sphinx-like smile of the surgeon.

NOW HERE SHE was, back in his Beverly Hills office, in a room with cream cabinets and bonsais cut into the shapes of coolie hats, watching him shine a light down her throat. "Inflammation," he said and his dark, moist eyes looked into hers.

"I will be able to sing again?" she asked in the only voice she had, a whisper.

"Perhaps your high notes—"

"But I'm a soprano."

"Yes." He must have heard the terror in her squeak. She heard it too, the screech of a frightened bat. It froze her spine.

His manner changed. He became energized, business-like. "I have in mind a speech therapist for you. She is the best. I will arrange it."

"I hope she's on my plan."

He took her cold hands in his warm ones. "I will take care of you. Send the bills to me."

Was this usual? Or was she terribly special?

She felt afraid to leave the room with the bonsais, the coral seahorse on the wall and ceiling lights with a warm pink tinge. Procedures might be done here. Hope could keep its feathered head above ground. But the surgeon was leading her out and away, holding her arm as though, despite her athletic frame, she might fracture, past the beautiful assistants with their shiny, long hair, down the pristine, celery-shaded corridor and into the waiting room. The floor to ceiling window flashed bright as a beacon. Was the glass shatterproof, would you need a running start to smash through it? The surgeon's hand was on her elbow.

The receptionist looked up from a swirl of black granite. One of her cheeks was badly scarred. Her hair was lustrous.

"Miss McDonnell needs an appointment for ten days please." The dark eyes, ringed with heavy lashes, again held Dani's. "Eat well, the best foods. And sleep. And exercise . . . "

He seemed to want to say more, something encouraging, and she held her breath, but an assistant called for him. "Get a whiteboard," he uttered and was gone.

THE TEN DAYS proved near unbearable. She felt as though the anesthesia never left her brain, making her stupid. At Ralph's supermarket, she set a carton of eggs, two tomatoes, a block of cheddar, and a bundle of scallions on the conveyor. When the cashier asked "Paper or plastic?" she scribbled "Paper" on her just purchased whiteboard. The cashier squinted, wrinkled her brow and showed it to the adolescent bagger. He shrugged. The manager was summoned. Head down, Dani repeated the word in a tiny voice.

"Can you speak a little louder?" he boomed.

The Roto-Rooter man in line behind her banged his checkout divider on the belt.

Dani's head felt sweaty with shame. She fled the store, leaving behind the ingredients for her omelet.

In the parking lot of her favorite coffeeshop she hunched against the car window and, with great care, marked her order on the whiteboard. The willowy barrista glowed when she saw it. "Are you taking a vow of silence? That is so cool. I want to try it." She comped the cappuccino.

Dani drank it in a dark corner and delayed going home as long as possible.

"I CAN'T HEAR you," her mother cried when Dani finally called her. "Can't you speak any louder? Are you going to sue the surgeon? Are you in pain?"

"No pain." Which was true in the physical sense. She wished her mother off on one of the long voyages she was always taking. Mars or Orion might be far enough. "Sue the surgeon." Typical. Her mother had never been a comfort, never understood a damn thing about her.

None of her relatives had. Dani was not a loner; she needed to be part of a tribe, just not the one she was born into. The music world, they were her people. They had made the calls to her.

Nevertheless she was not ready to face any of them, not yet, and was horrified when Al and Grace, two members of her choir, showed up on her doorstep, bearing daisies and a tin of Greither's Pastilles for "throat and voice." She had to let them in.

Her apartment had grown dingier in the days since the operation. Dust bunnies scurried across the floor. Stuffed animals, nighties, and insurance forms cluttered the yard sale furniture. Her visitors pretended not to notice. Grace, the choir director, a large earth mother and soprano like Dani, maintained a beatific smile, gave her a hug and bustled into the kitchen to find a vase. Al, a pale tenor, six years younger than Dani, slumped against a bookcase that dwarfed him. They'd slept together twice, months ago. She knew he'd like to again, but he was too newt-like and squishy for her. Now he folded his arms across his narrow chest and mumbled, "The soprano section's nothing without you." In the kitchen, Grace choked. Dani saw how red Al's face had become, how he was holding back tears. Smiling so her jaw ached, she patted his arm and saw them out with a whispered thanks and assurances she'd call when better. Only when their feet clanged on the exterior staircase did she allow her face to crumple.

"Zzzzzz . . . zzzzz," INSTRUCTED Monica Rand, the speech therapist, smiley in a jaunty beret. Dani had begun to see her twice a week in her office at Cedars-Sinai.

"Pretend you're watching a fly." Monica demonstrated, bobbing and twisting her head. A photo of Monica and the surgeon, both in evening dress, hung on her office wall. Dani studied it when the therapist went to the bathroom. The surgeon was handsome, something she had not realized when she met him at the pre-op. He had seemed ordinary then, bland almost. Not anymore. Not since he changed her fate with a flick of his wrist.

He would take care of her. The thought of him made her throat tingle.

She did the fly exercise, "eeehed and ahhhed," stretched her tongue so it met her chin, then her nose and, through teeth clenched around a straw, hummed the octave and a half range of "The Star Spangled Banner." Later, at a sex shop on Santa Monica Boulevard she bought a small vibrator and rolled it over her throat and vocal cords, to which she apologized, just as Monica had instructed. It felt good to be doing *something*.

In her bathroom, late at night, she examined the bandage that protected her incision and smoothed a fraying edge. But then she made the mistake of attempting a few bars of "Red, Red Robin." The wobbly, scratchy notes that emerged from her throat had her banging her head against the chilly tiles. She sounded like a crone with a cold.

Unable to sleep, she slipped on ballet flats, went down the stairs and headed toward the ocean. The few people she passed said nothing. A hideous raccoon, body hunched, ran out of the yard in front of her and across the street. It took a left and headed down Oakwood, zigzagging from sidewalk to sidewalk. Maybe it was rabid. She followed. He led her for blocks. Where was he taking her? The animal veered off. A short distance ahead, an enormous shape stood motionless under a streetlamp. Yes, she thought. Now is the time. Do it. She walked toward the mountain until it became a giant man in camouflage gear, staring at the trunk of a Palm tree. Her heart thumped so loud she was sure he could hear it. Before she could lose courage, she blurted, "You got a gun on you?" The man's head jerked back. His eyes—whites made yellow by the streetlamp—and nostrils flared, like a horse encountering a snake. He turned and ran.

Her breathing slowed. Excitement gone, her misery returned. She wandered from Venice into Santa Monica and back, but didn't ask the question again. Besides, all the other night-walkers had little white dogs, the kind that were taking over the neighborhood.

The next day she downed a protein shake for fortification and took the drive she'd been dreading, to a club on Robertson where she'd had a weekend gig singing jazz and show tunes. The owner owed her money. A warm, chatty fellow who she had always thought of as the father she never had, he kissed Dani on the cheek when she walked into the bar. But he wouldn't make eye contact. He led her down the dark hall to his office, a cramped space filled with Sinatra memorabilia, maintaining a meaningless string of chatter about his New York days.

"Buy yourself something nice, honey," he said and handed her the check (twice her normal fee), his eyes focused on a still of Nancy Sinatra in go-go boots.

Throat constricted so she couldn't even thank him, Dani started to write on the whiteboard that she would be better soon, but before she could finish the door burst open. It was Sabrina, a hateful crow with mean black eyes, surely there to replace Dani.

"Oh . . . hi!" said Sabrina. "Just keeping your spot warm till you get back."

Like the owner, Sabrina knew she wouldn't be coming back. The look in her eyes as she held the door open was unfiltered schadenfreude.

A hard rock of misery lodged in her chest, Dani waited at the curb for the little white figure in the crossbox to turn red. Then she started across. Cars screeched to a halt. A Porsche driver in a Dodger's cap yelled out his window, "Bitch! You want me to kill you?" If only she could have screamed: Yes!

On her Wonders of the World calendar, she exxed out the days until she would see the surgeon, fell into her bed and a deep sleep. She dreamed they were making love in a sumptuous, canopied bed with soft fabrics and bright curtains, like something from *Arabian Nights*. His sinewy body with its golden skin fit like a key into hers. As she rode above him, looking deep into his sympathetic eyes, from out of the air she plucked a scimitar and with it made clean, precise strokes across his neck. The expression in his eyes never changed, even as rivers of blood saturated the sheets. She woke, panting.

Finally, the ten days were up. Dani lined her red-rimmed eyes with kohl and slipped on her little black dress, low-cut and slim-fitting. Over it she zipped the new constant in her wardrobe, a fleece vest with high collar that hid her scar. The rope of lucky pearls from her cabaret act looked silly with the vest and she rejected them.

SWIVELING IN A WHITE leather chair, thyroids and larynxes like alien flowers flashing on a screen overhead, she studied the only other patient in the waiting room, a haughty blonde, in a vest like Dani, swiveling like Dani. Haughty or no, they were sisters in silence. The thought of it spread a balm over her heart.

She tried to catch the blonde's eye, to smile at her, let her know she wasn't alone. The woman fixed her with a gelid gaze and asked in a mellow tone, "Do you have the time?"

The clear voice jolted Dani like a live wire. She slid the book on Shar-Peis back onto a bronze slab of a coffee table. Her head dropped so the zipper of the vest grazed her chin, and the feeling of loss drenched her like a great wave.

One of the long-haired assistants called her name and led her back to the room with the bonsais, hoisted the chair and took her blood pressure. She started to feel better. She felt safe in here. A new acquisition caught her eye, a tiny mosaic of a peacock (the bird had the same liquid eyes as the surgeon, his dense eyelashes!) There was that pricking sensation in her throat again. She smiled for the first time in ten days. He was getting closer. When he entered, a honey-like warmth began to flow through her body. Her limbs felt heavy in a luxurious way, like she'd taken an opioid. She found her eyelids drifting down.

"Have you not been sleeping?" His voice rolled over her. What was that accent—Iranian? Egyptian?

"Not much."

Gently he pulled down the zipper on her vest. His fingers palpated her throat. "Have you been seeing Monica?

"Zzzz-zzzz," she replied.

"Zzzz-zzzz. Yes." He pulled the bandage off her neck. His heavy lids lowered as he studied the incision. "You're healing well."

"Am I?" She stared into the strong face that spoke of ancient civilizations.

"Oh, yes. I will make sure of it." She nodded. Yes. Yes.

"In two days you will start to massage. Like this please." He lifted his forefinger to the scar. Pressing his finger firmly on top of hers, he made small circles from one end to the other. She had the feeling he was enjoying the sensation, prolonging the touch.

"I'd like to see more of you." The words rushed out of her, faint, broken, but with great force, like the incoming tide hissing over the sand.

"Yes."

"Nobody understands."

"Except me." A barely perceptible smile wandered across his down-turned lips. "I know."

There it was. He knew. The nerve ends he'd reattached were fibers that held her and the surgeon together. Hence the vibration in her throat.

His eyebrows came together, deciding something. With a slow nod, he reached under his lab coat and pulled out a card. On the back was a number.

"Call me anytime."

She stared at the card. His private number. Would she dare to use it? Had he given it to the blonde in the waiting room? No. "When will I see you again?"

"Two weeks." She frowned. "Don't hesitate. Call me anytime."

And she did. After the first time it was easy. Mostly at night when the walls of the apartment moved in and her breathing got ragged. He always answered, not saying much, sometimes nothing at all. But she could hear him exhale, a whirring sound. She told him in a whisper how she'd never had the bump on her nose fixed, her chin was too pointy and she wished she was taller, but wasn't it true that the dullest songbird made the sweetest sound? And about leaning against the bathroom wall to stop from shaking. His "ahs" and "mmms" were great comfort.

And then, suddenly, they weren't enough.

His address sat in the phone book plain as pudding.

So on a night when a hot, dusty wind blew clouds across the stars, but not the near full moon, Dani drove the streets of Beverly Hills, hunting for the surgeon's house. It was hard to make out the numbers on the curb, but when she sighted the slabs of white and sand concrete, the copper cladding and tall bamboo next door, she knew she was home.

Her eyes were instantly drawn to the huge round window at the front of the house. Inside, light blazed from a modernist chandelier hanging above an oval table where the surgeon sat, eating a dish of noodles and drinking a glass of wine. The room was spacious, luxurious, like his office.

Her throat was tingling, the need to be closer filling her chest like a helium balloon. She pressed his number on her phone.

It was gratifying to watch him put down his fork, reach into the jacket of his cinnamon suit, check the caller I.D. and, without hesitation, answer.

"It's me," she whispered. He said nothing, but meticulously wiped his lips with a cloth napkin. "Sorry to disturb you while you're eating."

She thought the surgeon's mouth twitched. He raised his thick eyebrows and looked out of the well-lit room into the darkness beyond the window. She huddled in her car, glad he couldn't see her. "I love you," whistled out of her before she could help herself. Shoulders heaving, she hung up.

With opaque demeanor, the surgeon slipped the phone back in his jacket and resumed his dinner. After a few more bites he turned his head and called out. Was there someone else there? A dog maybe? A large frizzy-haired girl, a glass of wine slopping over her hand, lumbered into the room and cozied herself next to him. A fuzzy scarf wound round her neck like a caterpillar and she fiddled with its tassels. The surgeon offered her a small smile.

Immobilized, Dani took in the scene. She hadn't counted on this—there'd been no ring on his finger. The girl was too old for a daughter and had none of the silky tresses or lithe body he favored in his assistants. Why had he chosen her over Dani, who was small and slim and whose body fit his like a key in a lock?

She could see how comfortable they were together, how the surgeon leaned back in his chair, how the girl caressed his arm with one of her big hands. Dani watched in pain those hands massage his shoulders, saw his eyes close in pleasure.

She drove home, trying not to panic, forgetting to turn on her car lights.

Dani returned the next night, at the same time. Her spot had been taken by a white Mercedes, pearlescent under the now full moon. She parked behind it, but was dissatisfied with only a partial view of the table and a chunk of frizzy hair. The surgeon's long fingers dabbed a piece of sushi in what she imagined was wasabi paste and soy sauce. Had the girl hand-rolled the sushi herself?

The wide, tree-lined block was quiet with no one to observe her slide from her car or skirt the perimeters of the lawn. Unless some-one was watching from one of the dark portholes on the upper floor. She did not let the thought deter her and crossed the lush grass. That the surgeon was flaunting the water restrictions would have bothered her once.

Keeping clear of the sphere of light shed by the window, Dani sidled along the concrete façade until the surgeon and girl came into view. He was talking in his low, melodic voice, too low for her to get the words. Sitting next to him, the girl threw back her oversized head and laughed extravagantly, then reached for something on a side table.

A whiteboard.

Dani felt a scream enter her throat from high up inside her head, though nothing came out. She and the girl were the same. "No," Dani squeaked. "Just me."

Another woman entered, a tall, thin person with little cat glasses and hair tightly pulled into a bun on the back of her head. A black choker rimmed her long, thin neck. In one hand, she carried a flaming dish of flan, in the other—a whiteboard.

Dani could hardly breathe. In a fluid move, the tall woman replaced the surgeon's dinner plate and arranged herself on a chair, leaning over him like an affable giraffe. The girl poured wine for them all, spilling droplets of ruby red on the white tablecloth.

Dani rested her head against the cool concrete and breathed in the sickly sweetness of night-blooming jasmine, gardenia, and tuberose. White blossoms vibrated like eager stars in the darkness. When had that happened? They were everywhere. Small clouds of moths fluttered around the flowers and over Dani's head. From deep within the house a gong sounded. The light came on in the room above, then more lights, filling the lawn with golden spheres. She heard a humming from the upstairs rooms. Were others buzzing up there, following flies with their eyes? Gazing at themselves in mirrors, undoing scarves, fingering scars?

The sympathy calls to her cell had all but died out. Her mother didn't phone. Nor did the choir director or friends from the club. Only Al, the tenor. "Come back. I miss you," he crooned quietly to her voicemail. Soon he too would stop.

The tingle in her throat had become a constant throb. She pulled down the zipper on the vest. It was getting too warm to wear it. She would buy a scarf. A nightbird screamed from a pepper tree and something large rattled in the bamboo. The humming grew louder.

In the dining room, the three people had formed a tableau. They looked like they belonged to each other, like a family. A real family.

Like a rose blooming, the possibility of love opened inside Dani. With her fingertips she caressed the smooth glass of the window and began to tap, then rap, first with fingers, then knuckles, an increasingly frantic tattoo, watching, eyes wide, mouth open. Please, please, hear me, open the door, let me in, feed me wine and let me stay.

And then they were coming to the door, the tall woman and the girl. And they were smiling.

THE SURREY ALTERATIONS

Charles Wilkinson

————— ✦ —————

AFTER THE DEATH of Dorothy, Vernon Butts took to drinking with the early evening crowd at The Edge. Once a respectable roadhouse, albeit on the wrong side of the motorway, the property had been revamped on five occasions in the previous ten years. Its current incarnation aped the ambience of a long dead LA: movie posters of *The Maltese Falcon, The Long Goodbye,* and *The Big Sleep*; framed posters of Bacall, Bogart, and Sidney Greenstreet; furniture up-holstered in black leather. There was a small bar with a zinc counter and five high stools; burgers were served *à point* in an always half empty restaurant. The regular turnover of staff created an undercurrent of impermanence, some nights amounting to unease; Vernon named it Surrey Noir. Although it was three years since he'd given up his legal practice, he still wore a pin-striped suit.

"So one morning," he said, "I decided to get rid of the lot: the mobile phone, Dorothy's old crock of a computer, my laptop. Do you know the dear old thing even had a kettle that you could control remotely? Well that's gone," he told the two of them.

"You could call it a digital detox," muttered Greg Harris.

Three of the six o'clock regulars were perched on the stools. Harris, in tartan trousers and a florid flat cap, had Vernon's right ear, his good one. On his other side slouched Mick Merrihome, foxy-faced with foul little eyes.

"Yes, you could call it that—if you wanted to use a cliché," said Vernon.

"What about your emails?" Mick asked.

No one at The Edge knew for certain what Merrihome did; scrap metals, computer coding, and poaching, it was claimed. A quiz night enthusiast and conspiracy theorist, he mixed superfluous fact with paranoia and misinformation in equal parts. And was he or was he not growing a beard? Vernon leaned away from him.

"That's a point," Greg said. "How are people going to get in touch with you?" The colors in his tweeds were a touch too bright, as if his golfing never progressed further than a comic interlude at the first tee.

"If someone insists in communicating with me," said Vernon, "I'd rather it was done in the 18th-century manner: a scroll, sealed, delivered by a man on horseback wearing a tricorn hat. Failing that, I can still access my emails at the library. I also have a landline, although I answer it infrequently."

"What a mouthful!" Mick laughed.

"I'm sorry," replied Vernon, not deigning to glance in Merrihouse's direction. "I didn't catch that. I'm hard of hearing in this ear."

"They're closing the library," said Greg. "You won't last long without modern communications. Not these days. The landline's for fraudsters."

"They will not close the library; and while, to an extent, I agree with you about landlines, they are surely safer than relying on computers, which any crook from Khartoum to Karachi can hack into."

"Not with proper online protection, they can't."

Vernon elected to ignore this, despite the clear enunciation. Merrihome was a well known sponger and menace.

"End of the month, it shuts. That's what I heard," Greg continued.

"And your source of information is . . . precisely?"

"You need to get yourself some hearing aids, mate."

Vernon took a pair of horn-rimmed glasses out of his jacket pocket, put them on, and turned with a deep sigh towards Merrihome. "If I wish to take your opinion, on any matter whatsoever, I will be sure to let you know first."

"You can get a hearing test from the place on the lay-by. All this week," said Harris.

"What from, the hot food stand?"

"No that's gone. They've got this ... what's it ... instead ... audiology unit, they're calling it."

"Are you a Freemason?" asked Mick, tapping Vernon on the shoulder.

He must remember to avoid Monday nights. The more congenial members of the six o'clock crowd seldom came in. Harris he could endure; Merrihome's malice was quite another matter.

"Why on earth would anyone set up as an audiologist on a lay-by?"

"I'd say it was for Freemasons. Honk three times if you're a Freemason."

"I don't know. Perhaps they're trying to attract people who wouldn't normally bother to make an appointment," said Vernon, with a shrug.

"I'd get down there, Vern. Give them a funny handshake and they'll give you a free test!"

"Strange you should say that, Mick. It is free."

"There you go, Vern. You'll be able to hear what they're saying down at the Lodge and it won't have cost you a penny."

Vernon drained his pint. "Once I imagined I witnessed you with your wallet in your hand, Mr. Merrihome. But it was a dream. I'll bid the gentleman on my right good night."

It was still light outside. The early evening traffic streamed in both directions. Vernon's home was near the center of the old village, on the salubrious side of the motorway, with its tile-hung cottages and sturdy Victorian villas. If the inn on the green had not closed, he wouldn't have had to make his way over the bridge to The Edge, which had traditionally served motorists and the men from the estate beyond. Now that his wife was dead what was the purpose in pre-serving the six o'clock ritual, once a way of avoiding requests to set the table or keep an eye on the evening roast?

He opened the front door. It had been a long time since warmth and the smell of home cooking had greeted him. There was a pile of charity circulars on the hall table. Dorothy's illness had progressed in tandem with her increased generosity. Hardly a dog home or African orphanage had not benefited from her largesse. Vernon had decided to intercept the begging letters and deposit them unopened in the outside green bin. As soon as Dorothy realized this, she rescued every last one of them from recycling. In retaliation, the liberality of her donations increased. Months after her death, he was still finding letters from the Red Cross or the Salvation Army where he'd hidden them, in cupboards or under cushions. It was cold in the house and the leaves in the garden needed raking. He lit a fire in the sitting room. As soon as the blaze was over its initial spitting and crackling, he opened a pile of recently unearthed envelopes. The thin children, cancer patient, and feral cats curled and blackened.

THE SKY WAS a lighter blue in south Surrey than in the northern town where Vernon had been raised. In his mind, this was somehow connected to the sandy subsoil below his lawn. He walked along the edge of the motorway towards the lay-by, which was bounded on both sides by common land: heather, gorse, ferns, woody scrub; the coarser grasses now infringing on glades where delicate growths had once flourished. Beyond lay oak clumps and pinnacles of dark green pinewood. Before the nineteenth century this area had been rife with footpads, a haunt of highwayman. Here was desolation at odds with the stockbroker belt. During the day, dog walkers and riders used the common; at nights it was no place to stop.

As soon as he had a view of the lay-by, he saw that the food stall, where hotdog and hamburgers were served, had vanished. At this hour there would normally be a queue of lorry drivers and bikers, perhaps a few local youths; a bright green caravan was parked where the previous vendor's ancient Vauxhall had stood. Vernon was still reluctant to accept this was a mobile audiology unit. He crossed the bridge and went down to the lay-by, where he caught a whiff of burnt onions and axle grease, an elusive olfactory farewell. One thing was evident: the assumption that he was victim of the six o'clock crowd's joke was incorrect. On the front of the caravan *Harmony Invisible, Free Audiology Advice & Tests, Hidden Hearing Aids* was painted in an elegant italic script. Portable wooden steps led up to a door with a pointed arch. The design was antiquated and incompatible with an outreach project. The door swung open the instant he knocked. He'd expected someone standing on the other side, but there was only a small dark man wearing enormous glasses with white frames. Seated behind a desk with nothing on it, he stared straight ahead, apparently indifferent to Vernon's arrival.

"Good morning," said Vernon. "I'm hard of hearing, particularly in my left ear. I'd like to take advantage of the free test, if I may."

The man's gaze was directed in the region of Vernon's midriff. He remained disconcertingly still. Although his eyes were open, he might have been asleep or in a trance. There were no explanatory posters on the walls, only a reproduction of a painting that depicted the medieval idea of the cosmos, with the world sitting smugly at the center.

"Excuse me, I've come about . . . the offer of a test," continued Vernon. "Can you hear me?"

"Of course," said the man. "Everything in the universe emits a sound. You are no exception." His enunciation was exact without being prissy, each syllable weighted, the vowels and consonants perfect.

"And so I should continue standing here, talking to myself . . . is that it?"

"For the moment, if you please."

The man rose to slide open a drawer on the side of the desk. As Vernon took a pace forward, he saw a mineral glint, as from a tray of loose diamonds.

"Stay quite still, for a little longer," said the man. He held an irregular translucent object up to the light. "It's a question of aligning the most audible points within you to the wider harmony."

"You're not with the NHS, are you?"

"You may sit down now."

"Sorry to be frank, but I'm not sure about this. Not at all."

"Please, it will not take long."

The man took two of the pale objects from the tray; they were far too large to fit in his ears at all, let alone comfortably.

"I don't think those are ... "

"They adjust themselves to the shape of the inside of your ears."

The man moved from behind the desk. He was smaller than expected and his touch as he held Vernon's head was deft and gentle. There was no discomfort, only a refreshing coolness, in first one ear and then the other; something fresh and soothing, not quite liquid yet on the verge of fluidity and at odds with irritable wax, was cleaning the crannies of his ears. Then there was a shift in the audible. He could hear the hum of the halogen heater; a crane fly scuffling in the corner by the window.

"That's ... remarkable."

"There will be a period of adjustment," said the man. His accent was melodious but impossible to place. "To begin with it would be best to wear them for a few hours a day. The sudden increase in the volume of the world can seem a terrible thing."

Was it being implied the world was now larger? Vernon struggled to grasp his meaning.

The man must have observed Vernon's confusion. "Step outside for a moment. You will soon understand."

As he opened the door, the thunder of traffic was upon him, a tumultuous turning of wheels, so close as to seem tangible. But as Vernon flinched in fear of imminent extinction, the lorry sped benignly along the motorway. A sudden gust carried the tinny scrape of dry brown leaves across the lay-by, orchestrated the high pitch of strings in the ferns and grass. A squadron of wind droned in the woods, as if a whole flight of oaks were about to take off.

"I think," he said, slipping back inside, "these will need fine-tuning."

"You will adapt in a day or so. After a long period of hearing inadequately, it is inevitable that the world as audible presence will present itself as a physical force."

"Perhaps, but ... "

"Do you hear better now?"

"Well ... yes. Almost too ... "

"Then you must accept this gift. Here takes these." The man took out two small black boxes from the desk. "When you are not using them, place your hearing aids in these. It would be best to do that now."

"Do they need batteries?"

"No, once you wear them regularly they will be recharged by the energy within you."

The aids slid out smoothly. He handed them to the man who, having wrapped them in tissue paper and clicked the boxes shut, returned them. Something, no doubt the wind, blew open the door behind. He made his way out. Now the pounding, hissing wheels of traffic was muted once again.

THE HOUSE HAD been quiet since Dorothy's death, but when Vernon awoke the next morning the light through the green curtains had a submarine stillness, far from the movement of waves. If he opened his mouth, it would fill with brine. A single thread of cotton light fell through the crack. The black boxes were on the side table. As he lifted the first lid, he saw a silk lining; the second box was empty too. He took the boxes over to the window. In natural light, both of the hearing aids were visible, but they appeared to lack solidity; now they were shiny-bubble thin. Yet when he picked them up, they were quite firm. He popped them in. At once the sense of an invisible skin over the ear drums being stripped away. The creak of the floor boards and the tick of his alarm clock returned.

He drew back the curtains. Sunday walkers and dogs were emerging from the cottages around the green. The sky was a diluted distant blue, but the orange-red tiles on the cottages opposite added a touch of subdued warmth: a familiar scene, somehow softer this morning, the normally sharp lines of the church spire faintly blurred, the cross on the steeple no more than a gray smudge. It was almost as if a delicate after-dawn sea mist were still lingering, although the village was far from the coast. Then came the peal of church bells, so resonant they might have been ringing in his loft. A walk would enable him to escape the clamor.

By the time he was ready, the church goers were striding towards the lych gate. The boom of the organ began to compete with bells.

Vernon couldn't recall being so aware of the prelude of a service before. Even when he reached the village boundary he could hear the organ swelling, the voices raised to the highest pitch, the words of the hymn carrying clear until they merged with the roar of the motorway.

It was a relief to reach the stile that led to a bridle path through woods. Yet even in this customarily quiet spot there was greater activity; a rasp of creatures in the ferns and the birds more numerous: the wet crack of wings flapping overhead, the songs sharper; a crow cawing madly on the high stump of a pollarded oak. Even though the trees had only just begun to shed their leaves, the woods on either side did little to cushion the cacophony. Such sounds must have been present on his previous strolls, but he had never been so aware of them.

Once he'd walked as far as the heath, his attention was distracted by human figures: a boy flying a blue kite; a group of ramblers, bowed under their rucksacks like snails; two children throwing a Frisbee. In the distance, a man was moving in fits and starts across a landscape of gorse and heather. He was leaning back as though to prevent himself from being tugged onwards. Although Vernon deduced the presence of a dog, it was only once he was closer that he heard the panting that preceded it. Then he saw it: a low slung, broad-shouldered beast, with protruding eyes set far apart. At the far end of the leash was Mick Merrihouse, dressed in a surplus army shirt and trousers, a Parker and a Trilby.

"Why, if it isn't a member of my club. I say, shall we pop down to The Edge and crack open a bottle of champers, old boy?"

"I see you haven't quite got that creature under control, Merrihouse."

"So it's 'my man Merrihouse' now? You'd better understand this, squire: my pedigree hound what's accompanying me on my constitutional is not a domestic animal. In training, he is. For my own personal protection."

"Whilst I'm sure you're correct in your belief . . . "

Then a tilt in the angle of light. Merrihouse's face vanished for a second and when it reappeared his features had retreated into his skin, leaving only a shield-shaped head of flesh and a brim of shadow where his forehead had been. The dog too must be sightless, for its eyes had fled into holes beneath its fur.

"What's up with you, matey? Had a queer turn, have we? Not the first one since school surely?"

The voice was impossibly loud. It was also odd to hear the wind twisting round the gorse; the insects talking amongst themselves underground; the kite string, half a mile off, was sawing the sky.

BEFORE RETIRING TO bed Vernon realized he'd mislaid his hearing aids. Had they fallen out during the farce on the heath? His vision had returned to near normality and somehow he'd succeeded in extricating himself from Merrihouse. But the walk back was not free from anomalies. Even before he left the wood, he'd heard voices raised in a rousing rendition of the final hymn. All of which implied he'd misplaced the hearing aids later. In any case, it was now too dark to retrace his steps. He was in his pajamas. Should he check downstairs? He recalled wanting to turn down the volume of the television but struggling to find the remote. Perhaps he'd taken out his hearing aids instead? At length exhaustion bettered him and he tumbled into bed.

When he awoke the next morning, he was aware of having emerged from a place of shadow and malady; thin figures, barely discernible under blankets, although their feverish shivering was audible. He must have broken out in a sympathetic sweat, for his forehead was damp, the morning air cold against his skin. As he dressed hurriedly, the skeins of nightmare dispersed.

By ten he had searched the house several times; no sign of his hearing aids. But finding objects so small and translucent was always going to be difficult. How could he pick out their outlines against the pattern of the carpet? At noon he gave up. There now seemed little alternative to arranging a second consultation with Harmony Invisible. Yet shouldn't he research the company first? It might be possible to order replacements, which would save him a walk down to the lay-by and the embarrassment of confessing his loss. For the first time he regretted forswearing the internet. He would visit the library after lunch at the Edge.

As soon as he stepped outside, it was apparent some of the improvement in his hearing had been maintained. The sound of the motorway from his front doorstep, normally perceptible as a distant hum, was now textured with blare, screech, and hiss. But equally bewildering was a deterioration in his sight: the foreground visible but the middle distance and beyond blurred as if a watercolor had been put under a running tap. Had other clients of Harmony Invisible experienced similar difficulties?

Then he heard vast wheels and a prodigious engine behind him. As he turned, he saw a pantechnicon, painted the same shade of green used by Harmony Hearing, approaching. The air filled with exhaust; the rich taste of petrol was on his tongue. Once the lorry had drawn level, he observed, loaded onto the trailer behind, the prefabricated building that had housed the village library. The opening times were next to what had been the entrance. The driver stopped to wait for a gap in the traffic. Then as the trailer swerved onto the motorway, a book fell, with both facing pages down, from an open window. For a second it was a triangle on the tarmac before being flattened, first by a saloon car and then a van.

When Vernon reached the bridge that led over to The Edge, he stopped to peer down the motorway at the lay-by. Today he could no longer make it out. Beneath him the traffic snarled then vanished into the hazy gray-blue distance. It felt too far too walk down the lay-by unless he was certain the caravan would still be there.

As he walked up the steps to the entrance of The Edge, he glanced through the dining-room window: empty, apart from one waiter, moving between table and table—a solitary tiger fish in an aquarium. Inside, he was surprised to see the lobby and bar had been redecorated since the previous evening. The walls were painted the color of soft wet sand; the black leather furniture replaced by armchairs upholstered in pale yellow silk. Only the zinc counter and the bar stools remained unaltered. Greg Harris was the sole customer. Today, in an outsized floppy tweed cap and baggy plus fours, he was more than ever the vaudeville golfer or the cad on a dirty postcard, his tartan assigned to no known clan.

"Well, you were right about the library, Harris. I've just witnessed them towing it off down the motorway. It's a disgrace. What can they be thinking of?"

"It's all to do with 'The Death of the Visual'. That's what they're telling me."

"And who might they be?"

"The experts. You've seen one yourself."

"Harmony Invisible?

"That's right. The audiology boys."

"Since you mention it, I can't say I've been entirely happy with my hearing aids. Not that I can find them."

"Well, you wouldn't, would you? Not now."

Vernon realized that his hearing aids, far from being lost, had been absorbed. Yet even when they'd been at their most solid, hadn't he sensed a material instability, as if they were about to transmute from mineral to gel?

"I think I'd better make another appointment."

"You can't. Not today. They're having a conference. In the function room out the back."

Then the background music, of which he'd hardly been aware, stopped. There was a faint, repetitive swishing: oars pulling an open boat over quiet water or the empty revolutions before the end of the tape. Voices! At first a low moaning that almost matched the east wind; then overlaid with individual cries and shouts, recognizably human expressions of fear, hunger, rage, and pain.

"Listen. Can you hear them?" Vernon asked.

"Who?"

"People . . . shouting, crying."

"Oh them. They're always with us, so it's said. It's just that sometimes you don't notice."

Greg took out a pair of huge white framed glasses and put them on. "Yes, you're right. Their suffering's worse today."

"Did the audiologists give you those?"

"Of course, you see I've almost lost it, but not quite. Very good at keeping out the light, these are."

"And what are you about to lose . . . exactly?"

"My sight, of course. We're going blind. Don't you realize that? You must be well on the way if you can hear them without wearing glasses."

He would not panic or break down. Not in front of a ludicrously attired, purblind golfer. Yet the whole business was as unfair as it was preposterous. None of it had been explained.

"And you're going to tell me you're quite happy with your handicap?"

"I haven't actually played . . . "

"No, no, no . . . no! Your sight."

"The benefit will be considerable. When you lose one sense, the others improve to compensate. And then ... well, it's all about learning to listen properly."

It was important to sort out the whole matter quickly. Before his sight deteriorated any further. The sounds had worsened: a pitiful ululation; the approach of explosions; a wall falling onto the street; the hiss of the torturer's iron. If the evidence of his left ear was to be believed, someone was drowning, their arms flapping impotently before the final splutter.

He'd been to the conference room once before. A concert for some charitable cause followed by an auction. Dorothy insisted they should attend and then became angry when he'd refused to bid for anything. It was quite bad enough paying for the tickets without having to come away with a bottle of sickly sweet sherry or a bouncer-sized teddy bear. He pushed through the double doors at the end of the corridor. Once he'd stepped into fast forwarding hours, the light flickered, before fading to the edge of evening. The cries and shouts receded and Vernon became aware of the voice of a man speaking in a precise level voice. *The blind wage no wars; manufacture no weapons. Let us forgo light for the dark's black radiance. The loss of sight is the beginning of music and peace. Then there will be no noise to deafen us to the true harmony of the spheres.* There was a figure on the podium at the far end of the room, where the band had once played. As Vernon moved down the central aisle, he saw the upturned faces of the audience, unseeing behind their white framed glasses, yet angled to the new sun of sound. All his anger had gone now. If only he could find an ounce of charity within himself, the terrible cries would cease and he'd hear the crystal spheres turning. He sat down to wait for the end of the visible world.

ETERNAL ROOTS OF LANE COUNTY

J.C. Raye

———— ◆ ————

DOMINOS. MUCH LIKE the one and only set he'd ever laid his eyes upon. Packed into a sliding pine box, reliably stuffed into the pocket of Uncle Roy's overcoat, whenever the man would drop in for a visit. This was the image that swept through Cold McClurg's young mind as he fell back, hard, into the dust. Topple after unrelenting topple. Uncle Roy setting them dominos straight along a railing, or bound for turns around the curved runners of the porch rocker. Mesmerizing his nephew with scientific theories of thickness and energy and friction. All while using those finest peddler intonations and enunciations reserved for his most important of sales while on the road.

Now, digging his knuckles into the tender spot of tailbone onto which he'd so violently landed, Cold reflected on just how *very* much his panicked stagger rearward, the crash of lantern glass against the open barn door, and the screaming trill of startled hens as he tripped over them and into the woodpile, imitated those delicate rectangular tiles made of bone and ebony.

It was well after 11p.m., and the prickly warm wind had picked up considerably, wildly flapping his shirt collar and threatening to pinch his cap as he sat there, stunned, on the ground. The fence stakes and small trees lining the McClurg's barnyard seemed to fray around their edges in the murk of a chalky moon and powdery, dancing, plumes of topsoil which had been blowing about Lane County, Kansas, for as long as he could remember. By morning, this wind would stack more than forty tumblers against the north fence. Some big as barrels. Cold would need to haul them out first thing. It was a job that took three times as long without his pa, who was off in Dighton on a jackrabbit drive. But meat on the table was well worth the boy's aching arms and back. They hadn't had meat in ever so long.

Cold clambered to his feet in the darkness. The movement displaced a few of the still wandering hens, who chirruped their annoyance both with him and with the inner barn activity disrupting their roost. A sinister, involuntary shiver, had now settled decidedly between the boy's skinny shoulders and it reached up to grip his bottom jaw. And Cold knew it wasn't just plain old shock making his teeth rattle so. It was not as if he'd seen himself a ghost in the barn, or that Dracula feller he'd heard once on the radio after the Lee Overall Boys done their tune. After all, it was only his Aunt Eula back there. No reason to fear his own kin. Yes, true, the woman and her three children had been missing more than a month, and strangely, she hadn't come knocking to the house to let anyone know she was here. But *no,* these particular trembles had been borne of a completely different notion altogether. It was the chilly realization that his frightened hollers had brought *no one* to his aid. That sound, *any sound,* wood clatter, animal ruckus, would be always lost in this eternal raspy howl of the dust kicker, as it ravaged the flatland. The true extent of his family's hardship was, in this moment, becoming more clear to him. Because except for an exhausted mother, and useless, everlastingly hungry, three-year-old twins, Cold was alone. Here, in the dead of night, devoid of a lantern, or a weapon, living within the graveyard of a hundred abandoned farms, like it or not, Cold Daniel McClurg was *man-*of-the-house. Teeth puttering like a small engine or not, it was up to him to find out why Eula was hiding in their barn and why she looked the way she did.

HIS AUNT WAS no longer near the silo, in the center. Now, he would have to creep among the stalls. He knew she was still there.

Sporadic, ferocious gusts of wind blustered past the open door and wriggled up through the roof shakes, spawning a demonic chorus of hair-raising whistles. More air, moving through an empty haw mow, wound over beams and rafters. It cast a writhing web of snatching, black claw shadows across the boy's shoes and overalls. The barn door itself banged restlessly, as if calling out for him to close it. Open, the dust was sure to get in. *But closed?* Cold could not feel comfortable shutting himself in with her yet. At least until he knew what was what.

Then he spotted her. Four stalls back, hunkered down in the darkness and manure. Her back to him. The pink rosebud, flour sack dress she wore was frayed at the hem and torn up good in some places. Also, the garment was streaked with dirt. The same dirt which caked her unpinned hair and bare feet all the way up to the ankles. Her right hand was clutched onto the handle of an old metal tub. So tight was her grip, that even in the gloom Cold could see the blue veins in her hand pressing outward, as if threatening to burst from the woman's papery skin.

From what he could see over her shoulder, the tub looked to be made of copper, greatly tarnished and blackened over time. Decorative pieces of metal, shaped into vines and flowers and grasshoppers, were affixed around its sides. The tub didn't seem quite practical for bathing or for any other chore he could imagine. It was certainly nothing like he'd ever spied on a page of the *Montgomery Ward*, next to the fruit jars or skillets. Maybe she'd stole the tub, or was looking to trade it for food. He stepped in closer behind her, remaining still as death, watching her arms and shoulders furiously a-working on *something*.

Cold knew very little about what was happening to their family. Raggedy threads of detail, picked up while listening to his parents' low-talk some nights on the porch. That is, when his ma and pa weren't arguing about rain, or some town's fool idea to encourage showers by blowing up the sky with dynamite sticks tied to balloons. The boy remembered hearing how Uncle Donald got some sort of bank notice telling him that his family had to clear off, and Donald Trumbly outright refusing to do so. Making a stand on his property. Hitting a deputy with a piece of iron or some such other. Getting himself beat and thrown into jail. And Aunt Eula, following in his stride, not vacating the farm either. Hiding with her children out in the brush when the state came calling to take them. Of course, knowing a little more than these collected bits might have helped him talk to the woman in his barn right now.

Moonglow, squeezing between slivers of the boarded-up windows, shifted, and Cold could finally see what was in Eula's other hand. It was a sharp-edged white stone, about the size of an egg. She was using it to scratch a marking deep into the blackened copper. She must have been at it for some time because the stone was stained with her blood. He leaned in further, curiosity getting the better of him, and she suddenly turned, startled into a jerk. She dropped what was in her hands. In one swift movement, she stood and grabbed both his arms firm. He wondered then if his Aunt Eula was crazy with the prairie fever they'd heard so much about these days. He also wondered if she was of a mind to scratch something into his forehead next. Once, while repairing a fence, Pa said they'd built a round barn *to keep the devil out of the corners.* Cold hoped more than ever that Everett McClurg hadn't been beating his gums about nothing that day.

Eula got down on one knee and looked into his face. Through the tears in her dress, Cold could see rough patches of skin turned a buff-yellow on her exposed thigh. From what he saw, she hadn't taken a razor to her legs in a long time, and his face flushed with embarrassment for seeing it. As she held him fast, his other senses seemed more heightened. His ears picked up on the light *thump!* of the block and tackle against wall. Corn and buck saws juddered on their hooks. Then, there was that awful odor, emanating from the woman whose body was so close now. A strange, strong tang he couldn't quite place. All that running and sleeping in fields, he supposed.

"We don't have to leave, Cold," Eula said. Her hot breath smelled of wet bark. He did not know if the yellow stains on her teeth had always been there or not.

"Why, we're so much a part of this land, one hardly knows where the flesh ends and the dust begins." Eula let go and stepped back into the stall to retrieve the copper tub.

"Drought. Black blizzards. Plagues of grasshoppers." She continued talking while her hand was feeling around in the dust for the stone.

"Others. Running. Breaking up families." Eula found the stone and moved toward the boy once more, lifting his chin with her chalky hand. "We're tied here, boy. As sure as if by rope or chain. Surely you can see that? Surely your ma can. We got to stay somehow."

Cold knew his aunt was waiting on him to respond now. To say *something*. Though for the life of him, he could not think what. Did she want him to agree? Was she asking him if her family could move in here? He was terrified. Something very, very wrong seemed to be crawling across his Eula's Trumbly's face. And it was not a something one could see *plainly*. Later, after his aunt ran off, he'd try to describe it to his ma, but would fail miserably. A layer. A coating of sorts. Over the heat-cracked Kansas skin and the furrowed brow of calamity which everyone presented these days. Over that. More than that. But whatever *it* was, it had her in a state. All Cold could do was take the cowardly route. He wasn't even man enough to ask where her three young'uns, Myra, Dennis, and the baby, might be, or if they were safe.

"Aunt Eula, I'll get my ma," Cold sputtered. "Come to the house with me, and we'll get ma. And . . . she'll fix you something."

Eula let go of the boy's face and smiled. She closed her eyes. She bit her lower lip as if hearing music and trying to recall the lyrics of a childhood tune. Without warning, his aunt dropped down to the ground with a grunt, and once again, took up her strange carving.

"We have to endure," she said. "The land's going help us."

She was whispering this more to herself than anyone else. The last thing Aunt Eula said, the very worst thing, was what finally lit a fire under the boy and sent him tearing out of the barn, screaming for his mother, twin's peaceful slumbers be-damned. Eula said: *Just because you can't see them, don't mean they're not there.*

COLD'S FATHER REFERRED to the man as a noxious weed. A transplant. A government man, therefore a dangerous man. One who knew nothing about farming but had the power to choke out any kind of growth that might rise up around him. And now that very man was standing in the middle of their kitchen, one foot up on his mother's freshly wiped chairs, fanning his face with a wide-brimmed hat, asking a lot of questions, and acting as if he already knew all of the answers to them. Staring at Sheriff Frank Walter Winchell, Cold knew his pa had it right. He watched Winchell's eyes scan the inside of their home, take in walls quilted with bedsheets and yellowing newsprint, window sills stuffed with rags, the framed cross-stitch scripting his mother's favorite saying: *Make it Do, or Do Without.* He saw the man only half-listen while staring at the twins, occupied in brushing each other's hair, residue of their dive into the last of the peach preserves dappling their cheeks with sticky amber. Cold witnessed the man's distaste settle in quickly. As if living this way was a choice the family had made.

Telulah McClurg had her back to Winchell. She was kneading dough inside a drawer of the cupboard, under the cover of a huckaback towel. Red and green partridges were sewn into the hem. Barrettes fastened the towel in place and a slit opening in the middle was just large enough for Cold's mother to slide in her slender hands and do the work. This method was her best of late, but it could never remove all the grit from their bread. The dust would prevail. The kitchen was stifling with windows and doors shut. His ma had plugged in the fan on account of company, but the blades might as well have been constructed of flower petals for all the relief it was providing.

"You sure about that, Telulah?" Winchell said. "She just *took* off? Didn't even give you a hint where she and the kids might be holed up? Now, that don't make a lick of sense."

"I was never one to say my sister's actions made sense Frank," she said.

Winchell snorted as if someone had offered him a stick of chewing gum for a twenty-dollar bill.

"Forgive me," he said. "But that just don't sound right. You sure she was here? You said you never did see her for yourself." He took his foot down from the chair and leaned over to dip his index finger inside the rim of the preserve jar. He brought a taste of the peaches to his lips. Winchell then used the tip of his tongue to mash the goop up and around his front teeth like it was a cleaning paste. The Sheriff turned and looked dead at Cold.

"Now young man," he said, "is your mama telling me all there is to know? Was Eula really here and run off? What do you say? She give you even a hint of where she's living?"

Winchell took a long pause, still staring at Cold. He sucked preserve from between the spaces in his teeth. The sound was nauseating.

"I mean, you wouldn't want your ma to be obstructing justice now," he said.

Cold's ma instantly pulled her hands from the drawer and slammed it shut. Everyone in the room jumped. She crossly brushed her hands down the sides of her apron and turned to face Winchell. Even awash in flour and sweat, his mother was a beauty and there was just no getting away from it. Flawless, fair skin, the color of bone, seemingly impervious to damage from heat or dry wind. A cascade of cocoa brown curls, escaping their pins at every opportunity. Wide set green eyes with the flickering of something cagey, but resolute. Cold's father often referred to it as *the spark of life*. It was the reason why Everett McClurg had asked her to dance that first night they met, and then later, why he had fought with another boy, much bigger than himself, over taking her home. Cold simply adored when his pa told stories of their courting days. Ma too. She'd jump right in and tease back about how he danced like an electrocuted grasshopper.

But right now, Telulah McClurg wasn't dancing or courting. She was fuming.

"Now Frank, the *McClurgs* are honest people," she said. "Do you think for a moment I wouldn't go fetch my nieces and nephew right now if I knew where they were at after all this time?" She folded her arms and stretched her thin nose high, as if preparing for a scrap.

Winchell's eyebrows raised in surprise and he lifted a hand as if to calm her. But Cold's ma just kept on.

"And you *saw* the tub," she said. "Think that belongs to *me*? Think my husband would have ever made such a wasteful purchase? Proof enough that my boy's not lying."

Winchell sniffed and rubbed his knuckles under his nose. He lowered his head and stepped around the table a bit, a few steps closer to her. Particles of dirt and dust crunched under his boots.

"Well, I don't know too much about what a man buys his wife or doesn't buy his wife," Winchell said. "Seems like that might be a right nice washtub for a woman with your slender figure." He moved closer still, within arm's reach of her, and set his hat down on the table.

Cold didn't really like the way the sheriff was looking at his mother. Kind of like she was a chocolate cake fresh out of the oven. And his voice was different now. Warm. *Wrong.*

"But your sister, ma'am, whether she's laboring under a sudden attack of insanity, or whatever folks around here call it, she's on the run from the law, and trespassing on that property now, and her kids are missing. They might be sick or hungry. Probably real scared. And I think a good-hearted, loving woman like yourself would want to help me find them."

The kitchen door opened and Deputy Lockridge stepped inside, speaking as he did so. "Looks like we're all clear, Sheriff," he said. "If she's out there, then she's disguised as a bush."

Winchell quickly stepped away from Cold's mother. He scooped up his hat with some degree of aggravation. Nott Lockridge, one of Winchell's newest and youngest deputies, was coming in from searching the property for Eula. The young man carefully closed the door behind him, respectfully tipped his hat to Cold's ma and scraped his boots on the small rug just inside the threshold. The move was more about good manners than any real hope of not tracking more dust into the home.

Nott stepped away from the door to stand near the table. He smiled down at the twins and said, "Might have to be next in line for my hair combing. The wind gave it quite a turn out there." Then, to prove it, he vigorously ruffled his fingers through his short curly hair and blew loud bubbles of air through his lips, imitating a car motor. Grace and Sylvia giggled with delight and gave over their brush as if to trade it for more amusement.

The deputy caught Cold looking at him and added, "And boy did we have a real kicker the other day. I heard one fella in town say he saw the crows fly backward just to keep the dust from getting in their eyes!" The man was trying to lighten the mood. Cold's mother was much too worn out to offer anything but a weak smile. Winchell, however, let out a loud cough. It seemed to Cold that the action was less of a physical necessity and more of a scolding to his junior deputy for daring to speak.

"Well, since there's not much else we can do here, ma'am," the sheriff said, pulling on his watch chain to feign a look at his gold Mackey, "we'll need to be getting on our way." Winchell slapped his hat on the edge of the table before putting it on. A small cloud of dust floated up over the twin's heads. Sylvia coughed.

Lockridge looked at the family apologetically and then back at Winchell, who was already half out the door without another word.

"We'll make inquiries and be in touch," the deputy promised. He flattened down his hair and scooted out, deeply shamed by the telling of such a lie.

A FEW HOURS before dawn, Cold sat up in bed. It was the music that woke him. Delicate. Tickling. Inconsistent. Like the fizzle of a pop bottle under his nose. His ma must have left the radio on in the back parlor for the second night in row. He was certain she did this to drown out her own weeping. With the dust storms increasing over the last few days, it just wasn't possible for her to walk out away from the house to do her grieving.

But as Cold sat there, very still, so as not to creak the springs and wake the twins, something felt different to him. He was noticing the strange glow of his fingers atop the quilt, and could clearly make out the cream-colored blocks in the pattern of it. He spotted other items too, brighter than he ever remembered for this time of morning. The handle of chipped cup on the far dresser. The unevenly hung calendar near his head on which Grace had drawn a stick figure assortment of farm animals. Looking towards the window, the newsprint nailed there was lit up silver. It was the moon. And more. Over the faint chimes that had teased him from slumber, another sound. Katydids. Crickets. The sounds of life and a clear night.

THE RADIO WAS off and the living room was empty. The moon was so brilliant through the tall windows that the boy did not need to turn on a lamp to see. The kitchen still had not been tended to. Normally, in such a circumstance as this, neighbors would come from far and wide to cook for the family, and relieve them of the burden of daily chores. There would be coffee. Young children playing in the yard. Old people dozing in chairs. But there were no neighbors now. Not a one. And the sole donation of food that had arrived was a basket of apples and cakes from Nott Lockridge's sister, who came with her brother to deliver Everett McClurg's wrapped body home. Cold and his sisters had finished off the apples and some of the cakes almost immediately yesterday, as their ma was not of a mind to do any cooking. Not that there was much to cook with. Half a prune cake was still left on the table, only partially covered by a striped towel. Dishes and cups were scattered about, and the sugar tin had been carelessly tipped over, leaving a small mound of its precious powder on the dusty oil cloth.

Motion in the towel caught Cold by surprise and he jumped. The other half of the loaf hidden under cotton was not, in fact, prune cake. It was a large, hideous jackrabbit. A buff-colored beast greedily nibbling away at tomorrow's family meal. It jerked colossal ears in Cold's direction, but did not panic nor zig-zag off in a tempest of flying china. It simply stared at him with yellow ochre eyes, lifting its nose high in the air. The boy wondered if this one could be related to the rabbit that had most certainly killed his father.

NOTT LOCKRIDGE HAD not been present when Everett McClurg's accident occurred. A deputy from Healy relayed the story to Lockridge in this way. Something had gone wrong with the jackrabbit drive. That the army of small beasts, five-thousand strong, and a plague to every crop in their path, simply refused to be driven into the fenced enclosures at the sound of banging pans and car horns. That in fact, right before reaching the pens, dead ends which would result in a violent clubbing, the hares turned on their heels and began to run *at* the crowds. Chaos ensued. Many folks were bitten, and some of the elderly trampled. Cold's pa was seen to have a black-tailed jackrabbit the size of a small pig hanging on to the back of his neck by its teeth. The man was turning round and round in tight circles, as if caught in a steel trap, beating backwards with his arms, trying to force the creature to lay off. Blinded by fear, or by pain, McClurg backed into a wagon team and startled them. One of the horses rose up high. As it descended, one of the animal's heels wiped out Everett's lower jaw, and its other leg stomped the man's throat flat.

The officer from Healy did not say if Cold's father died instantly. The boy supposed that meant his father did not. Lockridge seemed to cut the story short, and offered to dig a grave. Telulah would not allow it, thanked the deputy and his sister for their kindnesses, and sent them away.

THE DARK SKY was the clearest it had been in months. There was a breeze, but it was clean. Cold couldn't remember any other time seeing so many stars as he crossed the yard to the barn. His mother was sitting on the ground next to her husband's corpse. She'd pulled it down from the boards set over two kitchen chairs which Lockridge had arranged before leaving. She'd untied the wrapping and splayed out the limbs. The head and body were still covered, but the white cloth around one hand had been folded back, revealing purpling digits, enclosed around an object. A stone. His ma followed his gaze to Everett's swelled hand.

"I had to help him," she said. "You're *allowed* to help them."

His mother moved to a crouch, not caring that her white shift dragged along dirt. Telulah McClurg smiled at her son and patted the patch of dirt next to her as if to indicate he should sit. Cold was afraid, but did. Close, next to her, the source of the strange melody that had woken him was then revealed. It was the copper tub. Meandering breezes were traveling in and along the metal vinery affixed to it, creating vibrations. The fine variations in the copper curls and designs poured out an odd but evocative series of tingles and chimes. The sound seemed to linger over their treeless flatland.

As the uncanny lullaby drifted out over the chirping of the crickets, Cold was now staring at the cloth which obscured his father's head. The boy was trying, for the life of him, to recall the features of his father's face, and was having a hell of a time doing so. So far, he could only picture those deep wiggly lines in his pa's forehead which always made him look a bit amused. He could also envision his pa's thick brown hair, chopped to an awkward tuft at the hands of his wife.

His pa's haircuts were a long-standing joke in the McClurg household. Soon as the man's hair so much as tickled his ears, Ma would be chasing him down with her nickel-plated shears. Sometimes he'd even pretend to hide from her. Once, he even scaled the windmill to stay out of her reach, all the while hollering about how she couldn't cut a straight line if her life depended on it. Cold always knew his parents put on this show entirely for his amusement and joined in by holding up the hewing hatchet and promising to do a better job of it if his father would come down.

His mother's loud jagging cough pulled him off his pleasant thought. She'd moved to the edge of the barnyard. Facing the field. He was not sure how she'd managed to get so far so quickly. He watched her bend over, her shoulders jerking repeatedly as she gasped for breath, pounding at her own chest as if it would do any good at all to expel the grit. It was nothing he hadn't seen a hundred times before. The helpless routine of a person slowly being strangled by prairie topsoil.

Cold kept her company for some time. Just before sunrise, he kissed his mother on the forehead and went back to bed, hoping to catch a few hours of sleep before the twins stirred. She did not follow him in.

ON THE SIXTH day of an ungodly black roller which blew coffee-colored snow and blocked out the sun, Cold and the twins were still trapped inside the house. Their ma had not returned, not in the six days, and the boy feared the worst. Tiny particles of dust viciously scratched at the windows day and night. And those bits which did gain entry dredged the four-room farmhouse; a churned-up fog, never seeming to settle for the wiping, greedily caking the hands and faces of the girls. Cold put out buckets of the dust every day. *Buckets.* This activity was a constant, and maddening, and it deprived him of sleep. But the alternative was unthinkable.

Adding to the misery of being completely shut in, having no working electricity, and living off boiled carrots and a few onions stuffed with peanut butter, the family now fell victim to rather size-able pieces of silt and paint that would occasionally drop from the ceiling. A little too often onto Sylvia or Grace directly. In the first few days of the storm, whenever this occurred, the injured party would wail so loudly that Cold thought folks could plum well hear the gal over in Dighton. Then, true to form, the unexpected outburst of one sister poked a hornet's nest in the other. Cold thought about dominos then too. Howling and sputtering, faces pinched up tight, shaking their heads to and fro with wild abandon, the twins set each other off till both were completely inconsolable. Sylvia, always especially adept at her tirades, would stomp the floor and turn over whatever item her little digits could reach, and that included turning over Grace when she had occasion to do so.

Yet the worst of it for Cold was not having to helplessly watch dirt sift onto the tots' heads, remembering that when clean, those mucky curls were the sweet color of bright sunflower. Even their confused cries over hunger and in the missing of their ma was tolerable, barely. It was when Sylvia and Grace *stopped* making noise that he was most afraid. Stopped crying. Stopping pleading with him for another onion. When a sizable dollop of dirt to their forehead resulted in nothing but a soundless shiver. That was when Cole McClurg was most like to lose his mind.

ONLY ONCE HAD Cold had ventured out. Only once. Drawn by the sound and remembering. Not knowing why, but believing the having of it might make them all feel better for a while. Wrapping his face and eyes in cloth, he pried open the kitchen door, just enough so as to squeeze his skinny frame through. Whirlwinds of soil beat on his exposed skin. Feeling his way down the porch and slowly crawling along the yard, he reached the barn. The doors had been left open, most likely by his ma, so even inside, the wretched brown blizzard was almost as abrasive and blinding. Using hands for eyes, he edged his way along the stalls. Cold had a terrible moment when he thought he had put a hand on the cloth covering his father's body. And when that happened, he screamed to high heaven and was quite sure his heart had burst open inside his chest. But, in the end, it turned out to be only the bottom of his own shirt, unbuttoned and blown forward in the current of air. A few feet more and his hands found what they were looking for, and there was a warmth there he did not expect.

Dragging it back was harder than he thought, and he lost his way several times, but the carcass of a dead hen, crossed over before, directed him back towards the farmhouse. He thought he was almost home, but then hit his head, *hard*, on the edge of the bottom porch step. It hurt and his lips involuntary parted as he yelped. A flying handful of dust seized the opportunity to coat his teeth and gums with grit. Then, feeling wetness drip down over his eye, Cold panicked and became disoriented all over again. For a while more, he crawled around in circles, crying. Eventually, it was the creaking of the tied-up porch swing which helped him find the house again.

EACH NIGHT (he was no longer keeping count), after shaking out bedding and soaking washcloths to tie over faces, Cold would string the copper tub to hang outside their bedroom window. Battering gusts of wind and sand through the ornate metal vines and grasshoppers would render the strange soothing melody and lull his sisters into a blessed, deep sleep. He'd lay next to them on his parent's bed, listening to their labored breathing. He'd then turn over in his mind all the roads he travelled with Pa in the pickup before it got sold off, desperately trying to recall any structure where he imagined his ma might have taken cover, or found water or food. Where could she go? The Duckett farm, Kalls, Leens, even the McKibben's place. All those folks were long gone. Driven out by blizzards or banks. No matter which road Cold tried to follow in his mind's eye, the ruminating always seemed to end in the same nightmarish thought. A nagging, plaguing, just plain terrible, notion. The possibility that Sheriff Winchell had picked her up in his car and finally got to have that piece of chocolate cake he pined for. Cold shook the thought free and simply focused on the comforting melody of the tub as earth and air wound through its cavities and creepers. Somewhere in the knells and light jangles, he could hear a chorus of voices. A chorus of the people he knew.

BY DUSK, COLD had taken each of his sisters' hands in turn and helped them scrape the first initial of their names into the metal. They barely put up a fuss, weak as they were. Grace's eyes could open barely a slit. Dirt, muddled with her tears, slowly welding them shut. Cold then crudely scratched the shape of a domino into the copper. All the while, he was feeling the stone grow heavier and more difficult to manage.

ALMOST IMMEDIATELY AFTER finishing, he could no longer hold the rock using the five toes of his densely furred front foot, and it dropped to the ground. His long ears and nose, now in constant movement, were analyzing the air current for every sound and scent. An unmistakable aroma of bluestem grass, quite near the house and a few feet underground, was what finally drew him away from the open kitchen door and from the two small jackrabbits by his side. Rabbits that looked like twins.

WED

Brady Golden

———◆———

BY THAT POINT, *my daughter's bad dreams had become a monthly event. Her screams had woken me up enough times that I should have known what they meant, but as I rushed down the hall to the girls' bedroom, still half-asleep, all I could think was that she was in trouble. Visions flashed in my head of a bed engulfed in flames, of a strange man hauling himself through a jimmied window. When I got there, I found the same thing I always did—my girls, painted blue by their butterfly nightlight, safe and alone. Alyssa was only just stirring awake in her crib, a shadow crowned with blonde curls. Lorah, upright in her twin bed, clutched her quilt to her chest with both hands. She wasn't looking at me, hadn't even registered my presence yet. Her eyes were fixed on something just past me in the corner of the room.*

"Don't let her get me!"

I'd tried before to get Lorah to tell me what her nightmares were about. She'd never given a clear answer. Upon waking, she'd be too traumatized to speak, unable to get a word out between sobs. After I'd sat with her for a while, rubbing small circles on her back with my palm, she would settle down enough to talk to me in a hoarse, fragile voice, but by then, the dream would have slipped out of her mind.

Maybe it was because this is the closest she had ever come to naming her boogeyman—her—or maybe it was the way her gaze didn't falter, but a certainty struck me all at once that there was someone else in the bedroom with us, a fourth person standing just behind me. I spun around, ready for something terrible.

Of course, there was no one. That not-alone feeling didn't go out of me right away, though. Lorah's fear had infected me. It stuck around.

Lorah's screams were degrading to hyperventilations. I had to take a moment to steady myself before I could go to her. Alyssa had pulled herself to standing, was watching me through the bars of her crib. "Dadda, Dadda, Dadda," she babbled as I passed.

THE WEDDING TAKES place at a winery an hour north of the city. At least, they call it a winery. So far, I haven't seen much in the way of grapevines, just an array of lawns, gardens, and picturesque footpaths. The scattered buildings are all of a vaguely Italian design— eaves and corbels, low-pitched roofs covered in red ceramic tiles, everything with a deliberately sun-bleached look. The ceremony is held on a lawn beside a duck pond. The officiant is a bearded man about my age, a non-denominational minister, some old friend of the groom's family.

Alyssa wears a sleeveless dress textured like braided rope. With their yellow hair, pink cheeks, and a general doughiness, she and Theo are a matching pair. They look enough alike to be related. Back when they first started dating, I used to find that a little unsettling. Sometimes I still do.

Four groomsmen stand at his side, five bridesmaids at hers. Lorah, at the end, is the odd one out. She has on a flimsy summer dress instead of the melon-colored gown the rest of the girls are wearing. This morning, she insisted she didn't have the money to join the rest of them at the hair salon, and refused to let me pay her way, so she is the only one up there not coiffed and styled.

Until a week ago, we didn't know Lorah was even coming. Alyssa had sent her an invitation months before, but had never received anything in the way of an RSVP. Lorah had gone dark again. Her phone was disconnected, and she wasn't answering emails. It happens often enough that I wasn't worried, but it did mean there was no way to get a definite yes-or-no answer from her. We'd assumed *no*. We'd assumed she would emerge from wherever it was she'd vanished to this time when she was ready.

Then, after months of no contact, she called to tell me she'd bought a bus ticket, and to let me know what day and time I should pick her up from the Greyhound station. She didn't bother to ask if it would be all right if she stayed with me while she was in town.

It took some work convincing Alyssa to include her sister in the wedding party. It wasn't just that she didn't want to throw off the bridesmaid-groomsmen symmetry. Her bridesmaids have been with her not only for the past year of planning, but for her entire life. They are her oldest, closest friends, and she didn't want to include her sister in their ranks. I was sympathetic. I only had two arguments of my own—first, I'm paying for the wedding, and second, it's what her mom would have wanted.

Later, when I met Lorah and her single overstuffed piece of luggage at the station, I said, "I should probably let her tell you herself, but Alyssa's going to ask you to be in the wedding."

"That's ridiculous," she said. She still smelled of her cross-country bus ride. "There's got to be twenty people she'd rather have up there than me. Tell her not to ask."

I refused to have the same argument twice in less than a week. "If you don't want to do it, you're going to have to tell her yourself," I said.

She didn't. Lorah feigned surprised when Alyssa asked, and Alyssa put on a show of delight when Lorah accepted. My girls don't have much in common, but they share a talent for acting.

The ceremony ends, as they do, with a kiss, applause, and a record-ing of Mendelssohn's "Wedding March." Afterwards, the photographer takes people in batches to the far side of the pond to have their picture taken with the bride and groom. The afternoon light is turning from blue to gray, and the photographer seems increasingly harried each time she comes back with a new list of names to summon. Finally, Alyssa's family gets called over—Lorah, me, and a cousin of Mary's none of us have seen since the funeral. It occurs to me that the same could be said for Lorah, for all the times she's visited.

We stand together in a clump around Alyssa and Theo and wait while the photographer fiddles with her camera. Lorah says, "Everyone pretend to be happy."

Alyssa is not one for big reactions, and emotions can sometimes be hard to read on her round, smooth features, but I spot a flicker in the smile she's been wearing all afternoon.

Dinner is served in a reception hall. Someone has propped open the double doors to let in the summer warmth. Tiny lights strung from the ceiling give the impression of a cloud of fireflies hovering above our heads while we eat. I sit with Mary's cousin and a few friends from work. Without staring, I keep an eye on the wedding party's table at the head of the room, counting each glass of wine Lorah drains. Over the noise of twelve tables' conversations, I can't hear the things she's saying to her sister, but the commentary seems constant.

Eventually, Alyssa shifts to look her sister in the eye. Whatever she says makes Lorah's cheeks go bright red. Theo pretends to be too engaged in a conversation with his groomsmen to notice what's happening, but the bridesmaids are gaping with barely disguised shock.

Lorah stands. She snatches a purse off the table and stomps to the exit. More than a few guests watch her go. Excusing myself, I follow her outside. I find her around the side of the building, sucking angrily on a cigarette.

"You've got to keep it together," I say.

"I am keeping it together. Tell her to keep it together," she says. "Do you know what she just said to me?"

"It doesn't matter what she said. Weddings are stressful. She gets a pass. You don't."

"I never do, do I?"

"Cut the drama, for once in your life."

We aren't alone. A woman has come around the corner and now stands nearby, watching us. Embarrassed at having been caught in an argument, I flash an apologetic smile, which she doesn't return.

She's old, older than either of my parents ever got, and they made it into their eighties. Her hair is stringy and long. It has a faint yellow tint that makes me think of urine-stained bedding. Her mouth hangs open slightly, and her breathing makes a papery sound. I might think she'd wandered away from some kind of facility, but I can't imagine there are any places like that out here in wine country. Anyway, she's clearly dressed for the wedding, in a silky, high-collared dress.

Without a word, Lorah goes back inside, leaving her half-smoked cigarette smoldering on the ground. The woman watches me grind it out with my toe. I try another smile. It gets ignored as thoroughly as the first.

THE FEW OTHER *parents in the toy aisle weren't looking at me, but I could feel their judgment, and I couldn't shake the feeling I deserved it. Their own kids were able to browse the shelves of bright plastic without falling to pieces. That mine couldn't clearly pointed to a failure of my parenting. I'd never meant to bring Lorah to such an overstimulating spot—we were at Kmart for bathroom supplies and cat litter—but a turn down a wrong aisle had deposited us here, and now she was in full meltdown, on the floor, on her back, squeezing the packaged doll I wouldn't buy her tightly enough to bend the cardboard. The parenting book Mary had asked me to read said I shouldn't raise my voice at her when she got like this, but how else could I get her to hear me over her own wailing?*

Alyssa was in the shopping-cart seat. Her jelly-sandaled feet kicked idly at the air. Another two-year-old might have taken her big sister's tantrum as a cue to throw one of her own, but not Alyssa. She was a calm kid, staid.

I warned Lorah that if she didn't calm down, I would leave her in the toy aisle. Then I turned my back on her and started to push the cart away. I braced myself for everything to get a whole lot worse, but instead Lorah abruptly went silent. Trying not to let my relief show, I slowed down enough to give her a chance to catch up. When she didn't, I glanced back.

Lorah was gone. The patch of linoleum where a moment ago she'd been flopping around was now empty, save the pink box that had been so important to her. I looked to the other parents standing nearby for help. They didn't look back. I wheeled the cart to the nearest intersecting aisle. There was no sign of Lorah, but I headed down it anyway. At the next intersection, I lingered only for a second before selecting a direction at random and taking it.

I went from toys to electronics to groceries to hardware, picking up speed as I moved. My head worked on a swivel, but I didn't know how much I was actually seeing for all the questions running around inside my head—Where could she be? How could I have been so stupid to turn my back on her? What was I going to tell her mother? I found a manager and breathlessly explained the situation. She asked me what Lorah was wearing—I couldn't remember—and how long it had been since I'd last seen her—I wasn't sure. She instructed me to stay by the front entrance in case Lorah tried to go out into the parking lot. I was too terrified to ask how we knew that hadn't happened already.

While the manager bustled off to search the store, I followed my orders. I took note of every kid who passed. None of them were her. An amplified voice called down from the ceiling, instructing Lorah to go to the customer service counter, or to find a store employee and ask for help. The voice made no mention of me or of how old Lorah was, but I was sure every shopper in the place understood what was going on. To the people who saw me at my post by the exit, how obvious was it that I was the negligent father who'd misplaced his poor little girl? A few minutes later, the announcement repeated.

Alyssa slapped at my knuckles on the handle of the cart. "Home?"

Later, the manager returned with a walkie-talkie in one hand. She informed me that they'd found Lorah, but something in her face made me think it was not entirely good news. She led Alyssa, me, and our box of Fresh Step to an aisle of camping supplies. Several other staffers in uniform vests waited for us there. They had their heads tilted back to look at something high, high up. I followed their line of sight.

At the top of a shelving unit, balanced on her hands and knees, was Lorah, sobbing and trembling. Tears and snot glazed her face. She was clearly terrified, and I couldn't blame her. The shelves were twelve, maybe fifteen feet high, and the strip of metal she was balanced upon couldn't have been more than a foot wide. I told her not to worry, that I was here and that everything was going to be okay.

To the employee nearest me, I said, "You guys have a ladder or something in back, right?"

The manager looked uncertain. "Maybe we should call the fire department? Insurance—"

"Just get me a goddamned ladder!"

My raised voice only made Lorah cry that much harder.

"Who was that?"

"Who?"

"Outside. That woman. Do you know her?"

"No. One of Theo's relatives. A grandmother, maybe." Picturing her face, I wonder if I should have added at least one *great* to that sentence.

Lorah doesn't look satisfied with my answer. She's sunk into a loveseat, tapping at her knees like at invisible piano keys. We're in a dressing room in the back of the reception hall that Alyssa and the girls used to get ready earlier. Clothes hang over the backs of chairs. Tubes and containers of beauty products are scattered on the table. A polished-off champagne bottle lies on its side in the middle of the floor.

"Jesus. What am I even doing here?" She looks wearily to me. "How about a ride home?"

I don't point out that it's been half a decade since she last lived in the house she just called *home*. "Of course not."

"Can I borrow the car, then? You could catch a ride back with someone else."

"You've been drinking. And you can't have money for a cab, so don't ask," I say. "You're not ditching your sister's wedding."

"She doesn't want me here. She told me how you guilt-tripped her with a bunch of Mom-talk. Alyssa hates me, Dad. She has ever since we were kids. She hates my fucking guts. So why don't you give us what we both want and *let me leave?* And please God, don't start talking to me about Mom."

If she wasn't rubbing her eyes in a demonstration of exasperation, she would have seen me flinch at that.

"I don't care if you spend the rest of the night holed up in this room by yourself. You're staying at this wedding until the last guest is gone."

When I get back to the reception, people are already eating dessert. I missed the cutting of the three-tiered cake I bought. I can only hope the photographer I hired captured the moment. Alyssa and Theo are going from table to table, thanking people for coming. I'd planned to make a toast at some point, and wonder if I missed my chance for that as well. I have to wait my turn to catch Alyssa's attention and pull her aside. I keep my voice down as I explain where Lorah is. "She's feeling insecure. Threatened, maybe. You know how she gets," I say. "Can you go talk to her? Convince her you don't hate her. Tell her you're glad she's here. It'll take five seconds."

Before she can answer, Theo appears at her side. He snakes an arm around her waist and nuzzles her neck. He's not usually this affectionate with her in front of me. Is he feeling carried away by the occasion, or is this just how things are going to be now that they're married? He asks how we're doing.

"Fine," Alyssa says, but she's not talking to him.

She twists away from Theo. I feel his puzzled gaze on my back as Alyssa and I hurry through a side door. We go down the corridor that leads past the bathrooms to the dressing room. Alyssa knocks twice and pushes open the door, then looks back at me. The room is empty.

THE WAITING ROOM for the security offices was small and air-conditioned. The woman at the front desk hadn't said anything to me in a while, and I'd lost track of how long we'd been there. Alyssa, sitting cross-legged in one of several upholstered chairs, was ignoring me as I paced, too focused on the melting popsicle that a sympathetic zoo employee had given her.

The door opened with a chime and Mary strode in, no makeup, hair unbrushed. I'd promised her a day of relaxation in an empty house. That had barely lasted three hours.

I went to her. "I don't know what happened. I only took my eyes off her for a second." The words spilled out of me. "We were fighting. She wanted to watch the penguins some more. I told her we needed to get moving. Then she was gone. She was just gone."

"It's not your fault," she said. I nodded, but I doubted she really believed that. "What's going on? What are they doing to find her?"

"The police are here. They're searching the zoo. And the zookeepers are checking the animal enclosures in case she—" My voice trembles.

She cut me off. "It's going to be fine. What can we do?"

"They just want us to wait here in case they need to find us."

From her chair, Alyssa let out a dismayed squeak. Her popsicle was in the process of detaching itself from its stick. It happened slowly, but not slowly enough that any of us could do anything about it. The large chunk sagged, then toppled. It splatted on Alyssa's chest and slid down her T-shirt. Mary knelt in front of her. Wadded paper napkins appeared in her hands, seemingly from nowhere, and she used them to mop up the smear. "It's okay, honey. Just a little spill." To me, she said, "Did you bring any spare clothes?"

"Yeah, I did." I had to think for a minute. "They're in the car."

"Can you go get them, please?"

I felt no shame at being dismissed. I was back on solid ground, assigned to a task I could handle—an Alyssa task, not a Lorah one. It was late summer, and the sun was oppressive as I navigated my way to the zoo entrance. Families moved around me in clusters. Parents pushed strollers with a tortoise-like lethargy while their older kids ran orbits around them, occasionally darting away to check out some animal or exhibit, then yoyoing back. When I reached the parking lot, I blanked on where I'd left the car, but only for a second.

The canvas backpack I'd loaded with supplies for the day—clothes, snacks, sani-wipes—was in the trunk, where I'd stowed and forgotten it. I hoisted it out, slung a strap over my shoulder, and slammed the trunk shut. As I was about to turn away, a shape in the backseat of the *car caught my eye. It was barely visible through the sun's glare on the rear windshield. I stepped around the side of the car for a closer look.*

It was Lorah, slumped in the seat. Her eyes were closed. At first I was too stunned to react. How did she get here? Why did she come? Weren't the doors locked? Sweat glistened on her skin. Her tank top was soaked through. Panic rose up within me. I tried the door, but it was locked. Frantically, I dug the keys of my pocket and hit a button. All four doors clicked at once. When I finally got the door open, a furnace heat rolled out.

I pulled Lorah to me and held her in my lap as I dropped to the asphalt. She was slick and dripping. In my arms, she felt rubbery, inorganic. I repeated her name over and over again, until her eyelids started to flutter.

ALYSSA SAYS, "IF she wants to go, let her go. She's an adult. She can do what she wants."

It's the truth, but it doesn't convince me. I picture Lorah on the side of an unlit road with her thumb out. No busses run out here that I know of. Most of the cars on these roads at this hour are headed back from an afternoon of wine-tasting, their drivers buzzed and as likely to plow Lorah over as pick her up. At twenty-four, after six years of living on her own, she's still making these decisions.

"She's got to be here. It's important," I say.

"Important to who? Not to her. Not to me."

"To your mom. It's what she would have wanted."

"You're always saying that," she says. "You're always telling me what Mom would have wanted. But you don't know. She's not telling you, and you don't get to speak for her."

I swallow. "I'm going to find her."

"Don't. It's almost time for the father-daughter dance."

"I'll be right back. She can't have gotten too far."

"Dad, don't go to her. I mean it."

I give the most reassuring smile I can manage, then head outside. An evening breeze is stirring, and the air carries the smell of grapes on the vine. A number of cobblestone paths snake their way through the winery. I take the one that leads to the parking lot. The lamps lining the path have come on. The murmur of conversations coming from the reception sounds like a pen overcrowded with animals. After a few turns of the path, I can't hear it anymore.

In a little while, I reach the parking lot. It's full past capacity. Drivers have wedged their cars in at odd angles to make them fit. A few, opting to skip the lot, have driven their cars onto the mowed grass that surrounds it. Any damage caused by the tires will, I'm sure, show up on my bill. I begin to walk around one side of the lot, but stop when I spot Lorah on the other side. She's on her knees, with her hands pressed to her face. She's crying. Her shoulders tremble with each sob. Someone's with her, standing beside her. At first, I can't make out who.

"Hey! What's going on here?"

Lorah doesn't react to the sound of my voice, but the other one turns towards me. It's the woman from before, the one who came upon Lorah and me outside the reception. Her eyes land on me with a sudden, heavy weight. There's a threat in them that I don't understand and can't account for. I start across the lot.

"Your little girl needs you," the woman says. Her voice is startlingly resonant.

"I'm right here. Lorah, honey, are you okay? What happened?"

The woman sneers. "Not this one."

With a sweep of a bamboo-thin arm, she knocks Lorah aside. Lorah lets out a wounded-animal sound and collapses in a sprawl. The woman steps over her and advances on me. Her legs seem to stretch and shorten with each step, giraffe-like one instant, frail and stumpy the next. Her whole body swells and bends like an image captured on burning celluloid. My head swims at the impossibility of what I'm seeing. I feel my balance going out of me, and I almost fall, but she reaches me and grabs onto both my shoulders before I do. Her grip is tight, her hands so cold that the sting penetrates my jacket.

"Who are you?" I manage to say. "What do you want?"

"The one who takes care of her. The one who loves her the most."

"Her. Lorah?"

"No!" The rebuke is sudden and ferocious.

"Alyssa?"

At my daughter's name, she sighs, a dry, exalted sound. "She is precious. You understand that, don't you?" She clucks her tongue. Something shiny and black wriggles in the back of her mouth. "She deserves devotion, from her own father more than anyone. But you let yourself be distracted. It's cruel. Your inattentiveness is cruel. Do you need me to help you focus? Should I clear away your distractions?"

I can't see Lorah. The woman blocks my view. "Leave my family alone," I say.

"Your family *is* my family. The piece of it that matters, anyway," she says. "Now, there's somewhere you're supposed to be."

She starts to press down on me, as though trying to push a stake into resistant soil. Her strength is uncanny. Pain screams up my legs. I think my shins might snap under the force. She opens her mouth to show me the black thing again. It stretches out, a parachute deploying. I try to scream Lorah's name, but it wraps itself around my face, sealing itself against my mouth, my eyes, my ears. For a while, there is only muted darkness.

THREE DAYS. THAT'S *how long it took Lorah to get around to calling to tell us where she'd gone. The lack of consideration was typical. We spent the time believing she'd been kidnapped or worse.*

It turned out that when she left the house, instead of walking up the street to catch the bus to school, she'd gone to a coffee shop two blocks over to meet a boyfriend. Her suitcase was already stowed in the trunk of his car. She'd been packing it gradually for weeks, one or two items at a time so Mary and I wouldn't notice. They'd left town after breakfast and driven six-hundred miles up the coast to start their new lives as high-school dropouts without a dime between them.

Mary blamed herself, blamed her diagnosis—too scary and stressful for Lorah, who had always been so sensitive. She blamed me, too, for always being so hard on Lorah. But it wasn't my fault any more than it was hers. Lorah ran off because that was who she was, who she had always been. She'd been gearing to leave us for her entire life, practicing for as long as I could remember. She'd just turned eighteen. There was nothing we could do to stop her, and she knew it.

Mary may have been heartbroken, but I was furious. That she would choose right now for this stunt made all previous attention-hungry antics pale in comparison. The results of Mary's biopsy had just come back earlier that month. We were in a transitional state, still reeling, but also readying ourselves for what was coming next. Ovarian cancer had killed Mary's mother and her grandmother. We knew what the treatment would entail, and its likelihood of success. This was going to be the most difficult thing we would ever face as a family, but Lorah had once again found a way to turn everyone's attention to her.

I couldn't tell how Alyssa was taking things. She was fifteen now, and as she'd cruised into teenagerhood, her emotions had only gotten that much harder to gauge. When we were alone, I asked her how she felt about her sister taking off.

Without hesitation, she answered, "It's better."

"What do you mean?"

"You know how Lorah is," she said. "All the freak-outs and the fights. Any time things don't go her way, she loses her mind. She's exhausting. I don't think she can even help it. She sucks energy out of everyone. Right now, we need all our energy. Mom needs us to be strong for her. If Lorah was still here, we couldn't. She wouldn't let us."

I didn't like how she was talking about her sister, but it wasn't like I could scold her for it. I'd asked how she was feeling, after all. She was only answering my question. Anyway—and as I realized this, I experienced the first bit of calm I'd felt in weeks—she was right. What Alyssa was saying was absolutely right.

MY LEGS BUCKLE beneath me and I collapse. I claw at my face to tear away whatever's there, but there's nothing, just my own skin. I can see again, but my mind's still spinning, untethered, and nothing makes sense. Time has passed. I can't tell how much. The pressure against my face made me feel drugged, sleepy. I might have passed out for a while. I'm back inside the reception hall, in the dressing room, alone. I can't imagine the skin-and-bones woman being able to drag me anywhere, until I remember her strength. There's no sign of her now. That doesn't do much to calm me down. My chest hurts. I worry I might be on the verge of a heart attack. Then I worry I might have already had one.

Nearby, music starts up—a piano, playing gently. The melody is familiar, but I can't place it until Elvis Costello's throaty warble comes in. The song is "She." One of my favorites. I picked it for my dance with Alyssa. She'd had something else in mind, a boy-band ballad that she'd loved in high school, but I refused. If I was paying the DJ, I got to choose the song.

I stand and run my hands down the front of my tux in a weak attempt to smooth out the wrinkles. A two-inch gash in one of the sleeves exposes the shirt underneath.

I follow Costello's voice into the main room. The guests hold champagne flutes and watch me come in. Their smiles are glossy, their eyes bright. At the front of the room, the tables have been pushed aside and the crowd has parted to make room for a dancefloor. Alyssa stands at its center. She has to help me get my hands in place. Around us, cell phone cameras click and flash. She looks at me expectantly. The song's still playing. She applies a gentle pressure with her hands, something just shy of a shove.

"Like we practiced," she says.

We dance. At first, it takes concentration and will to get my feet to move, but eventually the song catches up with me. I don't have to think about it quite so much.

Her mouth barely moves when she says, "You shouldn't have gone after her. I told you."

We turn in a slow, swaying circle. When the second verse ends, I spot a shadow moving through the darkness outside towards the propped-open doors. She's limping and clutching a bent arm to her chest. Dead leaves and bits of grass cling to her dress. Soon the guests notice her as well. One and two at a time, they turn to her. Muttering voices threaten to drown out the music. Several people gasp. Someone says the word "ambulance." I force myself to keep my eyes on Alyssa. We don't stop. The lights strung across the ceiling find only her.

THE VALLEY

Casilda Ferrante

————◆————

THERE WAS A GAME I liked to play with my daughter, before she was taken.

I brought very little with me when I moved to the valley. Left a house full of books and shoes and kitchen appliances behind. The one thing I could never part with was the old suitcase that held her things.

When she returned, we played the guessing game again. It helped to draw her close to me, draw her back.

Every day I brought out one of her toys. We sat on the living room floor, the suitcase open between us like a mysterious portal, pulling out memories one by one.

I peeped over the lid at her. She giggled, hugging her knees, waiting patiently.

"Who's this? Come back here, you!"

I wrestled with a toy inside the case.

Two cloth ears poked over the lid, then a bunny appeared, dancing in the air.

She reached for the bunny, squeezed it in her little hands.

"Billy!" she said "Hello, Billy!"

My eyes stung with hot tears. Billy had been her favorite.

"Do you remember Billy?"

She nodded.

"Do you remember we used to take him for a ride in the pram to the park?"

She stared at me then shook her head no.

"You used to sleep with him every night. Sometimes you even took him into the bath and we would hang him to dry on the clothes line by his ears!"

She laughed.

"Funny Billy!"

"Billy has missed you a lot," I said as I took the toy from her.

I stroked its mottled dirty fur. It smelt of her baby skin and of another life, of chocolate milk and bubble bath.

"Billy was very lonely without you. But I took good care of Billy for you and Billy is so happy you have come back to him."

I smiled at her and handed the bunny over again, and she clutched him against her chest.

"Miss you, Billy," she said. "Miss you, mama. I want to go home." She looked up at me, eyes wide with sadness.

"This is our home now, honey."

I scooped her up, held her as tight as she held Billy.

I CAME TO the valley to be alone, away from all the people in my life who had become strangers. I couldn't bear their loaded glances, their careful words. I wanted to grieve in private. I didn't mean to touch forces I didn't understand. There are spirits in that valley, angry and wild. Ghosts of convicts and bushrangers, child slaves, and cunning women. The ghosts of those brought to this colony in wooden ships hundreds of years ago who still wandered, alien and displaced. They have never been appeased.

The house was at the end of a long dirt road, surrounded by forest. Among the eucalyptus trees, their thick trunks as white and smooth as bone, I pleaded, I hated. I'm ashamed of those moments when I lost myself completely, digging at my skin with fragments of glass. It eased the pressure in my head and the pain in my heart. I clenched stinging palms. Blood dripped on dry earth, mixing with tears as I wept; a dreadful brew. I didn't realize they were listening. The spirits claimed the blood for themselves, as an offering, a pact. They took me on my word and what they gave me in return was my daughter.

I made her favorite foods to welcome her home. Blueberry pancakes for breakfast, cut into stars and stacked with layers of jam and cream.

In the evenings I made ham and pineapple pizza, pumpkin ravioli, potato wedges with sour cream, chocolate mousse for desert. A banquet spread out before the two of us. We sat by candlelight; it always felt like a special occasion. After dinner, we curled up together and watched movies.

At first my daughter was quiet and withdrawn but slowly she opened up to me. I knew it would take time to ease her back into this world. I can't imagine what she'd been through. There was so much I wanted to say but so much that couldn't be spoken. Or questioned. Perhaps in the future, when she was much older, we would talk about it.

Many things about her were the same; her dimpled smile, her pensive frown. The way she played with her toys so thoughtfully, never with malice or anger. Even the way she colored and the stick figures she drew.

Some things about her had changed. Her once blue eyes were now hazel. Her long hair was darker blonde, almost brown.

Two years had passed since she was taken from me. She hadn't aged at all but for a few fine lines around her eyes and mouth. As if death had left its mark and claimed a little of her purity. It didn't matter if she looked a bit different; she was with me again.

We went walking in the bush, spotting lizards, picking native flowers, hunting for fairy mushrooms.

It was how we passed much of our time.

She stopped to point at white cockatoos. They shrieked high in the gumtrees, their yellow crests standing on end.

"Pretty birds up there."

"Aren't they lovely?"

I held her hand as we stood and watched them.

"You know, the traditional owners of the land believe the white cockatoo carries the spirit home."

But she had already lost interest, her hand slipping from mine as she trotted ahead. I stood a few moments longer, thinking about the birds. The cockatoos gathered around the house during the day, bickering loudly, and they followed us when we went out walking, flying from tree to tree. They were always close, keeping watch. Their friendly chatter reassured me everything would be okay.

I took a deep breath and followed my daughter.

I avoided the darker hollows, still tainted with blood shed, with deep sorrow. We walked along sunny paths, down to the creek to paddle in the water, or up to the flat rocks where we gazed across the valley and snacked on nuts and fruit.

SHE WANDERED OFF one day when I was baking. I called out to her, no answer. I checked the rooms, empty. I ran outside, circling the house, shouting her name.

A helicopter was flying overhead in the distance. Sometimes they appeared, scanning the bush for stray tourists or for bushfire checks. I hadn't seen one in a long while.

Cockatoos screeched and scattered as I rushed through the trees, my panic building. I found my daughter nearby, standing alone in a clearing. She was staring into the bush, her face pale and blank.

"What are you doing here, honey. Didn't you hear me calling you?"

She looked at the ground and shrugged.

"Don't do that again. Mama was very scared."

I gripped her shoulders as I knelt beside her. She burst into tears.

"I want to go home."

"Come on, let's go back in, I've made some cookies."

"Where's my daddy?"

I softened my grip and smiled sadly.

"Daddy left when you were a little baby."

She stared at me and then cried some more.

I cuddled her, looking up at the sky. The helicopter had passed but it worried me.

"Come on, we've got to go inside. Cookies? Chocolate chip. Your favorite."

She rubbed her eyes and nodded. Such a brave little girl.

I carried her home. I didn't know how to truly comfort her. Although we shared happy moments there were times when she was so distant. Like a part of her was still missing. I felt I just couldn't get through to her, that we hadn't fully reconnected. I hated the feeling of being alienated from my own child. But who could I talk to about it? Who could I ask for help? Children are not meant to return from the dead, to leave your life all of a sudden and then walk back in one day. If people knew, they would take her away again.

I TRUSTED THE birds of the bush. There was meaning in their song and flight. They told me of coming weather, they warned me of things to come.

The visit from the neighbor was marked with peels of laughter. Two kookaburras sat in branches nearby, cackling loudly, sharing a joke. They are cunning birds. Their sudden outburst set me on edge. I called my daughter inside and shut the door just as I caught a glimpse of the woman strolling up the road. I drew the curtains and sent my daughter to play quietly in her room.

I watched the woman through the dirty lace, hovering out of view. She was a pretty woman in a simple floral dress and heavy boots. She knocked loudly, then again, then three times. I held my breath. She held something in her hand, which she left at the door. She began to leave but turned back to stare at the house before finally going away. I opened the door an inch to see what she had left. A jar of homemade jam.

When I moved to the valley I had no desire to meet anyone. I went into town only when needed and avoided getting into conversations. Since my daughter had come home I had forgotten about the outside world altogether.

I glared at the jar of jam, anger bubbling, and the kookaburras laughed some more. I threw the jar in the bin.

IT WAS THE kookaburras who told me where to find my daughter, after the pact was made in the bush. Thin red scars flashed across my palm, my fate forever altered, a new destiny etched by desperation and sheer will.

I woke to their boisterous song and felt like going shopping. The nearest mall was on the Sydney outskirts, two hours down the mountain.

She was waiting for me in the car park. I was getting in the car when I looked up and saw her standing alone by the lift. The lift opened several times, people walked in and out, rushing past her as if she wasn't there.

My little girl is an angel now.

It was a happy thought. In a daze I waved at her, I called her name. She looked over at me and waved back, smiling.

I took a few slow steps then I ran towards her light.

When our hands touched I was shocked to discover she was real, of warm flesh and blood.

THE APPEARANCE OF the neighbor bothered me. I couldn't sleep that night. I paced the house. I drank a bottle of wine. She would probably come back. Friendly with nosey questions, wanting to know all about me and my daughter. Maybe she had children of her own and would invite us over. And the helicopter. Another intrusion. My stomach churned, my thoughts raced.

I peeked on my daughter, sleeping peacefully, Billy tucked in beside her. Her plump little face, her thick curled lashes and rosebud mouth. Maybe she really was an angel just visiting for a while and would have to return.

Often I sat at the end of her bed watching her sleep. My fingers knotted tightly, squeezing until my knuckles turned white. She lay so still and serene. I was afraid that she wouldn't wake in the morning, that she might slip away in the night and I'd be left with her empty body again.

I sat outside on the steps and drank some more. The moonlight illuminated the forest, casting the trees in sharp silhouette. They stood like tall and wise beings waiting patiently to see what I would do.

I found myself walking into the bush, stumbling through the shadows, branches catching me in their stiff hold then spurring me on. Creatures rustled in the undergrowth and frightened me, but I kept going. I wanted to return to that dark magical place, to speak to the spirits, but I was soon disorientated, turning in circles. I fell in a heap and burst into sobs, weak fists clutching dry earth.

Please, please let me keep my daughter; please don't take her away again.

I woke up on the couch, my daughter standing beside me.

"I'm hungry," she said

I fumbled around the kitchen preparing her breakfast. She sat quietly eating porridge, and I nibbled at a slice of toast.

Something didn't feel right and it wasn't the hangover. I went to the window, looking out suspiciously. The day was sunny, the bush vibrant and calm. I scanned the trees; it was too quiet. No kookaburras, no cockatoos, no movement. But there was a large magpie, slick and black with white tipped wings, perched on the balcony railing. It peered at me, tipped its head this way and that. It spoke in a sharp voice, lyrical, mocking. It seemed to ask me the same question over and over, then it took off into the bush. I understood. I began to prepare.

We left the next morning. I packed only the bare essentials and as much food as I could. We were headed through the valley, to the other side of the ranges. I was leaving everything behind again but this time I had my daughter. We would find a new place to settle. It was the only way forward for us. We couldn't go back, into the world of people and things. We had to travel deeper into the wilderness.

By early afternoon we had to stop. We were both so tired. I had carried both her and the backpack for a while.

I set up our tent. We spent the rest of the day playing in the creek.

We sat wrapped in our sleeping bags by the small fire I had built, eating sandwiches. I kept her entertained with stories and games but as darkness fell and the mist swept in, the valley grew icy cold.

"I want to go home," she said

I poked at the fire with a stick. It cast little light or warmth against the looming blackness of the bush.

"We're going to find a new home."

"Why?"

"Time for a change. We'll find a lovely new house to live in."

"Where?"

"I don't know yet. Someplace nice."

I tried to sound cheerful. She sulked.

We crawled into the tent to stay warm. She turned from me and went to sleep hugging Billy.

We didn't get very far the next day either. She didn't want to walk and I couldn't carry her any more. The nights were freezing but the days were hot.

"I'm tired." She whined as we walked slowly.

"Just a bit further today, honey, and then we'll stop. I promise we'll be there soon."

"I want to go home."

"Stop saying that! I've already explained to you. Come on, just a bit further."

"No!"

I was about to snap at her when I heard the helicopter. I grabbed her and ducked under the trees.

"Why are we hiding?"

"Shssh!"

I couldn't see it, but it was close, circling above. I held her still. She tried to push me away.

"Stop it!"

"Let go! *Mama!*"

She burst into a tantrum. I held her tightly.

We sat in stillness until the helicopter finally moved on. I breathed out in relief. She was curled in a ball, wouldn't look at me.

"OK, we'll stop for today. Let's find a good spot for the tent. You know I packed lots of yummy snacks for us."

She didn't speak to me for the rest of the day. She sat under the tree pulling Billy's ears.

It would be okay soon, I told myself. We just needed to keep going. Maybe two more days of walking and we'd reach the western range. I was rationing our food carefully. I glanced around the forest, hoping for some kind of sign, but there were no birds to be seen. They had all deserted me.

In the tent that night she shivered and cried softly. I tried to cuddle her, but she pushed me away.

"I'm sorry, honey. I didn't mean to get angry. I'm just tired too. We'll be there soon, I promise. When we get over the hills we'll visit the next town. We'll have some fun. Can you hang in there a bit longer? For Mama?"

"Okay."

I smiled in the dark, so proud of my girl. I had to be positive, be strong for her, and we would make it.

Sleep came slowly, in the form of nightmares. I was walking towards the coffin. The floor was scattered with white rose petals, they swirled as I walked through them. Her small body was immaculate and beautiful on a bed of white satin. She opened her eyes; they were blue again, and she spoke to me.

I'm going back to heaven now, Mama.

In the background dogs were barking.

Panic jolted me from my sleep. They were close, no time to pack anything.

I grabbed my daughter, scrambled out of the tent and tried to run.

She was heavy, still asleep. The early morning mist was thick and wet around us. I couldn't see too far ahead, I stumbled forward. Dim spots of light appeared through the trees like watching eyes. My daughter woke up and began to shout.

"Billy!"

She struggled in my arms. I stopped and clutched her, tears beginning to spill down my face, rising from the deep well of fear in my chest. The lights grew brighter, hovering in the bush, surrounding us.

Men burst through the mist, shouting over barking dogs.

"Get down! Get down!"

They tore her from me, they stole her out of my arms. I was face-down in the wet dirt, guns aimed at me, hands cuffed.

My daughter was carried away, she was crying. I shrieked for her. I tried to tell her I would find her again, that I would never let her go.

MY CELL IS blank and empty. The bars are ice cold against my cheeks, a rare moment of sensation, of indulgence, in this barren place. The extra time I had with my daughter was worth it. I don't regret it. Beyond the bars there is nothing but white walls and endless hallways. And armed men. I am shuffled between men in uniform and men in suits. Men who can't accept the unknown. They ask me questions, the same questions over and over again, but they don't listen to anything I say.

I close my eyes and picture the lush and feral valley, the wild bushland where justice is metered by different laws. I think of the spirits, restless and hungry, waiting in tree hollows and rock crevices. Did I not shed enough blood? They heard my prayers once before. They will again.

SITTING SHIVER

Adam Meyer

———— ◆ ————

HELEN HESITATED AT the front door of the house she grew up in, shifting her suitcase and turning to find Goldfarb looking up at her from the base of the stoop like a tired old mutt. "I'm sorry," the lawyer said. "It's just . . . for a moment you looked so much like your mother."

She supposed the appropriate sentiment was "thanks," but she just forced a smile and said nothing. Her mother had been small-minded and vain, a vindictive woman who felt that other people always had the things she herself deserved. Helen had spent her life trying to make sure that she was as different as she could be from the woman in every way possible.

Goldfarb still hadn't moved, holding down his hat against the sharp wind. "Maybe I'll see you at shul tomorrow night? It's just, we used to count on your mother for the *minyan*. Without her . . . " He shrugged his thin shoulders, barely even lifting his heavy trenchcoat.

She pressed her lips together, trying to find a better excuse than, *I just don't feel like it.*

"All right, sure."

Goldfarb seemed to shrink further inside his baggy coat, his heavily-lined face sagging with relief. "See you then."

Watching him go, Helen pushed the key into the lock and stepped into the livingroom—the room where her mother had died—and braced herself for the shock of being here again after so many years. Strangely, she felt the comfort of the familiar. There was the same old couch on thick mahogany legs, the oil painting of a mountaintop wrapped in its dark frame, the lamps with gold tassels and yellowing shades. Helen dropped her purse on a sidetable—where her mother used to snap at her for leaving her backpack after school—and started toward the kitchen. But she stopped halfway there, noticing the black cloth nailed up to the wall.

"What the . . . ?"

She touched the cloth, thick and heavy, and studied the line of silver nailheads zig-zagging across the top. She pulled up a corner of the black sheet and saw a mirror beneath, her own look of confusion reflected back at her in the glass. What was going on? Her mother was the last person in the world who'd ever cover a mirror. She was the kind of woman who always liked to make sure her lipstick was just right, her hair combed perfectly, even when she was just going out to get a newspaper.

Helen headed for the bathroom off the main hall, and sure enough, there was another black cloth nailed over the sink. What had her mother been up to? She hadn't seen anything like this since—

Of course. Since her father died. Covering the mirrors was part of sitting *shiva*, the Jewish mourning ritual. But Helen wasn't going to be faithfully carrying out the old Hebrew tradition, which included spending a week not showering or looking at her reflection just so that she could focus on her grief. She hadn't talked to her mother in fifteen years, and she hadn't stepped foot in a synagogue in at least twenty.

Of course, that didn't answer the question: why had her mother covered the mirrors in the first place? To *force* Helen to sit shiva? Helen wouldn't put it past her, except that Dorothy had died of a sudden heart attack and wouldn't have had time to prepare the house. Besides, getting all those nails in the wall . . . the woman was pushing eighty. It would've taken her hours to put up those coverings. Maybe days.

No, it must've been Goldfarb, the lawyer. First the pressure to come to temple, now this. Ridiculous.

Helen pulled out her phone to call Goldfarb but no, she restrained herself. For now she just wanted to take a quick look around and get over to the hotel on Queens Boulevard.

She climbed the steps to the second floor, her fingers trailing lightly over the worn banister. In the master bedroom, she saw that as in the livingroom, nothing here had changed. Well, almost nothing. On the dresser was a large mound covered with a black cloth. Helen snapped the sheet away like a magician, revealing her mother's TV, a massive old Panasonic with a converter box on top.

What the hell was Mom up to? she wondered, noticing the slightly warped image of herself in the curved black glass.

This time, she didn't hesitate. She pulled Goldfarb's number up but the line just rang and rang. The old man wasn't back at his office yet, and of course he didn't have a cell phone. She wadded up the dark cloth into a ball, hurled it into the corner, and sat on the edge of the bed.

The sheets smelled of her mother's perfume and some other, muskier scent. Was this where her mother had been when she first felt the chest pains? Helen felt tears on her face, the first since she'd gotten the news. Soon sobs wracked her body, rippling up through her chest and coming out of her mouth. She lay back on the bed and inhaled her mother's rank smell and pulled a pillow to her chest, pinching out tears that tasted like seawater.

SOMEHOW HELEN MUST'VE drifted off to sleep there because when she finally opened her eyes it was dark. She fumbled around for a light, got her fingers on the tiny nub of a lamp. She still felt drunk with sleep. It took her a moment to remember where she was and then it all came back: her mother was dead and she was here, the home she'd vowed never to return to. She remembered what it had been like growing up, her and her mother locked in an endless battle of wills. *Don't wear that dress, it makes you look fat. I told you to study harder for that test. I don't like that boy, I think you should break up with him.* Helen usually ended up doing what her mother wanted. It was easier than trying to resist. But she became more and more expert at hiding things, camouflaging them. Her mother criticized that, too. *You're so secretive, you never tell me anything.*

She felt like her whole life had been one long battle of wills with Dorothy, and that was why she'd stayed away for so long. Her mother trying to force her into a box, Helen fighting to climb out. In the end it had been easier to stop fighting and just keep her distance.

Helen started to get out of bed, glancing at her reflection in the TV, and froze at what she saw. Her cheeks were puffed out like she'd just come back from the dentist, bloated as party balloons, and her right eye was squinched shut as if she'd been punched. She didn't feel any pain, and when she ran her fingers along her cheek she couldn't trace any problem. She ran straight into the bathroom but of course the mirror was covered over. She tried to pull down the cloth but the nails were hammered in so tight she had to whip up the bottom right corner of the draping and stick her head under.

What she saw was that her face was fine.

Her cheekbones were visible beneath smooth flesh, her eyes wide with concern but otherwise normal. She stroked her flesh slowly, making sure she wasn't missing anything. But no, she was okay.

She must've still been dreaming for a moment, even though she'd thought she was awake. She laughed but the sound of it in the empty house just unsettled her further. She had the strongest urge to get out of there but when she checked the clock she saw that it was three a.m. All right, might as well just get some more sleep. This time, however, she bunched up the blankets and carried them with her down the stairs, headed for the couch.

HELEN HAD TROUBLE falling asleep on the lumpy sofa but once she was out she didn't wake up until a quarter to nine. She found some wheat Chex in the kitchen and munched on that, then spun in a slow circle around the musty livingroom. She tried to imagine her mother waking up here, day after day, year after year. What a lonely life it must've been. Dorothy had never cultivated many friends, and the ones she did have she always seemed to drive away sooner or later. The local synagogue had been a lifeline for her, and Helen supposed that was why her mother had clung to religion so tightly. Or maybe it was just her fear of death closing in.

Helen crossed to the curtains and started to pull them apart but they wouldn't budge. She was confused at first and then frustrated. She pulled harder and finally managed to open a slight gap in the middle. Once she did, she saw the problem right away. Someone had used some kind of heavy-duty stapler to bind the curtains together.

Unbelievable.

Helen called Goldfarb again. When he didn't pick up, she left a terse message, ending with "I expect to hear from you soon." She then methodically opened all the curtains, prying apart the staples, making sure that every room was flooded with light. Then she pulled down all the black cloths from over the mirrors. It was no easy task, and she realized that she was making huge pockmarks in the walls where the nails had been, which might affect the value when she put this place on the market. She didn't care. She'd had enough of this nonsense.

She spent the morning finalizing funeral arrangements and getting in touch with various distant relatives to let them know the news. Everyone said how sorry they were and what a hard time this must be and Helen agreed, too ashamed to admit how much relief she felt. Yes, she felt bad that her mother was gone, but she couldn't exactly say that she would miss her.

By the afternoon, Helen was fully focused on packing. Few things in the house had any value, sentimental or otherwise. She found some boxes in the basement—her mother never threw away anything, even cardboard—and began to pack up old knick-knacks. Working felt good. She liked being busy, having a task, and when she looked around after a couple of hours she could see real progress. She'd get as much as she could loaded into boxes in the next two or three days and then hire someone to finish the job and cart everything out. Once the house was sold, that would be it. Her ties to this place—to her past—would be severed for good.

The thought produced a tightness in her belly. Was it sadness? Regret? No, it couldn't be. When she thought of what it had been like growing up here—her friends' parents or her teachers always commenting on how lovely her mother was—she wanted to scream. Her mother had been the ultimate conwoman, complimenting people to their faces, badmouthing them the instant they turned away. She'd spent her whole life trying to get away from that kind of hypocrisy and anger. She wasn't going to get nostalgic over it now.

She grabbed furiously at tiny figurines and pieces of dry pottery, stuffing them in nests of old newspaper. She was so busy working that she didn't look up for more than an hour. When she finally did stop, she was exhausted. She leaned back, trying to assess what to tackle next, and from the corner of her eye caught a glimpse of herself in the mirror over the sideboard.

Her face looked swollen again, and this time the skin was yellowish and pocked with dark red sores oozing with puss. Helen whirled to face the mirror head-on, but as soon as she did it was just her own normal face, staring back at her with wide-eyed surprise. She crossed to the glass, watching her image grow larger and larger. She raised her hand toward it, daring her reflection not to match her every movement. But of course everything she did, mirror-Helen did too. What she'd just seen—no, correction, *thought* she'd seen—was just her imagination.

Clearly she needed some rest. Not the curled up on the couch kind, but the kind she could only get in a nice cushy hotel bed.

Like her mother, Helen hated to leave a project half-finished, but that was how she left this one: the last box filled only a third of the way, a smattering of unpacked objects still in the room. She gathered her things, grabbed her suitcase, and called for an Uber. The weather was brisk but she waited outside. She'd had enough of her mother's house for today.

As HELEN ENTERED the temple that night, the sound of a man's deep voice chanting Hebrew wafted toward her.

Baruch atta adonoy...

She remembered coming here on Friday nights years ago and looking out at more than a hundred heads huddled over their prayer books. Now there were just a dozen, and she looked to be the only one under seventy, maybe even seventy-five.

She took a seat halfway back, nodding at the people that turned to greet her. A couple of rows up she spotted Goldfarb stuffed into a pin-striped suit, his arms sticking out like clumps of straw. He was so engrossed in his chanting that he didn't notice her. She looked down at the black book, the soup of Hebrew symbols. Although she couldn't read it anymore she found her mouth chanting the words, picking up on the rhythm and the sounds through instinct.

The rabbi—a relatively spry senior citizen with arms as big as Torah scrolls—paused in his chanting and looked down at her with compassion. "As we say our next prayer, I want to acknowledge the loss of one of our most devoted members, Mrs. Dorothy Levine."

Helen nodded. Her mother hated to be called "Mrs."

"Her presence here was a comfort to us all, and we are deeply saddened by her loss. However, we are quite pleased to have her daughter Helen with us tonight, and I ask that everyone please rise and join me in saying the mourner's kaddish."

Helen stood, surprised to see that her hands were shaking.

Yitgadal vyitkaddash shmeh rabbah...

Suddenly, Helen remembered how when her father had died, her mother chanted these words in the livingroom every night. Helen had only been five, too young to really understand what was going on. Her mother had explained about the car accident and that her father wasn't coming home again but all Helen wanted to know was why not. Because he didn't love her?

...dekol bet yisrael...

Helen wasn't allowed to go to the funeral but she remembered the week after, her mother wearing all black, sitting on the hard wooden box, people coming by with Jell-O molds. *Your father's gone,* her mother had said for what seemed like the hundredth time. *We're sitting shiva for him.* All Helen could do was cry and dumbly repeat the words. *We're sitting shiver. Daddy's gone.* Yes, her mother said proudly, as if she'd just learned to tie her own shoes. Yes, you've got it. But the truth was Helen didn't have it at all.

. . . *viamru amen.*

When the service was over, Helen was accosted by a group of old women dressed in black, murmuring their condolences. Helen wondered if they had dressed that way in honor of her mother or if it was just a fashion statement. The old ladies led her to a smattering of food in the back. Flat soda, stale cookies. She took a bite of an oatmeal raisin, sipped from a waxy cup of RC Cola, smiled and nodded as the women told stories about her mother. They talked about how kind she was. Clearly none of them had known her well at all.

Finally, Helen excused herself to get another cookie. The rabbi muttered his condolences and gave her a big hug, and when he pulled away Goldfarb was waiting. Watching her.

"I've been trying to reach you," she said.

He nodded. "Yes, I'm sorry. I've been praying a lot . . . and then it was Shabbat, so I couldn't call." But he didn't meet her eyes as he said it, and she had the distinct impression he'd been trying to avoid her.

She smiled thinly, trying to hide her frustration. "Anyway, I just wanted to ask you something. This might sound silly but did you . . . that is, were you the one that covered my mother's mirrors?"

He looked at her strangely, as if he had no idea what she meant and yet wasn't totally surprised either. "Mirrors? No, I . . . I wasn't aware she had done such a thing. But . . . it makes a certain kind of sense, I suppose."

"How exactly?"

"As I said before, we did rely on your mother to help make the minyan here but . . . she hasn't actually been to services in months. I'd call to check in but she almost never answered. Then one day she came to my office, maybe two months ago. She wore these big sunglasses and her face was all wrapped up in a scarf, which struck me as odd because . . . well, it was probably sixty degrees outside. Truth be told, she seemed a little *meshugana.*"

"What did she want?"

"She said she wanted to talk about her will, what she was leaving to you. As far as I knew, all she had was the house and its contents and a few bank accounts. And I told her that as far as I knew the will was complete."

"But she wanted to make some kind of a change?"

"Yes and no. What she wanted . . . she asked me if I could add a line in the will to make sure you got *everything* that was hers, but I told her it would only be redundant. I also explained that according to Jewish law, there's no need for a will, really. When a widow dies and has but one child, everything goes to her or him, automatically. That seemed to put her at ease. "

Helen turned this over in her mind. What had her mother been so concerned about Helen getting? A stash of hundred dollar bills under the floorboards? Or something more sentimental, like old pictures of Helen's father? But no, sentiment wasn't her mother's style. She glanced over at the stained glass image of Moses, a bold image in red and blue and white glass, so dark that it cast no reflection.

"Did you find anything unusual she might've left for you?" Goldfarb asked.

"No," Helen said, shaking her head. "Nothing at all."

"Just as I suspected." Goldfarb sighed in relief, adjusting the yarmulke on his head. "Looks like this 'everything' was really nothing at all."

HELEN WENT FROM the shul straight to her hotel. She wasn't going back to the house, not tonight and hopefully not ever. Goldfarb could ship some things to her if she decided she wanted anything, but at the moment she couldn't think of what she might want to keep. Let him sell everything and send her a check. As for the funeral, she would take a pass on that, too. She didn't want to spend another minute here, in her mother's world. Maybe she was being ridiculous—of course she was. What she'd seen in the house, that was some kind of a trick she was playing on herself, or more accurately, that her mother had played on her. All that old programming getting into her head and making her see things that weren't there. But she wasn't going to be a part of it, not anymore.

All she wanted was a good night's sleep and to get on a plane back home.

If she had dreams that night, she didn't remember them, and she woke feeling refreshed and calm. She'd changed her flight online before going to bed and just wanted to go downstairs and have a quick breakfast before heading to LaGuardia.

She headed out into the hallway, feeling herself tense as she passed a wall mirror, but when she looked over, there she was, hair pulled back in a ponytail, looking surprisingly youthful without makeup, her smile wide with relief. She was leaving all the bad memories of her childhood behind, and that made the smile bloom even bigger.

She stood at the elevator doors, checking her cell for the Facebook condolence messages. She had started to tap a reply to one of her coworkers when she looked up at the silver elevator doors and saw herself, her face misshapen, the sprouts of wispy gray hair, the puss-filled sores. No, she said, backing away. She stumbled into the staircase, ran down five flights to the lobby. This wasn't happening, this wasn't real. She looked around frantically at whiny kids tugging at their mother's hands and couples smiling over suitcases. Sunlight streamed in through the sliding doors out front and everything was normal, and then she turned, spotting a wall-length mirror beside the front desk, and there was hag-Helen, staring back at her.

It was just as she'd feared.

Everything. Her mother had left her everything. Even this. This was her mother's curse, not hers, but she'd wanted to make sure she passed it on.

Helen staggered to a table, a decorative vase perched on top. She grabbed the cool ceramic and hurled it at the glass. The mirror shattered, splintering into tiny pieces, but some of the glass still clung stubbornly to the wall and she could see herself in fragments, not her actual self but this other self, this monster.

Helen wrapped her arms around herself, rocking back and forth, her eyes closed. Words sprang into her head. *Yitgadal vyietkaddash shmeh rabbah* . . . The Jewish prayer for the dead. She repeated it to herself, over and over, but the words didn't bring her any comfort at all.

One For the Wolf

M. Lopes da Silva

———◆———

"Leave one for the Wolf," Ma told her, pointing with the long knife. And the youngest obediently took one of the small cooling buns from the basket and carried it outside, to the wood chopping stump, and placed it there. There was a stain in the center of the stump, uncommonly dark and red. The youngest took a moment and stared at the stain dappling the severed rungs. There was a transparency to the color that reminded her of insect wings. Then the autumn wind burred and stung the youngest's face, so she toddled back to the warmth of the hearth as quickly as her stubby legs could take her.

The oldest stood beside the hearth, bouncing a little on her heels when Ma and Pa weren't looking. It was the oldest's turn to read from the Master Book, and she was not overly fond of reading aloud. The middle and youngest liked to tease her about it, but gently, when adults weren't around. Now the middle lit the two yellow tapers while Ma and Pa put their harnesses on over their nightgowns and knelt on the hard packed dirt of the floor. The children knelt beside them.

The well-worn, handsewn pamphlet was bulky in the oldest's hands. "Master Ansel Thomas blesses both the worthy and the humble: we the lambs who labor in the soil for our Savior, and the Master's Wolf who watches over us," recited the oldest in her best reading voice.

"Praise to our Master, praise to his Wolf," answered the adults and the children.

Outside the distant metallic clinking started, scraping and echoing in between the low log houses of the recently founded colony of New Anselton. The oldest hated this part. She cleared her throat a little and continued reading.

"This is an age of modern miracles! Master Ansel Thomas has guided us to a new pasture, just as our Lord and Savior Christ Jesus once guided his flock."

"Praise to our Master, praise to his Wolf."

The metallic sound was getting closer. They were forbidden from looking outside during the Ceremony, so the oldest looked at the printed words on the page in front of her. The middle and the youngest stared at the floor.

There was a panting, heavy and lupine, just outside the door. A bang as metal hit the logs of the wall caused everyone to flinch. Then the long, protracted rasp of a dragging chain.

"Merry are the lambs of God!" the oldest squeaked.

"We are merry indeed!"

A low growl muddled by the wind moved on.

THE HOUR WAS deep. All the fires in the houses were banked. The oldest sat up in her cot, her eyes taking in the faint starlight from gaps in the beams. She watched the youngest stir fitfully in the cot by her feet. The middle slept soundly beside them, his breathing grunting into an occasional snore. Ma and Pa slept in the loft above.

The oldest thought that she had heard something.

She waited in the dark, listening. She tried to remember the sound; it had been a whisper, the syllables without clear edges or definition.

She heard it again. The oldest got to her feet. It sounded like someone was whispering just outside. Quietly she crept along the wall, towards a particular wooden slat that had a hole in it where a knot used to be. The oldest knelt down and leaned her eye against the wall to look out of the gap.

There was an eye there, looking back at her.

The oldest screamed, sending the youngest and middle into a panic. After lanterns were lit and Ma and Pa came down from the loft, the oldest admitted that it was childish of her to wake up the household with her nightmares, and was required to recite:

With Master and Wolf and family near
There's nothing but Master and Wolf to fear.

THE OLDEST MISSED Baltimore, which the middle pronounced "Bal'moore" and the youngest had never known, and was on the whole skeptical about.

"I tell you there was a place in Baltimore that smelled like fresh wood and sugar, and had fish in barrels and cloth and tools, and if we were very good Ma would give us each a twist of the marzipan in paper, and it was the most wonderful thing in the world to eat."

"Better than bread and butter?" The youngest had retorted.

"Better than *raspberries*," the middle piped up, stunning the youngest into silence. Nothing was better than raspberries.

"What's this you're talking about?"

The children fell silent. They hadn't heard any footsteps approach the barn, but the steady, ponderous voice that had interjected itself into the children's musings could belong to only one individual: Master Ansel Thomas himself.

The man loomed like a pine tree, his eyes flashing red in the shadow of the barn. The children looked into the dirt, trembling. There was something hungry in Master Ansel, something monstrous that was keenly felt by the children but never mentioned aloud. The oldest edged herself in front of the middle and the youngest, her features grim.

"It's all my fault, Master Ansel. Please forgive me."

He sank the fingers of his hand rigidly into the oldest's shoulder, a smile twisting his lips. "I think it's time that you witness a Miracle, oldest of Builders."

Anne Fallen was not like most of the people who had founded New Anselton. She was one of the three Fallen women, who "fell from the grace of their families" when they joined the movement, but unlike Sarah or Hester Fallen it was rumored that she had once been married. Where her husband was, no one would tell the children, but despite Ma's vague warnings to "have a caution", the oldest liked her most of all. She knew it was a sin to have a preference, but Anne Fallen knew how to make reed whistles and corn husk dolls, and never said a word about false idols or idle hands.

Anne Fallen once told the oldest a story.

"There was a preacher who wanted more than anything else to talk directly to God. He thought that if he did good works and spread God's word, that God would take a shine to him and want to talk. So he took his humble fortune and devoted himself to his parish. The years went on, but God remained silent.

"And one day that preacher set himself after a seamstress that everyone in town said was a witch, but no matter how he thundered and pleaded, she would not give up her witching ways and attend his church. He finally threatened to fetch the bailiff for a witch trial when she lost all patience and said: 'Why should I listen to the secondhand words of your god when I can hear mine directly?'

"After hearing that, the preacher demanded an explanation, and wore her down until she eventually said that there was a Wolf that came by her house every night, and if he stayed on that evening, he'd see all that he needed to.

"The preacher stayed on, waiting by the hearth until the moon was just over the tip of the blasted pine, and he heard the Wolf howl. That howl sent shivers up and down his spine with all the feeling of divinity, but it wasn't enough—he had to see for himself. So he went outside and saw."

At that point, Anne Fallen went quiet, as if listening—but no one was near. Eventually the oldest prompted: "What did he see, Anne Fallen?"

"Someone who wants to tame the world will see a different thing entirely from someone who just wants to live in it," she replied. "I do not know what he saw, but the preacher's reputation was ruined after he was witnessed leaving the witch's house early the following morn. Mostly he paid no mind: he was obsessed with what he'd seen that night, and determined to have the Wolf for his own.

"But no matter how he begged or threatened her, the witch would not tell the preacher how to catch the Wolf. So he kept an eye on her cottage and waited until she had to take a trip to another town. Then he snuck inside and stole her book of spells.

"The preacher read the book from cover to cover. Then he took the remains of his meagre fortune and bought silver, and went to the smithy with a special order. That order was for a certain length of chain to be made. And with that, and a few other things, he caught the Wolf for himself! But the Wolf changed the preacher, as much as the preacher tried to change the Wolf. Impoverished and mistrusted by his flock, he was cast out of town, and forced to start anew."

"What happened to the witch?" the oldest asked eventually.

Anne Fallen smiled wryly. "It's a difficult thing to be a witch without spells."

The story was a secret. The oldest hadn't even shared it with the middle or youngest. She knew, somehow, that Anne Fallen had meant it as a present just for her.

Now Anne Fallen stood across from the oldest, her eyes lowered. She seemed so far away.

The oldest had never been permitted to enter the Miracle House before. She did not like it. The air was hot and close, and reeking with a heavy, musky smoke. Everyone wore long, black shifts except for Master Ansel, who wore bright red, and the oldest, who still wore her dirty undyed wool. Flames rose from a brazier in the center of the room. The oldest could feel the fire's heat against her skin.

Anne Fallen spoke the opening lines from memory: "Master Ansel Thomas blesses both the worthy and the humble: we the lambs who labor in the soil for our Savior, and the Master's Wolf who watches over us."

The oldest wondered, as she had often wondered, who was meant to be the worthy, and who the humble—the lambs or the Wolf? Her throat was dry.

"Praise to our Master, praise to his Wolf," said the voices of the harnessed families in the room. The Farmers and the Shepherds, the Butchers and the Weavers were all present. Even the Fallen were there. It was the oldest's family, the Builders, that were conspicuously absent.

"We have among us a Sinner!" Master Ansel Thomas roared. "The Builder's oldest still clings to the world of the past!"

There were murmurs among the families, but the soft response seemed to incense the Master.

"New Anselton is our home! New Anselton is our past, present, and future! Those who defile themselves with the outside world don't deserve the salvation of the Wolf!" he fumed.

Now there were some grunts of assent from the group. The oldest felt her flesh turn cold.

"But we are determined to save all of the lambs of God." He grinned, his teeth long and yellow in the firelight. "Even if our own children Sin and turn against us, we must try and save them. That is why this mere child, this Sinner, is here today. Like Doubting Thomas, she must be shown a Miracle for her faith to grow strong."

"A Miracle," the adults muttered to each other.

Master Ansel Thomas spread his arms wide, beaming. "Like the loaves and fishes before us, we ask for a Miracle of Feasts, so that we may fend off hunger, and never know famine."

"A Miracle of Feasts," the adults recited, anchored in ritual.

"Who is our lamb?" The Master asked the room. The smoke burned the oldest's eyes.

"I am," said Pa Farmer, stepping forward. The Master placed his hands on the Farmer's shoulders, and looked into his eyes.

"Are you ready to accept this Miracle?"

"I am," he replied, but there was a faint tremor in his voice.

The Master looked up and spat a phrase that the oldest could not decipher, and there was a heavy feeling, an intense pressure from above accompanied by a low growl, and Pa Farmer's body twisted with a gurgle, then again, then sagged limply to the ground.

Master Ansel Thomas held a knife. They all held knives, except for the oldest, who trembled where she stood. She held her lip between her teeth, trying to be brave. Then the Master struck down, stabbing Pa Farmer in the gut.

The oldest bit straight through her lip. Her mouth was full of blood. Pa Farmer sighed, then began to groan as more of the knives plunged into him. Blood was everywhere. The oldest turned, spitting. The adults dragged their knives through Pa Farmer's innards, removed pieces of him, and began to eat.

"Behold!" Master Ansel Thomas said, his mouth full of something pink and red. "Witness this Miracle, child!"

The oldest kept spitting, until the red she spat turned milky with vomit.

THE OLDEST THOUGHT that things were over once the adults had butchered Pa Farmer and neatly parsed his meat from his bones, but they still sat there, waiting. They watched the damp skeletal remains avidly. Ma Farmer, her mouth stained red, kept clasping and un-clasping her hands together. The oldest stared at all of them, silent.

That intense pressure returned, and for a moment the oldest thought she saw two yellow crescents in the dark, oddly reassuring, then gone. A gasp arose from the group. The oldest blinked, incredu-lous; she had seen something impossible. Then, the impossible thing kept happening.

The bones began to grow back their flesh, blood vessels and mus-cles and ligaments sprouting from the carcass like a miniature carnal forest. Praises to Jesus and the Master and the Wolf were shouted fervently to the ceiling, again and again. They were familiar to the oldest, who had heard the cries when she idled with her siblings out-side the Miracle House on Sundays.

Pa Farmer, skinless, raised his head and spoke: "Praise the Wolf!"

Anne Fallen knelt in front of the oldest, who cringed and looked away.

"You ate him," the oldest whispered in her lowest voice.

"So will you," Anne Fallen said, holding out a small piece of meat to the child. The oldest looked up, saw that the Master was watching them, and numbly took it.

"I can't do it," the oldest said softly.

"Yes, you can." Anne smiled. "You've done it before. Just pretend it's covered in gravy."

The oldest swallowed, her saliva uncomfortably, abruptly thick.

AFTER WITNESSING THE Miracle, the oldest became quieter. She performed her chores automatically, but dutifully. Her siblings pestered her for a while, then started to leave her alone.

The oldest couldn't stop thinking about the Wolf.

She stayed up later and later, listening for the whispering to begin as it did every night. The whispers had a pattern to them, a repetition—like a sheep bleating for a lamb, or a master calling for her dog.

Or a witch for her spellbook.

The oldest performed every chore she was given to the very best of her ability. Even Master Ansel Thomas noticed her diligence, and stated: "Behold! Our Sinner is a lamb again!"

She was assigned more chores.

The oldest searched every new space that she was allowed access to, unnoticed. She cleaned until blisters studded her hands, and grunted on through the pain. She closed her eyes every evening when she was forced to read aloud from the family's pamphlet and heard the lupine pants and whimpers beyond the wall, intermingled with the rasping of the chain. She ate her meals, and managed to keep most of them down.

She always left one for the Wolf.

One day the oldest was given the assignment of cleaning up the Miracle House floor. She dragged her mop and pail inside. The oldest made certain that she was alone, then began to search. She avoided looking at the fresh red gore on the floorboards, searching shelves and inside crates. Sweat beaded her forehead. She froze whenever she heard conversation or footsteps approach, her breath burning in her lungs.

She searched every corner frantically, scrubbing as she went along, but found nothing. Frustrated and in need of fresh water, she hefted up the pail and headed for the well. It was on the way back, as she lugged the clean water past the approving nod of Ma Butcher, that the idea came to her.

She began to clean the gore off of the floorboards.

The bucket water started to turn pink, and the wood beneath the scabby surface was revealed to have the right angles of a small square door cut into the floor. The oldest applied her short, torn fingernails to the wood, pressing and pulling as she searched for an opening.

There was a soft click, and the square opened outwards. The oldest reached into the secret compartment underneath the floorboards, her hand closing on the spine of the book lying there. As she pulled it upwards, there was a slight resistance, like the roots of weeds, that she had to fight. When it came free, she thought she heard a faint gasp.

It felt like something was listening, now.

The oldest had to be certain; she opened the book.

As the oldest read the words she felt a rush of understanding and confusion overwhelm her all at once, a feeling like running in a forest, barefoot and unafraid. A fragment of something unknown. She closed the book.

Her heart hammering rapidly, the oldest hid the book inside her shift and ran.

"YOU FOUND IT." Anne Fallen smiled. "I knew you would find my book."

The oldest's fingers tightened on the surface of the spellbook. "Can you help set the Wolf free?"

"Yes," Anne Fallen answered.

The oldest licked her lips. "And the Miracles—will they end? I can't—they can't hurt middle and youngest. They can't."

"Give me the book, and everything will end," she replied, her smile starting to flatten.

The oldest took a deep breath, then handed Anne Fallen her spellbook.

AFTER THE COLONISTS of New Anselton failed to make contact with any local townships for over eighteen months, a small expedition of do-gooders struck out to see if they needed any help.

New Anselton was found abandoned. Although there were no outright signs of violence, it did not appear that the colonists had moved. In fact, there were frequently signs that New Anselton had been abandoned in the middle of everyday life. A set of hammer and nails were found by a splintered fence post. Laundry hung dusty on a line. A butter churn was clotted with half-churned, rancid butter.

The expedition leader said that he saw a pack of unusually large wolves in the area—the largest at least twice as tall as a human being—with three pups in tow, but was discredited by locals and experts alike upon reaching civilization.

ABOUT THE CONTRIBUTORS

PATRICIA LILLIE grew up in a haunted house in a small town in Northeast Ohio. Since then, she has published picture books, short stories, fonts, and two novels. Her debut collection, *The Cuckoo Girls*, will be published by JournalStone/Trepidatio Publishing in April 2020. As Patricia Lillie, she is the author of *The Ceiling Man*, a novel of quiet horror, and as Kay Charles, the author of *Ghosts in Glass Houses*, a cozy-ish mystery with ghosts. Find her on the web at www.patricialillie.com or on Twitter @patricialillie.com.

DAVID MCGROARTY mainly writes strange stories. More of his fiction can be found in the anthologies *Caledonia Dreamin*, *Rustblind and Silverbright*, *Sensorama* (all from Eibonvale Press), *Strange Tales V* (Tartarus Press), *The Five Senses of Horror*, *A World of Horror* (Dark Moon Books), and (occasionally) on his blog at www.davidmcgroarty.net. He was shortlisted for the 2011 James White Award. David was born and raised near Glasgow, Scotland, and now lives in London with his wife and two sons. He has never been responsible for a garden.

SHANNON SCOTT is an adjunct Professor of English in the Twin Cities. She has published articles, book chapters, and reviews in Manchester University Press, Routledge, *Neo-Victorian Studies*, *Film & History*, and the *Victorian Network*. In 2013, she co-edited the collection, *Terrifying Transformations: An Anthology of Victorian Werewolf Fiction, 1838-1896*. She is currently at work on a collection of short stories.

SAMUEL M. MOSS is from Cascadia. He has work published or forthcoming in *decomP*, *Vastarien* and *Gone Lawn*. He cohosted Hespera, a quarterly reading series in Minneapolis concerned with the distant and ineffable. Currently he travels between, lives on and writes within North American public wilderness land. More at: perfidiousscript.blogspot.com and on twitter @perfidiousscri2

J.A.W. MCCARTHY goes by Jen when she is not writing. She lives with her husband and assistant cat in the Pacific Northwest, a place that inspires her dark tales. Her work has appeared or is forthcoming in numerous publications, including *She's Lost Control*, *Vastarien*, and Flame Tree Publishing's *Lost Souls*. Find her at www.jawmccarthy.com or on Instagram @jawmccarthy.

SEAN LOGAN's stories have appeared in more than forty anthologies and magazines, including *American Gothic Short Stories*, *Black Static*, *Supernatural Tales*, and *Twice Upon an Apocalypse*. He lives in Northern California with his wife, their newborn twins, and a giant white Kuvasz that may be part polar bear.

SAM HICKS lives in Deptford, south east London, but is often to be found wandering the forgotten paths of the lower Thames marshlands. Her work has appeared in *The Fiends in the Furrows* and *Best Horror of the Year Volume 11*.

SIMON STRANTZAS is the author of five collections of short fiction, including *Nothing is Everything* (Undertow Publications, 2018), and is editor of the award-winning *Aickman's Heirs* and *Year's Best Weird Fiction, Vol. 3*. His fiction has appeared in numerous annual best-of anthologies, in venues such as *Nightmare*, *Postscripts*, and *Cemetery Dance*, and has been nominated for both the British Fantasy and Shirley Jackson awards. He lives with his wife in Toronto, Canada.

M.K. ANDERSON is a writer living in Austin, Texas. Her day job is comparing balance sheets to one another while frowning. She enjoys writing about weirdos on the margins and sub-cultures bound to a particular place and time. You can find her work in *Nightscript III*, Alternating Current Press' *The Coil*, and on her website at www.mk-anderson.com.

DAN STINTZI received his MFA from Johns Hopkins University and currently lives in Wisconsin with his wife and dogs.

TRACY FAHEY is an Irish writer of Gothic fiction. In 2017, her debut collection *The Unheimlich Manoeuvre* was shortlisted for a British Fantasy Award. Two of her short stories have been longlisted by Ellen Datlow for Honorable Mentions in *The Best Horror of the Year*. She is published in over twenty Irish, US and UK anthologies and her work has been reviewed in the *Times Literary Supplement*. Her first novel, *The Girl in the Fort*, was released by Fox Spirit Press in 2017. Her second collection, *New Music For Old Rituals*, was published in 2018 by Black Shuck Books. More, including links to her fiction, can be found at www.tracyfahey.com.

M.R. COSBY lives in the Eastern suburbs of Sydney, Australia. He splits his time between running, looking after his family, drinking French wine—and writing strange stories. His first collection, *Dying Embers*, was published by Satalyte Publishing in 2014 and he has just finished the follow-up, *The Trains Don't Stop Here and other strange adventures*. Visit his website at www.martincosby.com and his blog at strangerdesigns.blogspot.com.au

MARY PORTSER lives in Venice, California. As a playwright, she has won the Otis Guernsey "New Voices in the American Theater Award" and has had plays produced in Dublin, Los Angeles, Toronto, and New York. She is also an actress, working in theater and television and showing up in such movies as *Passion Fish*, *True Love*, *The Italian Job*, and *Human Nature*, as well as the HBO series *True Blood*. Excerpts from her first novel, *Squawk*, can be read in the online journals, *Embark* and *Bartleby Snopes*.

CHARLES WILKINSON's publications include *The Pain Tree and Other Stories* (London Magazine Editions, 2000). His short stories have appeared in *Black Static*, *The Dark Lane Anthology*, *Supernatural Tales*, *Phantom Drift* (USA), *Bourbon Penn* (USA), *Shadows & Tall Trees* (Canada), *Nightscript* (USA) and *Best Weird Fiction 2015* (Undertow Books, Canada). His anthologies of strange tales and weird fiction, *A Twist in the Eye* (2016) and *Splendid in Ash* (2018) appeared from Egaeus Press. A full-length collection of his poetry is forthcoming from Eyewear in

2019, and Eibonvale Press will publish his chapbook of weird stories, *The January Estate*, in 2020. He lives in Wales. More information can be found at his website: www.charleswilkinsonauthor.com

J.C. RAYE's stories are found in anthologies with *Scary Dairy Press*, *Books & Boos*, *Franklin/Kerr*, *Chthonic Matter*, *HellBound Books*, *Death's Head Press* and *Jolly Horror*. Other publications are on the way with *Belanger Books* and *Rooster Republic*. For 20 years, she's been a professor at a small community college teaching the most feared course on the planet: Public Speaking. Witnessing grown people weep, beg, scream, and pass out is just another delightful day on the job for her, and the dark fiction she writes is just one more way to freak people out after hours. In her spare time, she covers walls with barnwood, makes excellent pecan brittle, and dreams of one day owning a goat who will be named Ben Gardner.

BRADY GOLDEN is an editor and writer who lives in Oakland, California, with his wife, crossword constructor Juliana Tringali Golden. His short fiction has appeared in *Mythic Delirium*, *DarkFuse*, and on the podcast *Pseudopod*. On Twitter, he is @bradiation.

CASILDA FERRANTE is an Italian/Australian author of horror and weird fiction. Her stories appear in *SYNTH: An Anthology of Dark SF #2*, *Spirits Unwrapped* (Lethe Press) and *Vastarien: A Literary Journal* (forthcoming).

ADAM MEYER is a novelist, filmmaker, and television writer. His short fiction has appeared in many anthologies and magazines including *100 Wicked Little Witch Stories*, *Prisoners of the Night*, and multiple volumes of *The Year's Best Horror Stories*. He has written documentaries and TV series for Fox, CBS, Discovery, and National Geographic Television.

M. LOPES DA SILVA is a bisexual author and artist from Los Angeles specializing in hope, punk, and horror. Her fiction has been published or is forthcoming from *Mad Scientist Journal*, *Glass and Gardens:*

Solarpunk Summers, and *A Punk Rock Future*. She likes to put fairy and folk tales in everything she makes. Currently she is working on a tragicomic personal memoir and a feminist slasher novella. She tends roses and cats alongside her partner, a film critic.

C.M. MULLER lives in St. Paul, Minnesota with his wife and two sons— and, of course, all those quaint and curious volumes of forgotten lore. He is related to the Norwegian writer Jonas Lie and draws much inspiration from that scrivener of old. His tales have appeared in *Shadows & Tall Trees*, *Vastarien*, *Supernatural Tales*, and a host of other venues. *Hidden Folk*, his debut story collection, was released in 2018.

———— ◆ ————

For more information about NIGHTSCRIPT, please visit:

www.chthonicmatter.wordpress.com/nightscript

Made in the USA
Monee, IL
08 January 2020

20003407R00141